I0668440

THE REALIZATION
of Grayson Deschanelle

a
pine bluff
novel

NANCEE CAIN

Serrated Edge Publishing

The Realization of Grayson Deschanelle, Copyright © Nancee Cain, 2020
All Rights Reserved. Except as permitted under the U.S. Copyright Act of 1976,
no part of this publication may be reproduced, distributed, or transmitted
in any form or by any means, or stored in a database or retrieval system,
without prior written permission of the publisher.

Serrated Edge Publishing
PO Box 969
Jasper, AL 35502
www.nanceecain.com

First published January 2020

This is a work of fiction. Names, characters, businesses, places, events and
incidents are either the products of the author's imagination or used in a
fictitious manner. Any resemblance to actual persons, living or dead, or actual
events is purely coincidental

ISBN: 978-0-9995362-6-1

10 9 8 7 6 5 4 3 2 1

Editor: Jessica Royer Ocken
Line Editor: Coreen Montagna
Cover Design by Shannon Lumetta
Interior Book Design by Coreen Montagna

Printed in the United States of America

For Marie & S.R.
Thank you for your help and inspiration.

Chapter One

Five years ago

TRAGIC DEATH CAUSED BY BROKEN HEART

Fifteen-year-old Lissy Carlton mulled over the headline sure to be splashed across social media by tomorrow morning. Would her dumbass boyfriend even be sorry? Make that *ex*-boyfriend. She slammed her fist into her tear-soaked pillow, wishing it was his face instead.

Her bedroom door opened, interrupting her crying jag. *Great.* No one could possibly understand the depth of her pain and humiliation. Without looking up she mumbled, "Go away and leave me alone. Can't you see I'm dying here?"

The door closed.

"You look fairly healthy to me, *ma chérie*," rumbled a deep, delicious French accent. "Whatever the problem is, Santa Claus will be here in a few days to fix everything."

"Oh brother. I haven't believed in Santa since I was six." She opened one eye and peeked through her tangled hair. An expensive pair of men's black dress shoes approached.

Scrambling to sit up, she swept the tears from her burning eyes. The skies had parted and a heavenly being had descended to Earth. *And in* my *bedroom, no less!* No mere mortal could be this beautiful. His hair was a rich dark brown, and a flawless five o'clock shadow graced a square jaw with a slight cleft in the center. Beautiful blue eyes framed by dark lashes stared back at her. Perhaps she needed to rethink believing in Santa. This man was definitely a gift of some sort.

He was dressed completely in black, and she could tell his clothes were custom made. They hugged his broad shoulders and lean hips too perfectly not to be. Even without the sexy foreign accent, she would've known he wasn't from this godforsaken hick town.

He pulled a cigarette out of a sterling silver case, lifting a brow and motioning to see if she wanted one.

Lissy bit her lip and shook her head, peering at the closed door behind him. "Y-You can't smoke in the house. Mother doesn't allow it."

His startling blue eyes crinkled, and his mouth curled into a smile. "Ah, well, then it will be our little secret."

The smooth, deep voice zipped a warm tingle through her body.

"Okay, uh, sure. Wait—let me at least open the window. Even though Daddy smokes a pipe, I don't fancy getting in trouble." Lissy scooted across the bed and threw open the window.

Taking a deep breath, she straightened her shoulders and turned around to face the French god. She stared at his long fingers as he held out his hand in introduction.

"Grayson Deschanelle."

Her eyes snapped up as she placed her hand in his. "*The* Grayson Deschanelle?" she squeaked.

No way. She blinked and wanted to pinch herself to see if she was dreaming. Grayson Deschanelle was in her bedroom? She'd seen his photographs in her beloved fashion magazines and read about his love life in the tabloids. He'd once been involved in a huge scandal involving twins!

"You know my parents?" *Why do I have to sound like I just sucked a helium balloon?* Her parents were affluent, but even this was beyond the realm of possibility, wasn't it?

"George and Patsy? We just met. And you are?" Warm lips tickled the top of her hand, and her toes curled inside her borrowed shoes. He stepped back, seeming oblivious to his effect on her as he took a long draw on his cigarette.

"Lissy, er, I mean, Alyssandra Georgina Carlton." There was something about that accent that made her want to sound more grown-up.

"A beautiful name, *mon chaton*. So why are you up here alone and crying when there is a party downstairs?"

Crying? Her muddled mind scrambled for the reason. *Oh, right. Michael the dickhead.*

She sighed. "My life is over. I can't face those people. *Everyone* saw my reaction when I caught my asshole boyfriend making out with Gabriella. She's hated me since first grade and did it on purpose to embarrass me. And it worked. I mean, really? They had to do it at *my* house at *my* sister's party? Oh! Is that why you're here, to photograph Jessica and Frank's we-eloped party? I don't think Mother will ever forgive her for not having a big church wedding."

Lissy was pretty sure she wasn't the only one counting down to see if a baby appeared in less than nine months.

"Yes, that's one reason."

"That's amazing. How do you know Frank and Jessica?"

"Frank and I share an interesting history." He smiled.

I wonder if Jessica knows about this... She dabbed at her eyes. "I don't understand. I thought Michael cared about me. Why would he make out with someone else? What's wrong with *me?* My braces will be off soon."

Grayson frowned, and his gaze swept her from head to foot. Fidgeting under his scrutiny, she picked at her chipped nail polish.

His mouth curled. "Come with me."

Lissy hesitated a moment before taking his hand. She stumbled in her sister's stilettos, falling into his arms. Which wouldn't be so bad, except she didn't want to be seen as a clumsy kid. Steadying her, he looked down at her shoes for a moment as his breath hissed through his teeth. With a quick turn, he guided her to the Jack and Jill bathroom she shared with Jessica. A firm hand pushed her to sit on the bench facing the mirror. Grayson's presence and personality seemed to fill the bathroom as he loomed behind her.

A tremble of anticipation shivered up her spine only to be replaced by a jolt of embarrassment when she caught her reflection in the mirror. Black mascara had tracked down her cheeks and mingled with red lipstick smeared everywhere but on her lips. To top it off, she'd used so much gel and hairspray trying to make her hair hold a curl, it now resembled the Bride of Frankenstein's — without the gray streaks. Grayson Deschanelle photographed the most beautiful women in the world, and she looked like the Joker.

Muttering under his breath in French, he rummaged through the bathroom closet. Lissy died a thousand more deaths as he moved the box of tampons to find a washcloth. Nonchalantly, he proceeded to wash her face as if she were a child with a chocolate moustache. His lit cigarette dangled from his lips as he worked. Laugh lines etched the corner of his eyes, but there wasn't a hint of gray in his hair. She wondered how old he was.

When he'd finished, he grabbed her chin and turned her face left and right. Appearing satisfied, he tapped her nose with his index finger. "You are entirely too young to wear that much makeup. You have beautiful skin and lovely eyes. When the braces come off, be sure to wear your retainer." He took a draw on the cigarette and flicked the ash into the sink.

Her mouth felt like it was full of sawdust, and she swallowed the whimper of teenaged hormones welling in the back of her throat. He turned her back to face the mirror again where his gaze met hers.

Her heart raced under his frank perusal, and she jumped when his hand brushed the back of her neck. *Holy cow!* It hit her that *the* Grayson Deschanelle had just washed her face and was smoking a cigarette as if they'd just had *sex!* She was glad she was sitting; she didn't think her legs would hold her up, especially in the six-inch heels.

Picking up her hairbrush, he began brushing the shellacked snarls out of her hair. His strokes were mesmerizing and surprisingly gentle. When it was free of tangles, he smoothed her hair into a sleek ponytail. Cocking his head to the side as he stared at her reflection, he took another draw off his cigarette.

"Much better. Now, a little—and I do mean only *a little*—mascara, and a pale pink lip gloss. Nothing more, understand?"

Lissy nodded and applied the makeup as instructed, turning to him for approval.

"Perfect, Alyssandra."

She loved the way her name sounded with that delicious accent. Her full name was usually the bane of her existence—only used by her parents when she was in trouble.

"Now, if I might have a moment of privacy, I came upstairs looking for a bathroom. The one downstairs was occupied."

Her heart stuttered. One dark eyebrow rose as he waited for her to leave.

"Uh, sure. Sorry." Lissy teetered back to the bedroom, mentally plotting how to get some more alone time with him. Spotting the box of tissues by her bed, she quickly stuffed some into her bra. Not satisfied, she grabbed a pair of socks and folded one into each cup. The toilet flushed, and she wasted no time positioning herself on the edge of the bed, crossing her legs and hiking her skirt up just a bit. She wished she'd had time to send a text to Michael or Gabriella. It would be perfect if they were to accidentally-on-purpose catch her in her bedroom with a French sex god.

He entered the room and paused. She kicked her heel flirtatiously and leaned back, so her now-enhanced breasts would appear perkier.

Leaning against her dresser, he stared at her shoes. "Those shoes are not for you. Put on some flats."

"But they're sexy and beautiful. My sister paid a fortune for them."

He crossed his arms and waited. Sighing, she got up and scrounged in her closet, where she found a pair of black flats and slipped them on. His nod of approval sent her heart into overdrive.

"Now, remove the stuffing. You're not a Thanksgiving turkey."

Heat infusing her cheeks, she turned her back to him and pulled out the socks and tissues. She hated men. All men. Especially devastatingly handsome French men.

"Alyssandra."

Squaring her shoulders, she lifted her chin and faced him, but her unshed tears made his face blurry.

"Listen to me, and heed my advice. Go downstairs and hold your head high. Learn your own value. You're beautiful just as you are. Outward beauty fades; it's inner beauty that lasts. And most importantly, protect your heart and save it for the man who deserves it—the man who will move heaven and earth for you."

She nodded, and her confidence inched upward a notch.

At the door he paused. "Someday, Alyssandra, I would like to photograph you the way I see you." He slipped downstairs, leaving her alone.

Lissy sank back to her bed and hugged herself.

Holy Mother of Fashion, Grayson Deschanelle!

Six months later

"No, no, no!" Grayson barked at the set engineer.

He pointed impatiently to where he wanted the fan placed. Black didn't begin to describe his mood. This last-minute change in the ad campaign was his asinine stepbrother's fault. *And where the hell is Frank?* Grayson pinched the bridge of his nose. He knew he was a perfectionist and a control freak. He freely acknowledged that marketing wasn't his part of the business. But this latest harebrained idea was a waste of time and money for Southern Unmentionables, the family lingerie business.

In the corner sat the protective mother, knitting. The constant clicks of her needles further increased his irritation. He glanced at his watch.

"Where is the girl?" he hissed at his assistant.

Unfazed by his temper, she pointed. Alyssandra Carlton stood in the shadows.

Impatiently, he motioned for her. "Come, come."

Hesitating a second, she approached stiffly, holding her terrycloth robe closed with white knuckles. Wide gray eyes peered at him, and a tremulous smile lifted her full lips.

He could feel her nervousness and bit back a vile oath. This wasn't going to be easy. Although the girl was beautiful, she was untrained. The only consolation would be that the time wasted trying to get a decent shot would run them way over budget, and his father would blame Frank.

"Ready, Alyssandra?" He hoped his smile appeared warm and inviting, not pissed.

"Yes, of course," she croaked. She handed an assistant the robe and immediately tried to cover her body.

He pointed to her mark, and the makeup artist and hairstylist finished touching her up.

"Ya got this, Liss," Frank hollered, approaching the set.

Her mother put down her knitting and moved closer to watch.

"Relax, and remember, we need to see the underwear, not your hands," Frank instructed.

Lissy bit her lip and moved her hands. Her body was stiff, her shoulders hunched.

Grayson glared at his stepbrother but spoke to Alyssandra. "Try shaking your hands and then place them on your hips." Behind him, Frank cleared his throat. Belatedly, Grayson added, "Please."

She did as told—and perfected the look of a deer caught in the headlights. Grayson could feel his blood pressure rising.

"All right, move a bit to the left, chin up. Do you know where the light is?" he asked.

"Uh, there?" She pointed overhead.

Grayson sighed and tried to control his temper. "Not physically. Do you know where the light is in relation to your face and body?" Under his breath he muttered, "Why didn't we hire a professional? My time is valuable."

Frank punched his arm and strode to the set, speaking quietly to his sister-in-law. Grayson assumed he was explaining what they needed, based on her nods. Arms crossed, she glanced over his way every few seconds.

Frank shot him a dark look as he walked away and mouthed, *Be nice.*

Grayson promised himself he'd try to be more patient. She was just a kid, after all. And she beautifully embodied the look and direction his father's company wanted to go—*if* she were a professional who knew what the hell she was doing.

They set up the shot, and this time he calmly gave her the instructions, but to no avail. Every picture revealed an awkward girl in sexy underwear, not one worth keeping.

"Clear the set," he instructed, moving toward her.

"I'm sorry." She hung her head. "I told Frank this was a dumb idea. I'm too short and fat, anyway."

Frank and her mother approached, looking concerned.

"I will take the photos of Alyssandra *alone,*" Grayson announced.

"You *can't*, Trip."

His stepbrother was the only one who still called him by his childhood nickname, an ode to being the third Grayson Olivier Deschanelle. Frank spoke a warning with his eyes and gave an imperceptible nod toward his mother-in-law.

Grayson turned to Mrs. Carlton and amped up the charm, taking her hand in his. "Of course if you object, I understand. It goes without saying, my assistant will remain to assure your daughter's interests are protected. But Alyssandra will never relax with this many people around. I just want to make her comfortable."

"I've told you it's okay to call me Patsy." The anxious mother looked deep into his eyes and stressed, "Remember, she's just a child."

"Mother!" The *child* rolled her eyes, and her face turned red.

"I know," he assured Patsy with a squeeze to her hand. "And we're family. I promise I will take care of her."

"You sure, baby?" Her mother scurried over to the teenager and rubbed her shoulder.

"God, yes. Just *stop*. This is embarrassing enough without you treating me like a two-year-old. I'm a grown woman."

"You're only sixteen—"

"Go!" Alyssandra stomped her foot.

Inwardly, Gray groaned. This was going to be damn near impossible. Patsy nodded and gave her a kiss on her forehead before leaving with Frank.

Makeup and hair touched her up once again and left. Gray motioned for his assistant to make herself scarce at the other end of the set.

When she scurried away, he took Alyssandra by the hand. "Let's talk."

"No, I'm fine. I don't want to overdraw the check or whatever."

"Don't worry about it. That's Frank's problem." He chuckled and guided her to the table of snacks.

She looked down and wrinkled her nose. "Celery and carrots? Yuck."

"Models. They never eat. Don't become one." He grabbed a bottle of water before leading her over to a couch. Opening his camera bag, he took out a chocolate bar and handed it to her. "Relax and have a sip of water and some chocolate." Grabbing his camera, he moved to the floor in front of her, watching her closely.

Pink bloomed in her cheeks as she took a sip and then nibbled the candy bar. "This isn't where you drug me or anything, is it? This tastes so good. I haven't had anything but water since yesterday to keep the bloat down." Her eyes darted to the assistant at the back of the room.

"No, I don't relish the idea of prison time. I'm too pretty. And starving yourself is ridiculous. Life without chocolate is worthless." He winked at her. "How is the asshole boyfriend?"

She grinned but quickly covered her mouth. "My braces won't show in the pictures, right?"

He smiled. "Not if you keep your mouth shut."

"I don't have a boyfriend. Boys my age are so immature. Especially in Pine Bluff. All they want to do is go mudding, talk football, and drink."

"Mudding?"

"They drive their oversized pickup trucks—which make up for their small you-know-whats—and race them through the mud. It's stupid."

He laughed. "I see. Not exactly the Grand Prix, I take it?"

"Nope." She looked at him. "I haven't seen you since the last family gathering. Were you as surprised as I was that Jessica wasn't pregnant when they eloped?"

"I never considered it my business. The last time we were together was Easter weekend when you beat me at tennis."

She giggled and shrugged. "What can I say? I'm good. I'm on my high school team. I saw in *The National Intruder* that you're dating what's-her-name, the newest Ford model. Last week you were with that actress. Are you seeing both?"

"Put the bottle down." She did and turned back around, more relaxed. He snapped a picture.

"I wasn't ready," she protested. "And you didn't answer me. Oh! And did you really get caught with twins, *at the same time?* And they were both married?"

"That was ages ago—I don't discuss my personal life. Quit overthinking how you look, and quit trying to anticipate when I will take the picture. Tell me what you're passionate about. What—how do you say—cranks your tractor?"

"That sounds ridiculous with your accent," she replied with a laugh. "I dunno." She stretched out on the couch and propped her head on her hand. "I love fashion."

"That's it?"

"Yup."

"How shallow."

She laughed. "I didn't expect you to say that. You're a fashion photographer. What are *you* passionate about?"

He contemplated her beauty through the lens. Staring back at him was a girl on the precipice of blooming sexual awareness, a young woman with more power than she realized. He shot another picture.

"Stop, I'm not ready." Laughing, she grabbed the pillow, covering her face. The position elongated her body, showcasing his father's newest bra and panty set for Southern Unmentionables: skimpy pieces of white silk with pink bows. The scraps of material left little to the imagination. And she was young. Too damn young.

Hearing the click of the shutter, she tossed the pillow at him, and he laughed, deflecting it with his arm. She ran a hand through her hair, and he damn near forgot to take the picture. The fact that she had no idea of her sex appeal made her even more attractive. This girl had an innate innocence he hoped she'd never lose.

"Come on, tell me."

"We're talking about you, not me." He unbuttoned his white shirt and tossed it to her. Her eyes bugged. "Put this on and stand over there on your mark."

"What?"

"Don't make me repeat myself." He fiddled with a setting on his camera.

After a moment's hesitation she did as she was told. "Okay, now what?"

"You tell me what you're truly passionate about." He watched through the lens of his camera.

"Well, I love walking in the rain, the smell of cinnamon, the sound of a purring cat, and the rush of winning a tennis match. And I love to sew. I even make my own patterns. Your turn. What are *you* passionate about?" she purred, looking closely at him, as if she knew he was hiding behind the lens.

"Women and art," he replied without elaborating.

"Ooh la la. How very French." She batted her eyelashes and winked at him.

"*Oui.*" He laughed, framed the picture, and waited.

"I want you to take some sexy pictures of me."

"It's an underwear campaign; did you think I would take un-sexy photos, silly child?"

"I'm not a child," she protested with a stomp of her bare foot. Her chin lifted in defiance, and that delectable lower lip puffed out.

Perfect. He snapped the shot. "Just a small smile—think of a secret, *mon chaton,* and make sure the panty and bra show." She shyly pulled the shirt open, and her look turned pensive as she gazed at him. It was the money shot.

"I don't think it's any secret that I find you very attractive. What do you see when you look at *me*, Mr. Deschanelle?" She turned away from the camera, dropping his shirt off one shoulder, looking back at him with hooded eyes.

He damn near dropped the camera. "Jailbait. We're done."

Her startled look was the final picture he took, and although it wouldn't be the one used in the ad campaign, it was his favorite.

Chapter TWO

Five years later

"Alyssandra Georgina Carlton."

Daddy meant business when he used full names. Lissy squirmed in the Chair of Reckoning as she faced her father across his desk. She and her siblings were positive that Yellow Mama, the State of Alabama's retired electric chair, couldn't have held much more fear than this chair did. A vague queasiness rose in her stomach, and she swallowed the rising bile.

She sighed, wishing Daddy would commence with the lecture so she could get this over with. Was it too much to ask that she be allowed to wallow in her misery in private? Stealing a peek at her father's red face, Lissy knew this was going to get ugly.

"You're flunking out of college. You were a solid B student until this last semester. Why should I waste my money on your education when it's obvious you don't give a damn about it? Who wants a nurse that can't pass anatomy and physiology?"

Lissy shrugged. *Oops.* Daddy hated shrugging. He considered it a sign of flippancy. She shouldn't have pushed that button.

"Have you considered spending a little more time *studying* and less time hanging out at the frat houses or the sorority house?"

She rolled her eyes.

His hand slammed down on the desk. "You dare to sit there, flunking out of college, *and roll your eyes at me?* I'm sick of your flippant attitude, young lady. Patsy!"

"Sorry, Daddy. I don't think I want to be a nurse. And I didn't mean to be disrespectful. I'm not in a *sorority*. Jessica was."

Jessica: her perfect older sister, married to the perfect husband, with the two perfect kids. They even had the perfect flippin' white picket fence.

"Don't get lippy with me; I'll not tolerate it. Do you understand me? You didn't want to be a teacher, either. You've changed your major how many times? Patsy!"

Here it comes. Time for the good cop/bad cop routine. Lissy stared at her hands in her lap, bouncing her leg. She bit her lip and stole a look at her father from under her lashes. His steel gray eyes snapped like flint striking metal. Pacing, he puffed on his pipe, a sure sign of his stress. He never smoked in the house.

He stopped before her and, using his prosecutor look, waited for her to spill her guts.

Which wasn't going to happen. *Ever.*

There has to be someone with the financial means to help me out of this mess...

Mother bustled into the room, wearing her signature look of worry.

Lissy suppressed the urge to throw herself into her mother's arms and weep. It wouldn't help. She wasn't three years old, and her mother's hugs couldn't solve this problem.

Her parents must never find out; she couldn't bear their disappointment.

Mother broke the uncomfortable silence in the room. "What's going on, Liss? Talk to us; we're your parents. This isn't like you. Is it Joshua, the pre-law student?"

Is Josh the problem? Lissy bit the inside of her mouth to keep from laughing hysterically and yelling *Bingo!* She wrapped her arms around her waist as her leg shook harder. A tear tracked down her heated face. She dashed it away, but too late.

Like a cat with a mouse, her mother pounced. "It *is* Joshua, isn't it?"

Despite her efforts to appear calm and indifferent, her hand shook as she pushed a strand of hair behind her ear, refusing to meet her parents' eyes.

"Did you have a fight? Break up?" Her mother's voice gentled, and she stroked her back.

Lissy was a little thrown by the change in her parents' roles. Usually her father overlooked her transgressions and her mother was the disciplinarian.

The tears started in earnest this time. "I-I can't talk about it."

And that was the truth. She couldn't. The pain was too raw, too fresh.

"You're failing because of some boy? Oh, for God's sake!" Her father shook his head and took a draw on his pipe. "Have you learned nothing from your older siblings? You need to stand on your own two feet and make something of yourself. I have the answer. You, young lady, need a job. Let me spell it for you, since you're *flunking* out of college. J-O-B. Maybe after trying to live off minimum wage for a few months, you'll decide it's time to settle down and crack open a book. As a matter of fact, you can go work for your brother at the bank. This is non-negotiable. I'm not paying for next semester. It also means you will *not* be accompanying us overseas for Christmas. I do not reward failure. You can spend Christmas here with Jessica's family."

Lissy flinched. She hadn't expected her father to be *that* mad. Their trip to London had been planned for a year and was to include three days in Paris, the capital of fashion. She gazed out the window, trying not to cry harder. Her heart beat so fast she felt lightheaded. She needed some fresh air.

"Are you done yet?" she asked.

"Oh, yes, I'm quite done. And you'll find out soon enough what done means when you're flipping burgers at the Mug and Cone for a living or counting petty change at the bank. Now, get out."

"Yes, sir."

Fleeing the room, she ran headlong into her sister, Jessica, and her family. Frank gave her a big kiss and handed her the new baby, Grace. Lee, their two-year-old son ran and stumbled, shrieking. Seeing the children made her heart flip and her stomach churn even more.

"What's Daddy in an uproar about?" Jessica asked.

From behind the study door, Daddy continued to pontificate about spoiled children.

"Wikipedia version: I'm failing. I just lost out on a trip to London, and according to Daddy, I'm doomed to flip burgers for the rest of my life or work at the bank, bossed around by our brother. I'm supposed to spend Christmas with you. I'm sure you're as thrilled as I am."

"What happened? Your grades were fine last semester." Jessica picked up Lee and bounced him on her hip. "Christmas will be fun with the kids! Travis, our bossy brother, and Grayson will be there, too. Lee will be so excited."

Frank's phone beeped. He glanced at the text and muttered, "We'll have plenty of room. It seems Trip's *not* coming for Christmas. He took me up on my offer and is headed to the cabin to get away from the paparazzi." Frank tucked his phone into his pocket and took the fussy toddler from his wife's arms.

The mention of Gray piqued Lissy's attention. She'd watched the tabloid media with keen interest yesterday when the news broke that Candie Fontaine had been caught cheating on Grayson Deschanelle with her director.

Spend Christmas with Jessica, Frank, their children, and Travis? No way. She loved her family, but Gray's idea of getting away sounded like a plan…a very good plan. Suddenly, Lissy had the answer to all of her problems.

She kissed Grace's forehead, rubbing her finger over her soft hand. The baby stirred, and Lissy swallowed the lump forming in her throat, quickly handing her back to Jessica. "I appreciate the offer, but since London is out, I'm going to go stay with a friend—one last hurrah before I'm indentured to Travis. But thanks for the invite."

Frank let out a melodramatic sigh and gave Jessica a swat on the butt. "Well, damnation, sugar. Liss just robbed us of our youth. We are, my dear, officially *old and boring.*"

Jessica frowned. "Yes, I suppose we are. Are you sure, Lissy? We'd love to have you. It will be Grace's first Christmas."

She squirmed under her sister's gaze. If anyone could get her to spill her secret, it would be Jessica. *Not. Going. To. Happen.*

Lissy pulled a smile out of somewhere. "No thanks. I turned my friend down when I thought I'd be in London, but this will be fun. Love you both dearly, but Frank's right. You think cleaning up baby poo is exciting. It's disgusting to be so crazy-ass in love with two kids."

"Okay." Jessica hugged her and attempted to look into her eyes. "Are you okay? You've lost weight, and I can tell you aren't sleeping. You always get circles under your eyes when you don't sleep."

Lissy bit her lip and nodded, wanting out. She'd never been good at lying.

The library door opened, and Lee squealed. Her parents pulled the grandchildren into their arms as Frank and Jessica followed them to the den.

As if she were a seasoned thief, Lissy rummaged in Jessica's purse and unhooked the key to the cabin from her keyring, slipping it into her pocket.

Grayson nodded at the doorman of his Manhattan penthouse as he stepped out onto the sidewalk. Yesterday, he'd been taken aback by the number of paparazzi hanging around his building, and he'd felt sorry for the unlucky bastard being stalked. Then the multitude of flashes had blinded him, and he'd realized with horror *he* was the unlucky bastard.

Although he'd had his moments making unflattering headlines, he'd kept a low profile for years now—ever since the twins incident. It wasn't worth listening to his father and grandmother bitch. And anyway, he despised being the center of attention, preferring to hide behind the lens. Today, he met the media vultures with a game plan in place: ignore them and act indifferent.

"How are you holding up?" Camera shutters clicked.

"Have you been in contact with Candie?"

"Where is Candie? Is she still in Rome with Antonio?"

"Have you seen the photos? Do you have a statement?"

Grayson refused to acknowledge them as he stepped into the limo.

Seated, he glanced at his watch and straightened the cuff of his black coat, his face devoid of emotion. Years of playing cards with his battle-ax grandmother, *Grand-mère,* now served him well. He'd arranged for a private plane to take him away from the spotlight in just over two hours.

Some would say running was the coward's way out, but so be it. He wanted to lick his wounds away from the watchful eye of the world. He and Candie had been growing apart for over a year. As a matter of fact, he'd become bored with their bicoastal relationship, but lazy when it came to actually ending it. Still, it was damn insulting to be dumped for her director. He wasn't even an A-lister.

Joining his father and stepmother in Paris for the holidays wasn't an option. He didn't want to subject himself to their oft repeated advice to "find a good woman and settle down" like his stepbrother, Frank. Even worse would be *Grand-mère's* unrelenting lectures about his hedonistic lifestyle.

Now that he was once again a free man, why on earth would he want to settle for one woman? There were so many to choose from, as long as he was discreet. He liked his relationships spelled out with certain expectations. If Candie had told him she wanted out, he would have complied, no questions asked. They'd had an understanding, an unwritten agreement.

No, he didn't blame her for leaving—it was the way she left. The public humiliation was uncalled for, but in hindsight, he should've seen this coming. Her last movie had tanked, and she was a media whore.

He shuddered. What he needed was a nice, quiet holiday alone at the cabin, tucked away in the scenic mountains.

Well, maybe not *completely* alone…

By the end of the day, Grayson was too damn drunk to drive home from the bar. But he wasn't too inebriated to turn down the invitation of the redhead who'd been rubbing on his dick for the last hour. Just after midnight, he'd closed out his tab as he watched her tie a knot in the cherry stem with her tongue. That act alone made it a done deal.

Being the sober one, she offered to drive, and he readily agreed. He'd pick up his rental car tomorrow. With the help of GPS, she navigated their way to Frank's secluded cabin. The nice thing about being in the backwoods of Tennessee was no one knew who the hell he was. He was just Grayson, not Grayson Deschanelle, infamous chump jilted by Candie Fontaine, star of a half a dozen cheesy paranormal movies.

The car came to a stop, and whatever-her-name-was walked around to the passenger side and opened the door for him. She giggled, and Grayson groaned. Not only did she have a nasal voice, she *guffawed*. In no way could that annoying sound be called a laugh.

Not a major problem, though. He'd find something for her mouth to do that didn't involve talking, *or* guffawing. He stumbled out of the car and managed to make his way up the steps. She steadied him by hanging on to his ass.

Unlocking the front door, he motioned for her to enter first. Some etiquette lessons he never forgot, even when wasted. He shoved his keys back in his jeans pocket and shrugged out of his coat, dropping it on the floor. Mindful of his manners, he took her coat and tossed it on top of his. He gritted his teeth against another annoying giggle.

Grayson pulled her close, fisting his hand in her hair and grinding his erection between her legs.

"I've been waiting for this all night," she gushed.

"I know."

Using his free hand, he lifted her skirt and cupped her ass. She giggled, and he kissed her roughly, silencing the annoying laugh with his mouth and tongue. With a jump, she wrapped her legs around his waist, damn near toppling them both. He managed to retain his balance and made his way to the dark leather couch, falling back on it.

"Oh babe, you want me, don't you?" she murmured as she straddled him.

Unsuccessfully, Grayson tried to pull her name from his scotch-soaked brain, but decided it didn't matter, because in truth, he didn't give a damn. "*Oui.*"

"Oh my God! Your accent is so hot."

The redhead slithered to the floor next to the couch, shedding her clothes on the way. He managed to keep from rolling his eyes, trying to hold on to some semblance of politeness—she was, after all, about to give him a blowjob. Nothing about her was real, from her expressionless Botoxed face, to her fake nails, bottle-red hair, and cantaloupe-sized breasts.

"Say something else in French!" She guffawed again, this time with an added snort.

Ah! There you go—the sound that could serve as a foghorn—that was painfully real.

He shifted and stretched out on the couch as she unzipped his jeans. What's-her-name climbed on top and attempted to take his clothes off, but he dissuaded her by pushing her head lower. Closing his eyes, he settled in and immersed himself in her thorough and talented ministrations. *The girl could suck a golf ball through a straw.* He relaxed somewhat as she worked her magic. If he had the energy when she was done, he'd fuck the hell out of her as a thank you.

"When you're finished, may I have a word with you?"

Grayson's eyes flew open as he turned to face the stairway. There stood Alyssandra Carlton. He blinked and rubbed his face, confused by the alcohol-induced hallucination just as he climaxed deep into the redhead's throat.

When the blood worked its way back to his brain, he realized he hadn't been dreaming. Alyssandra was actually here and had just watched whatever-the-hell-her-name-was suck him dry. *Sonofabitch.* Stunned, annoyed, and not thinking, he said the first irrational, inappropriate thing that came to mind.

"Care to join us for a *ménage* à *trois, mon chaton?*" he asked, eliciting an outraged shriek from what's-her-name.

"No thanks. You know me better than that. I'm a spoiled youngest child. I've never liked sharing my toys."

Surprised, he hurried to make himself presentable to keep from laughing. Alyssandra didn't blink, look away in embarrassment, or blush as he zipped his jeans. Grayson gave a cursory glance at the irate redhead struggling into her tight dress.

"You didn't tell me you were married." The lipstick smeared around her mouth almost matched the fury-tinged color of her face.

"I'm not."

"Or that your kid would be here."

Grayson winced. Now that was a low blow. *I don't look old enough to be Alyssandra's father...do I?*

"She's *not* my kid."

"Whatever. You didn't tell me anyone else was here, you...you..." She glared at Lissy as she zipped her dress and slipped into her heels.

"I think *fuckwad* fits," Lissy offered with a smirk.

The redhead grabbed her coat and stormed out, slamming the door in her wake.

"Don't you need a cigarette or something, *Daddy?*" Alyssandra sat on the staircase, one arm propped on her knee, her chin resting in her hand.

In her Hello Kitty pajamas, with her face scrubbed of makeup, she looked much like she had when he'd first met her. How the hell old was she now? *Nineteen? Twenty?* He couldn't remember.

Upon closer inspection, she didn't look well. Purple smudges shadowed her eyes, and he could see the definition of her ribs below her collarbone. Her hair hung in a tangled brown mess of waves well below her shoulders. He glanced away, reminding himself she was off-limits. He'd always kept a respectful boundary with her, aware of her teenaged crush on him, their significant age difference, and the fact that she was his sister-in-law's younger sister.

"Very funny. I quit smoking years ago. How did you get here?"

"I drove. My car's in the driveway."

He'd been too drunk to notice. Stretching back out on the couch, he rested his head on his hands, keeping his eyes closed, praying this was just a nightmare. "Why are you here, Alyssandra? Did Frank and Jessica send you to check on me? If so, as you can see, I'm fine." He opened one eye and smirked. "More than fine—she was damn good."

"I should've taken notes. I suck at blowjobs. And no, Jessica and Frank don't know I'm here."

Silence engulfed the room. Grayson stared at her, unnerved. She always said the damnedest things. The thought of her giving him a blowjob both unsettled and excited him. He pushed the fantasy out of his mind, attributing it to the excessive amount of alcohol in his system.

"I need a huge favor, but you have to promise not to tell…" She paused and whispered, *"Anyone."*

"Intriguing. Is what you're going to ask me illegal, immoral, or fattening?"

"Depends on your point of view, but definitely not fattening."

Grayson sat up and patted the couch. She hesitated a moment before gracefully descending the stairs.

"You have my attention."

She stood before him, looking at her feet, twisting her hands together. For a brief, unguarded moment, her pain and anguish shone clearly, and he longed to haul her into his arms and offer to slay her dragons, whatever they might be. Instead, he waited.

"Promise not to tell. Cross your heart." Shifting from foot to foot, she looked very young and vulnerable.

Mildly disturbed by her intensity, he gestured dramatically. "Cross my heart and hope to die, stick a needle in my eye. I promise not to tell."

"That's a little extreme." She looked away, chewing on her thumbnail.

"I'm merely reciprocating the melodrama."

"I need six or seven hundred dollars." Her eyes met his for a second and her lower lip quivered. "I'll pay you back, of course."

"Of course." He stood and moved to the kitchen to get a bottle of water and some ibuprofen. "And may I ask why you need the money?"

She followed him and sat at the table. "I, uh…may need a ride tomorrow, too. You don't have to stay. I'll call you when I'm done."

He ignored the tinge of hysteria in her voice. She'd always been a drama queen.

"Tattoo? Piercing? Did you run up your credit card? Paying off a gambling debt? Need a new pair of shoes?" He smiled at her. She was such a kid, probably worried over nothing. He took the ibuprofen and chugged the water.

"I need an abortion."

Chapter Three

Grayson choked and gasped, wiping his mouth with the back of his hand. That was so far off the radar of what he'd expected her to say, he wondered if he'd misheard. One look at her distraught face told him otherwise.

"An abortion?"

She nodded.

He gentled his tone. "Are you okay?" *What an asinine thing to ask.*

"I guess. You know, aside from being preggers, unmarried, and almost broke. I've got some money saved, but not enough. My appointment's tomorrow. Cash would be best — no paper trail."

She looked fragile as glass, ready to shatter into a million pieces.

Grayson put on a kettle of water to make tea, using the mundane action to keep from hitting the wall with his fist. "What about the father? Who is he? What does he have to say about it? I take it he's broke, too?" Unable to quite contain his anger, he threw a spoon on the counter and slammed the drawer shut.

Whipping around to face her, he clenched his teeth. "What kind of bastard makes you go through this alone?"

"I dunno." Her long hair curtained her face as she ran a finger over the grain in the wood table, back and forth.

"What do you mean, you don't know? You have to tell him, Alyssandra. You shouldn't go through this alone. Plus, he has a right to know—"

"I don't know who the father is," she interrupted. Her eyes slowly rose to meet his, silently daring him to pass judgment on her.

"*Excusez-moi?*"

Lines of worry etched Gray's brow, and sadness filled his eyes. It only made him more beautiful. She'd loved him and hated him for five years. Mostly loved—she couldn't blame him for his rejection of her pathetic seduction when she was sixteen. Over the years, they'd developed an easy friendship at family functions. He kindly never brought up her silliness and treated her like Frank did, as a younger sister. He always called her Alyssandra instead of Lissy.

Besides her best friend, Eddie, he was the only person she could think of who'd help her without passing judgment. Lord knows, according to the tabloids, he'd been no saint. Eddie would've been her first choice, but he was always broke and also inordinately stressed over school this semester.

"I don't know who the father is." Stating the truth out loud made her feel even more ashamed.

She lifted her chin, trying to seem nonchalant, but her heart pounded and heat rose in her cheeks. The teacup rattled in the saucer as she accepted it from Gray. He was so stuffy at times. She would have used a mug.

Sitting next to her, he dropped a teaspoon of sugar into his tea, and they both watched as he swirled the spoon in the cup round and round.

His hair now held a touch of gray at the temple and was gloriously mussed after his stint on the couch. She suppressed the urge to finger-comb it.

"I see." He pursed his lips and held his teacup suspended in the air as he thought. He lowered the cup back to the saucer and looked at her sharply. "Were you raped?"

"No, I don't think you'd call it that." She bit her lip to keep it from trembling and blinked back her tears.

Not really.

Sort of.

Kind of.

Maybe, probably not.

I don't know…

"Are you sure?" His firm-but-gentle tone pulled the truth from her like a magnet.

"I went to a party at my boyfriend's apartment. I drank too much, I guess…Josh took me to the bedroom and, well, things happened…"

Grayson's breath hissed between his teeth, and he rubbed his furrowed brow. "What *things* happened?"

"I passed out. *I don't remember.*" She met his piercing gaze and somehow managed not to flinch.

"So, this *Josh* didn't use protection? Why aren't you proactive with your birth control? This is very irresponsible, Alyssandra. Why didn't you go and get the morning-after pill?" His jaw hardened, and he tapped the table with the teaspoon.

Thwack, thwack, thwack…

"I *am* on birth control pills, but sometimes I forget," she admitted. "Just occasionally. As for the morning-after pill, I dunno…I was too much in shock, I guess. I just went back to my apartment and didn't leave for a week. And yes, w-we used condoms, but one must've busted." *Whose? That was the million-dollar question.*

"I'm not following the story. If this Josh is involved, why isn't he handling it?"

Lissy jumped up and slammed her fist on the table. "Because apparently, I pulled a train, okay? Do I need to fuckin' spell it out for you? There were at least seven damn condoms scattered around me when I woke up. One of them must've busted. I don't even know the name of the other guy who was in bed with Josh and me. My *so-called* boyfriend's friends were all snickering and whispering when I walked the hall of shame the next morning.

"So there, are you satisfied with that explanation? *Not only am I pregnant, I'm also apparently a fuckin' whore!*"

She didn't add that Josh had been laughing, too. That's what hurt the most.

Her stomach lurched, and the room spun as waves of nausea rolled over her. Running to the bathroom, she sank in front of the toilet and expelled the contents of her near-empty stomach. When she was done, her muscles ached. Tears streamed down her face, and her heart thundered in her chest. She wondered if it was possible to die from humiliation and prayed it would happen. She couldn't go on like this. Another wave of vomiting commenced.

The door opened behind her and capable hands scooped her hair away from her face. She was hard-pressed to decide which was worse: Gray knowing she was a slut, or Gray watching her throw up. He wet a washcloth and hauled her to her feet, sitting her on the counter. Gently, he began to wash her face, just as he had all those years ago.

"So here we are, full circle, with you washing my face again." She slowly raised her eyes, relieved when she didn't see revulsion in his.

"At least you don't look like a raccoon this time," he murmured. "You've always had beautiful skin, Alyssandra. And appalling taste in boyfriends." He pulled open a drawer and handed her a new toothbrush and toothpaste. "Tell me, did you consent to this 'train,' as you called it?"

She sighed. She didn't want to talk about this. Why couldn't he just give her the money? Her humiliation was almost more than she could bear.

She shrugged and hopped down from the counter. Brushing her teeth, she spoke to his reflection in the mirror. "I don't remember. Probably? I mean, surely my boyfriend wouldn't…" She rubbed away her angry tears. "Regardless, I've come to a conclusion. I think sex is way overrated. After the abortion, I'm going to become a nun. Will they accept me, or do you have to be a virgin to join a convent?"

He shook his head. "I don't see you taking to the vows of silence. Stop avoiding the question and answer me. If you hadn't been under the influence, would you have consented?"

The mirror swam with her tears. Pregnancy had made her so damn emotional. She blinked them away and leaned over to spit out the toothpaste. "N-No."

Launching a string of French expletives, he stormed out of the bathroom to the living area. She found him a few moments later, pacing back and forth in front of the couch where the redhead had sucked him off not an hour ago. Still cursing, he threw his arms up, punctuating his words with his wild gestures. At this moment, he looked very much like his father, Olivier. She would have laughed but didn't want his anger directed toward her.

When he noticed her, he pointed to the couch. "Sit." It was a command, not a request.

Once she had done so, Gray squatted in front of her and grabbed her chin so she could not look away. "You were raped, my darling girl."

She lowered her lashes, unable to speak. A portion of her brain registered the term of endearment and filed it away to ponder later.

"What the hell are you doing?" he continued. "Why are you shouldering all of the blame? You may have made a mistake in your choice of so-called friends, but you are *not*, and I repeat, *not* a whore. I never want to hear you say anything like that again."

She attempted a small, grateful smile as emotions surged and ebbed through her like a tidal wave. Unable to stop herself, she launched herself into his arms, throwing him backward into the coffee table.

He did not resist her but held her tight, settling them both on the floor. As she wept, he murmured in French. Whether he cursed her, comforted her, or chided her, she had no idea, nor did she care. For the first time in weeks, she felt safe.

Holding the devastated young woman, Grayson whispered in French—silly things, like how she felt like a limp doll in his arms, how her wet nose felt like a puppy's, and how her tangled hair resembled a bird's nest. *Why am I spouting such ridiculous things to her in a language she doesn't understand?*

To hide the overwhelming anger boiling inside, he answered himself almost immediately. He wanted to tear each and every one of those prick college boys apart.

"Will you help me? And not tell?" Her soft voice broke through his murderous thoughts.

"Why didn't you report this to the police?" He stroked her back, trying desperately not to think about her warmth, her smell, or the hard nipples poking through her thin pajama top.

She snorted. "Like they would do anything? I willingly went to a party at my boyfriend's place." She'd made air quotes with her fingers around the word *boyfriend*.

She sniffled, and Grayson dug in his pocket for a handkerchief.

"Thank you. Who carries a handkerchief under the age of eighty?"

"I do. It comes in handy when I'm rescuing damsels in distress. You were raped. You should've reported it. They need to pay for their crimes."

"No. It's too embarrassing. I would've been known all over campus as 'poor little Lissy, the girl who cried rape.' Plus, I'm sure those guys would've testified against me, saying I was a willing participant. Who would take my word against all of them? I don't gamble, but even I know those odds are stupid." She shook her head and looked at the floor. "I got what I deserved."

"Don't be ridiculous. Why do you insist on downplaying this reprehensible crime? Have you not been following the news? If those assholes did this to you, they may have done it to other girls." He was so angry he wanted to punch a hole in the wall.

His phone rang, and he yanked it out of his pocket, recognizing the ring. For one second, he contemplated not answering it, but decided Candie would be a good one to vent some of his anger and frustration upon. After all, she deserved it.

"Go to bed. We'll discuss this in the morning." He dismissed Alyssandra with a wave and answered the phone with a clipped, "Candie."

He paced back and forth, running a hand through his hair as he listened to his ex's pathetic excuses, and without thinking, fired back a response in French. He stopped pacing.

"I know you don't speak French. Maybe I should have spoken in Italian?" He hung up the phone and threw it across the room, swearing profusely in three languages.

He turned when he heard laughter from halfway up the stairs.

"Sorry. When you swear, it sounds so much classier."

"Brat. Go to bed."

"Where? There's only one bedroom."

"I'll sleep down here. What time is your appointment tomorrow?"

"Nine."

"Do you need anything?"

"No, I don't think so."

"Good night."

"Good night. And thank you, Gray."

Her shoulders slumped as she crept up the stairs, and his heart clenched. There had to be something more he could do for her.

Gray had agreed to help her. She didn't deserve it, but she was grateful. And he hadn't looked disgusted, just concerned. Lissy stared at the dark ceiling, hands behind her head. *Am I doing the right thing?*

She hated to admit it, but he was right. In hindsight, maybe she should've returned Josh's calls, pushed him for details of what happened that awful night. Shame had frozen her into a shell of depression. All she'd done was feel bad and sleep. Never in a million years had she thought something like this could happen to her. *I'm just one more college statistic on date rape.*

Josh's part in it stung the most. She shuddered, angry and repulsed all over again. Mostly she hated herself for being so gullible. She rolled over to muffle her sobs in her pillow. Why did she cry all the damn time now? And at times her heart would race and race until she thought she'd pass out. Stupid pregnancy…stupid baby… *God, I'm an awful person thinking like this!*

She swallowed the lump in her throat as her thoughts wandered to her niece. Grace was adorable and smelled so sweet. *Well, most of the time.* Lissy loved how her little hand would grip her finger, and she loved to kiss her adorable, tiny toes. Lee was fun, too…

Stop! She punched the pillow with frustration. Thinking about Grace and Lee wasn't helping. In her heart, she knew she wasn't ready to be a mother at twenty-one. She wanted to finish college—just not in nursing like her parents were pushing. But regardless of her career path, that wasn't going to happen for a while. Now she was going to have to work until she could prove to her father that she was responsible. Tears streamed down her face.

God, what's wrong with me? She sat up and scrubbed them away. Pulling her knees to her chest, she wrapped her arms around her legs and rocked. Her chest hurt so badly she couldn't breathe.

Lissy's stomach did another somersault. Dear God, how did women survive pregnancy? Holding a hand over her mouth, she bolted for the bathroom again. What dumbass had labeled it *morning* sickness? She was sick all damn day.

A few moments later, she closed the lid on the toilet and flushed it. Brushing her teeth again, she felt like she'd just run a marathon, so she slid down to the floor. *I'm dying. I'm going to die and be found lying next to a toilet. How gross.*

Grayson heard the retching. How could she possibly be throwing up again? What if she's dehydrated? *Should I take her to the emergency room?*

He wanted to call his stepmother and ask her advice. Or Jessica — she'd know; she'd been through this twice. Surely this wasn't normal. Wasn't it supposed to occur in the *morning?* He found his phone and started to dial but stopped, remembering he'd promised not to tell. Running upstairs, he decided to try to convince her to at least tell her mother. Patsy was a reasonable woman. And he'd insist she go to the ER.

Stopping at the door to the bedroom, he paused, unsure of his next move. *Jésus*, Alyssandra had always thrown him off balance…*Oh, the hell with it.* He opened the door and headed toward the bathroom.

"Alyssandra?" He peeked in and found her curled up in a fetal position next to the toilet.

"Go away. I'm dying." She rolled partway onto her back and draped the back of her wrist over her eyes. "Please cremate me and scatter my ashes around Triangle d'Or in Paris."

"That could be a problem, Sarah Bernhardt. I don't think I can book an affordable flight this close to Christmas, and Papa has the jet. Instead, I could take your ashes back to Pine Bluff and spread them over your father's cow pasture."

"Sometimes I really hate you." She moved her wrist and glared at him.

"I know you do. Now be a good little girl and go to bed. I need to bathe, and this is the only shower in the cabin."

"Don't mind me. It isn't like I haven't already seen your pride and joy." Suddenly, her eyes sparkled as she teased him.

Annoyed as hell, he folded his arms and glared.

"Fine. I'll go sleep on the couch," she announced. "You were here first, after all."

As she hopped to her feet, the color blanched from her face, and her eyes rolled back. He caught her just before she hit the floor. Gently, he carried her to bed.

"Alyssandra."

"Gray," she whispered, giving him a small smile.

"I swear to God you're going to give me a heart attack. I may seem old to you, but I'm too young to die," he chided, checking her pulse. It was a little fast, but steady.

"I think you're perfect." The look she gave him made him more nervous than his fear she was seriously ill.

"Alyssandra," he warned.

"Sorry. I'm fine, really. It must be a preggers thing. I'm okay, just really tired."

"Stay here. I'm going to shower, and then I'll get you some water if you need it. Or do you need anything now? Maybe I should take you to hospital?"

"No, I'm fine. It's just morning sickness. Or in my case, all day sickness. I'll go downstairs and sleep."

"Move from this bed, and I'll turn you over my knee," he warned.

"Promises, promises," she whispered, eyes closed.

Jésus, she's killing me. Grayson grabbed a pair of pajama pants and showered in record time. Opening the bathroom door, he peered at Lissy as he brushed his teeth. Curled up on her side with her back to the bathroom, she remained motionless except for her regular breathing. Good, maybe she was finally asleep.

He turned out the bathroom light and stopped to check on her before heading downstairs. With the back of his fingers, he brushed her hair from her face, and murmured, "Sweet dreams, *mon chaton.*"

"You always call me that. What does it mean?" In the filtered moonlight, her beauty was ethereal.

"*My little kitten.* Sleep well." He turned to leave, but she caught his hand in hers. Small and fragile, he could easily crush it. As a photographer, he saw life in visual metaphors. He prayed this wasn't one.

"Gray?"

"Yes?"

"Please don't go."

"I'll just be downstairs." He wanted to comfort her, but fear skimmed the surface of his conscience like algae on water.

"I don't want to be alone. Tell me I'm not a terrible person. Lie to me if you must…I just need to hear it."

She opened her eyes. At that moment, if she'd asked him to cut his own heart out and give it to her, he would.

"You're not a terrible person. You could never be a terrible person—you're not made that way. You don't have to do this, you know. You have other options. We can figure something out."

Her lip quivered as she turned away from him.

His breath hissed between his teeth. *I'm a dead man.*

Resigned to his fate, he pulled the covers back and crawled into bed. Without a word, she rolled over, placing her head on his shoulder and wrapping her arm around his waist.

"Thank you," she whispered as she drifted to sleep.

The warm body curled into his was the stuff of his dreams and now his worst nightmare.

I'm old enough to be her father, if I'd been careless…

Staring at the ceiling, he silently reviewed the multiplication table in English, French, Italian, and Spanish.

Chapter Four

Grayson woke up stiff as a board. *Everywhere.*

This beautiful, young woman—the one he was supposed to think of like a younger sister—was asleep on top of him and had him trapped with an arm and a leg. He swallowed and tried not to move, not wanting to wake her.

Eyes closed, he tried to remember the multiplication table again. But this morning he'd be damned if he could count. Even thoughts of *Grand-mère* weren't enough to kill the raging hard-on. A cold sweat beaded his brow. *What the hell am I supposed to do?*

Alyssandra stirred in her sleep and snuggled closer, purring like the little kitten he'd nicknamed her. Damnation, there was no easy way to do this. He had to get out of here fast. Unceremoniously, he rolled over and sat up, waking her with a start.

She needed to go home soon. Otherwise, he'd be back to smoking three packs a day.

"What time is it?" she murmured in her siren voice.

"Early. Go back to sleep." He shot off the bed and into the bathroom.

After Gray left, Lissy sighed, wishing she could burrow under the covers and hide. It's how she'd coped for weeks. Adulting sucked. With a yawn, she made her way downstairs to start a pot of coffee for Gray and mentally prepare herself for a difficult day.

Ten minutes later, he appeared downstairs as she stretched into her sun salutation yoga sequence. *Good Lord, he's a beautiful representation of the male species.* As she continued her yoga, she stole another side glance. She'd dreamed about this man since she was fifteen years old.

"Coffee is ready," Lissy said as she rose into *Urdhva Vrikshasana* before finishing with *Samasthitih.*

He mumbled something incoherent and stumbled toward the kitchen. She grinned. He'd never been a morning person. Frank claimed no one in the family would talk to Gray until after the second pot of coffee. She followed him and hopped up to sit on the counter next to the coffee pot.

"What time did you say we had to be there?" He yawned and ran a hand through his hair.

"Nine. You look like hell. Did I snore?"

He was eyelevel with her breasts and stared at them, his coffee cup poised midair. Something in her stomach coiled, and her cheeks felt hot. She squirmed, and he looked away. The hand holding his cup trembled as he took a sip.

She hopped down from the counter, not sure what to make of his reaction, or hers. "Do you want some breakfast? I can't have anything, but I could pour you a bowl of cereal or something." She glanced over her shoulder and noticed he looked uncomfortable and red-faced.

"No, coffee is fine. And you don't snore, maybe just purr a bit." He smiled, and her heart flip-flopped. "Are you okay? Ready for today?"

The concern in his voice moved her, and she struggled to seem indifferent by shrugging. "Guess so."

He frowned. "I really think you should talk to your parents. This is more serious than, say, getting a tattoo…"

"I want to get a tattoo, but Daddy nearly stroked when Jessica and I got our ears pierced. Maybe I should just do it and tell him I got my nipples pierced instead. That way, when I say I'm kidding, the tattoo won't seem so bad. What do you think?"

A strangled noise came from the back of his throat. He pinched the bridge of his nose and closed his eyes. "I'm being serious."

She sighed. "Look, I'm tired of talking about me. I'd kinda just like to think about something else, at least for now."

"Ignoring a problem doesn't make it go away."

She knew that, but ignored him anyway. "Tell me what really happened with Candie. I never thought she was good enough for you. She's a lousy actress, too. Wanna know my theory? That director banged her just to get some expression out of her for his film. She always has that insipid look on her face." Lissy made a blank face and batted her eyelashes.

He stared at her, his face unreadable.

Guilt washed over her. "Shoot. I'm sorry, Gray. That was mean."

His blue eyes crinkled as he took a sip of his coffee. "You may be right. She *is* a terrible actress." He paused, and his face fell. "Although now that I think about it, she might be better than I've given her credit for. She certainly fooled me."

Lissy looked at the floor. "Sorry. Who am I to judge anyone, right?" She shoved a lock of hair behind her ear. "I guess I'll go shower." Looking out the window at the gray clouds, the gravity of the day squeezed her heart. She wondered if she'd really be able to go through with her decision. Maybe Gray was right and there were other options. Her stomach knotted, and she shoved the thoughts away.

Grayson put the coffee cup down and looked at her. "I hate to keep nagging, but are you sure you're okay? Won't you consider talking to your mother or Jessica? Or even my stepmother?"

"No. I can't. I'm fine," she mumbled, blinking away tears. God, she was so sick of this emotional rollercoaster.

He pulled her into his arms and held her, stroking her hair. "You don't have to do this, Lissy. I'll be here for you, whatever you decide."

She nodded. "I know." Pulling away, she looked up at him. "You never call me Lissy."

His brow furrowed. "I, well, uh…" He shrugged and stepped away. "I'm going for a run. Be out of the shower by the time I return. I'll need one."

What the hell? Lissy? I called her Lissy! Grayson ran out of the house as if the devil himself was after him. He'd never, ever called her Lissy. He'd always kept a level of formality between them. But the girl was barely hanging on. He wanted to help her but had no idea what to do other than be here for her. Or should he betray her confidence and involve her family? *What the hell am I doing?*

For the most part, he found girls her age shallow and irritating. But he'd always been fond of Alyssandra, enjoying her sense of humor and offbeat fashion style. Her family indulged her but had always treated her like a scatterbrained brat—the result, he presumed, of the considerable age difference between her and her older siblings. But the times she and he had talked about non-superficial issues, she'd shown some surprising insight. And she was no longer a kid...

He sucked in a laborious breath, whether from the run or his thoughts he couldn't tell. After today, he needed to pack her up and send her home before something terrible happened.

Sprinting up the hill, he pushed himself to the point of exhaustion. And then there was the Candie issue. Just a week ago, he'd lamented to his father that he was bored—bored with life, bored with his job, just bored. *Now my life is anything but boring.*

When he and Candie had first hooked up, she'd been fun and sexually satisfying—when they were actually together. But over time, she'd proven to be vain and career-obsessed—always looking for ways to stay in the public eye, something he abhorred. However, neither one had been interested in marriage, so she'd fit his bill: a perfectly workable, no-strings-attached relationship. They'd had an understanding...one she'd broken, and he wasn't really sure why. Was she in love? Or was this to garner attention?

Candie was the total antithesis of Alyssandra—in looks and values. Grayson stopped running and stood with his hands on his hips, taking in the view from the mountaintop as he struggled to breathe. That was an odd thought. He'd never put the two in remotely the same category before.

He closed his eyes a moment, hoping for clarity. Then he checked his watch and headed back to the cabin. Regardless of whatever craziness he was muddling through, there was no way he'd desert Alyssandra when she needed him.

Her leg bounced, and she chewed on her thumbnail as she stared at the clipboard. Gray's phone dinged, and he pulled it out.

"They're saying bad weather is moving in later." He pocketed the phone and frowned. "Alyssandra, staring at it won't complete the form. If you're having second thoughts, we can leave." He took the board from her and started filling in the blanks. "Middle name?"

"Georgina."

"Age?"

"Twenty. I'll be twenty-one New Year's Eve."

"Weight?"

She grabbed the board from him. "None of your damn business. I'll do it." Completing the forms, she stood and paused, unable to move. Her feet felt like lead. From somewhere far away, she heard Gray asking if she was okay.

What a stupid question. No, I'm not okay…

The pounding in her chest became so intense she couldn't breathe. Spots danced before her eyes, and a dull roaring noise flooded her ears. She closed her eyes for a moment and let the engulfing darkness pull her away from the hardest decision she'd ever had to make.

Two hours later, she sat in his car in stunned disbelief as he drove them away from the clinic. "I guess you need to take me to the nuthouse, because obviously I'm frickin' crazy. *Anxiety?* Seriously? Plain old stupid *anxiety* made me miss my period, throw up, feel ungodly pain in my chest, and cry like a baby over everything? This is insane. I'm crazy. Nuts. Looney Tunes. Cuckoo. *Loco in la cabeza.* How do you say it in French?" She attempted for the third time to buckle the seatbelt, but once again missed.

Grayson bit the inside of his cheek and tried his damnedest to keep from laughing at her. "*Tu es folle.* I would think you'd be relieved you're not pregnant." He buckled her seatbelt for her and then his own.

"Duh. Of course I'm *relieved.* But I'm, like, a little *distressed* that I'm a nutcase, ya know?" She blew a strand of hair out of her face.

"I guess your home pregnancy test wasn't accurate."

Color rose in her cheeks, and she stared out the window.

He knit his brows together. "Alyssandra?"

"Uh, well, I didn't take one. I was scared. I mean, I had all the symptoms…"

Grayson shook his head. "You're joking, right? Why not?"

"Someone for sure would've seen me buying it." She stared out the window, adding softly, "And it would've made everything so real…"

He sighed. "You were stressed. You talked to that counselor at the clinic, but perhaps you need more time to process everything. If you decide you want to talk to someone else, I'll pay for it. I think you can even do that stuff online—although I'd think in person would be better."

"You'd do that for me?"

Circling the bar parking lot, looking for where he'd parked his rental car last night, he answered without thinking, "Of course I would. I care about you—" *Fuck.*

Keeping his eyes on the road, he attempted to cover his slip. "I mean, I care about your mental state. After all, you're staying with me; I can't have you going UPS." He pulled in and parked next to his rental car. "Do you cook?"

"Go UPS? What's that? I can heat up stuff. I'm a whiz with a can opener and a microwave."

"You know…" he searched for the word "…crazy, shooting people—isn't that going UPS?"

She giggled. "Postal, not UPS. And nobody uses that saying anymore."

"Whatever." He pulled open his wallet, thankful he had cash. He used it to avoid leaving a trail while lying low from the paparazzi. "Stop by the store and pick up whatever you want to eat. Just make sure you include quality steaks and a nice red wine. Thankfully, I can grill. We'll celebrate your non-pregnant status. I'll meet you back at the cabin." He looked at her critically. "You need to eat and rest before you go home tomorrow."

"Cash? Who uses cash? I'm not old enough to buy wine."

Ouch. "I'll buy the wine."

"I'm not old enough to drink," she responded.

He shot her a dubious look, and she laughed. After all, he'd been the first to sneak her some champagne at a family party.

"Gee, thanks. Let me fight the Christmas rush." She unbuckled her seatbelt.

"The alternative is to leave now to be with Jessica and Frank for Christmas. I could bring your things with me when I come for New Year's Eve." He pulled out his phone and checked the weather. "Scratch that. I don't want you on the road. We need to hurry."

She wrinkled her nose and bit her lip, looking away. "Would you think me a horrible aunt to skip Frank and Jessica's for Christmas?"

He grinned. "No. The children are lovely, but…"

"Oh, thank God. I mean, the kids are great, but…" She looked down at her hands. "The truth is, I need time to think, reassess, and figure out what I'm doing. Thank you for letting me stay…"

She still had dark circles under her eyes and flushed cheeks. In her pink knit cap and matching muffler, she looked exhausted, vulnerable, and quite young.

He handed Lissy more money. Better to be safe than sorry.

"Get enough food to last for a while and any emergency supplies we may need, like batteries, candles. If it's as bad as they're predicting, the roads will be impassable by tonight. Don't waste any time."

"Do you really think it's going to snow? What are you going to be doing while I'm fighting for the last gallon of milk and loaf of bread?"

"The worst part will be the ice. I doubt sand trucks would come out to an area as remote as Frank's cabin. I have to get gas and arrange to get some more firewood in case we lose power. See you back at the cabin—be safe and hurry. We have a couple of hours before it moves in."

Not pregnant, not pregnant, not pregnant! Lissy wheeled the cart through the store, grinning widely and wishing all the grumpy shoppers a merry Christmas, which was only four days away. Sure, she felt incredibly dumb for not having taken a home pregnancy test first, but the relief far outweighed the feelings of stupidity. *Snowed in with Gray! Who said Santa isn't real?*

The store was packed with a combination of last-minute Christmas shoppers and those stocking up for the impending ice storm. The way everyone was yammering about it, you'd think it was the end of time. *Any* snow would be more than she was used to, so she had no idea what to expect. Maneuvering through the frenzied throng, she loaded food into the cart and hurried over to the craft side of the store. She found four skeins of soft, charcoal gray wool and knitting needles. It wouldn't be much, but she wanted to make something for Gray for Christmas. She looked longingly at the fabric but didn't have her sewing machine with her, so she moved on to get batteries.

Standing in the checkout line, she hummed along with the holiday music blasting through the sound system, happier than she'd been in ages. As she passed the rack of tabloid magazines, she stopped and backed up, causing the man behind her to swear. Eyes wide, she grabbed the trash magazine and added it to the rest of her purchases. *Poor Gray.*

Chapter
Five

Back at the cabin, Grayson plugged in the lights. When nothing happened, he swore, now understanding why Candie had always hired a professional to do their Christmas decorating. Hands on hips, he glared at the tree.

He had planned a nice, quiet holiday with no fuss, lots of illicit sex, and copious amounts of alcohol—until Alyssandra arrived.

Now, after arranging for a load of firewood to be delivered, he'd picked up some wine and his favorite single malt scotch. At the gas station, on a whim, he'd bought a rather straggly tree with a box of cheap ornaments and three strands of lights. It never ceased to amaze him how gas stations in the States sold a little bit of everything. In spite of his worry over being snowed in with Alyssandra, he felt a need to give her a semblance of Christmas. His memories of Christmas past were lonely—until his father had married Lynn Jaymes, Frank's mother. She'd brought joy to the holiday.

He tried the lights again, but nothing happened. Dammit, he didn't remember stringing lights being this difficult when he and Frank had helped *Maman,* as he called his stepmother. Maybe this was all a stupid mistake. He fiddled with the light bulbs to find the loose connection. They were brand new. One entire strand could not be dead.

"*Merde.* Stop it."

He plucked the small gray kitten from the tree. Here was yet another mistake. He didn't even like cats. But the damn thing had made eye contact with him at the gas station and meowed pitifully. Rubbing its head against his leg and purring, it had reminded him of Alyssandra: soft, pretty, and with plenty of attitude. Sleet hit the cabin's windows, and he glanced at his watch. *Where is she? I told her not to take too long.*

He twisted one last bulb, and the strand illuminated.

"Finally!"

He admired the lights and adjusted a few. Hearing someone pull up, he ran to the window, but it was just the truck delivering firewood. *Where the hell is she?* He tried calling her, but she didn't answer.

Sleet hit the windshield as Lissy drove like a ninety-year-old woman on the treacherous road. Either the forecasters had been off on their prediction of when the front would move in, or she'd taken too long shopping. She ignored the incoming call, concentrating on driving. Her car went into a skid, and she carefully steered into it, just as Travis had taught her. By some miracle, she managed to regain control. Her brother would be proud.

The breath she'd been holding hissed between her teeth as she finally pulled into the driveway. On the porch was a new stack of firewood. Gray dashed out the door, gesturing wildly and looking quite perturbed. She laughed and stepped out of the car, grabbing her purse and popping the trunk. She was pretty sure he was cursing in French. Ice made the walkway slippery, and they both stumbled. He caught her before she fell.

"My hero," she teased.

Stepping away, he busied himself with retrieving the groceries. "Where the hell have you been?"

"You try shopping with the threat of bad weather *and* Christmas. The lines to check out weaved all the way to the back of the store. Geez, Gray. Relax, will ya?"

She grabbed some of the plastic bags and followed him into the cabin. "O-M-G." Her eyes widened when she spotted the crooked

Christmas tree next to the fireplace. Dropping the groceries, she threw her arms around his neck. "Thank you! You have no idea… Now it feels like Christmas."

Grayson gave her a brief, stilted hug, still holding the bags of groceries. "It wouldn't be Christmas without a tree, Alyssandra."

Her heart fluttered. *God, how I love that sexy accent…*

Untangling himself from her arms, he muttered in French as he moved toward the kitchen. She did a happy dance as she moved one strand of lights a little lower before following him.

"Do you think we'll have a white Christmas?" She peeled off her coat and threw it on the back of a kitchen chair.

"It appears so." Gray yelped, and a tiny gray kitten with blue eyes peeked over at her, its claws embedded in his leg.

Her mouth dropped and she screamed, rushing over. The frightened kitten clawed its way up Gray's leg.

"Ouch. Calm down, both of you." Gray removed the kitten, whose claws were now in a danger zone.

"Who is this?" She took the kitten and snuggled it to her neck, laughing when it nipped her ear.

"Whatever you want to name it. Personally, I think *Trublion*—Hellion—would be appropriate. *Joyeux Noël*, Alyssandra. It would have been impossible to hide this bundle of energy until Christmas morning."

Apparently forgiving the hellion, Gray stroked the kitten. In the process, his fingers brushed her cheek, and her heart skipped a beat as electricity sparked between them.

Backing away as if burned, he spun around, slamming the groceries into the cupboard. Watching him, she wondered how he could make an old worn pair of jeans and a navy long-sleeved T-shirt look so damn good.

"*Merci beaucoup*." She peered around the cat's tail, laughing when she received a hiss. "I love her already."

"What will you name her?" He seasoned the steaks, appearing quite comfortable in a kitchen.

"Noëlle, of course." She hugged the kitten, still smiling. "This is the best present you've ever given me—even better than the pearl earrings you gave me for my eighteenth birthday."

Gray chuckled as he scavenged for a pan. "Better than Mikimoto pearls from Tiffany's? I could have saved a lot of money…"

"I'm sorry. I didn't mean to sound ungrateful. Of course I love those earrings. I even kept the box. Nothing makes a girl's heart sing like those little blue packages."

She didn't add that she had also saved every card and note he'd ever written her, and a tennis ball from the time she'd beaten him. And, in the back of her closet was a box of family photos and magazines featuring his work or news articles about him.

She laughed. "This kitten is too cute for words. Listen to her purr." She held the now sleeping kitten to his ear.

He smiled. "She's like a child: best when sleeping." Placing the steaks in the refrigerator, he wiped the counters.

"Don't let the family hear you say that. We're supposed to be the doting aunt and uncle." Stepping into the living area, she carefully placed the sleeping kitten on the couch. Suddenly overwhelmed by the gift and the tree, hot tears spilled down her face. *Everything is better. Why can't I get a check on my emotions? Why is there dread in the pit of my stomach?*

Taking deep breaths, she managed to calm down, and her racing heart slowed. This must be normal, she rationalized, wiping her tears away. After all, she'd been on an emotional rollercoaster for weeks. Now that the stress was gone, this exhausted feeling must be the result of crashing back to an even keel.

When she returned to the kitchen, Gray was chopping vegetables and tossing them in a salad bowl. Who knew he could cook? She could barely boil water.

"Need help with anything?"

"I'm almost done. Why don't you decorate the tree? Would you like a glass of wine?"

"Yes, but you know I'm not supposed to drink yet." She smirked, waiting for his diatribe on American views on alcohol.

He blew out an exasperated breath. "In France, you'd be able to legally drink. And there is no ridiculous age restriction on alcohol consumption in the privacy of one's own home. Even children are given a sip of wine. Wine is good for the heart. It can help protect the brain…"

Only half-listening, she finished putting the groceries away and came to the last bag, the one with the wool, knitting needles, and trashy tabloid. "Gray, you may need to go ahead and drink a glass, or maybe even something stronger."

He paused, his brows furrowed. "Why?"

"I, uh…She's awful. Trust me—no one will believe her…"

"Who is awful? Believe what?" He put the knife down, giving her his full attention. He frowned as she held out *The National Intruder* featuring Candie's picture on the cover with the caption, "Antonio is the Best Lover I've Ever Had."

He shook his head. "I don't read that shit. Buying this trash only puts money in their pockets."

"I'm sorry." She hadn't thought about that, but still felt like she'd done the right thing. He needed to know. "I think you should read it. Eventually the paparazzi will ask you about it. Don't you have a publicist or somebody who can make a statement to refute this?"

"Why would I need a publicist? I'm merely a photographer. I'm nobody important." He scowled as he finished chopping the vegetables. The knife hit the board with a little more force than before.

"Gray, you were her fiancé—"

"She was *not* my fiancée; I'm not a marrying man."

"Whatever. You're a famous fashion photographer; of course you're important. It's really bad—" Her phone rang, and she dug it out of the pocket of her jeans. Looking at the incoming call, she sighed. "I don't recognize the number…"

"Then don't answer."

"But what if it's something about the family?" She pressed the button. "Hello?" The familiar voice sent rage surging through her. "Who's phone are you using, Josh?"

Dropping the tabloid on the table, she walked out to the back porch, slamming the door.

"Quit calling me. Quit texting me. Why would you think I'd want anything to do with you after what you and your friends did?" She walked down the steps, needing to cool off.

"What? You still mad about that joke, Liss?" Josh's voice sounded chipper, as if nothing had happened.

She wanted to vomit. "A joke? You're truly a sick bastard. I should've pressed charges."

"Whoa, now—what the hell are you talkin' about?"

"You must've spiked my drink, and when I woke up…" She choked, so angry she could spit nails.

"C'mon, Liss, I've texted you that I'm sorry, and I've left you a ton of voicemails and emails. You've shut me out long enough. Just get over it. You promised to meet my folks at Christmas. I've got your present, and I want to see you—"

"Just get over it? Meet your parents? You're beyond twisted! You raped me, allowed your friends to—good God almighty, I feel sick." Her heart felt like it was going to explode. Mixed with stinging sleet, the snow was coming down harder.

"Liss…what the hell? You didn't truly believe anything happened, did you? It was a *joke*. You got punked, that's all. We set that shit up. Hell, it was egg whites in the condoms. Brock was tore up from the floor up, too. He didn't know at first, either. Neither one of you moved as we threw the condoms on the bed. You were both so damn drunk; it was fucking hilarious…"

A rush of sound like a wind tunnel rang in her ears, and the world around her spun. She wondered if she would ever be able to draw enough air into her lungs.

When she did, it exited with a scream. "A joke? *Hilarious?* Josh, do you have any idea what you've put me through? I thought…"

She grabbed the stair railing for support. "Never call me again. I hate you and hope you rot in hell!" She hung up and her knees buckled as white, searing anger flooded her body.

The hair on the back of Grayson's neck stood on end. When Alyssandra had walked outside to talk to that punk Josh, he'd respected her privacy and stayed behind. But the sound of her deep, gut-wrenching keening had him out the door in a flash. He found her at the bottom of the steps, on her hands and knees, sobbing—seemingly oblivious to the sleet and snow pelting her.

"Alyssandra!" He raced down the steps, slipping once and barely catching himself. "Come inside, my darling."

She continued to sob. Scooping her into his arms, he carefully made his way up the slippery stairs. Inside, he settled her on the couch, wrapping her in a blanket. Prying the phone from her hand, he placed it on the end table.

She pounded her fist on the arm of the sofa. "I hate him!" Her entire body shook. "Hate, hate, hate him!"

A throw pillow sailed past him. She picked up the box of ornaments. He quickly grabbed it.

Annoyed and concerned, he sighed, not sure what to do. He didn't like a woman out of control—unless it was his doing and in bed. When she remained hysterical, he picked her up, marched upstairs, and shoved her into the shower—both to warm her up and shock her out of her crying.

She crumpled to the floor of the shower. "Why?" she sobbed. "Why would he do that to me? The hell I've been through…" She gasped, holding a hand to her chest. "I can't breathe."

Her despair triggered every protective instinct within him. Stepping into the shower, he helped her to her feet and wrapped his arms around her as she wept.

"Shh, deep breaths. Calm down, my darling girl. You're going to be okay; you'll get through this."

"No. No, you don't understand. Josh said it was all a *joke*."

Grayson turned off the water, trying his damnedest to rein in his growing fury. How could that little prick think rape was a joke? He held her tight until her crying eased to sniffles.

"Let's get you out of these wet clothes."

"I bet you say that to all your women."

Bon Dieu, she always said the damnedest things. He guided her to the closed seat of the toilet. Handing her a towel, he said, "Dry off. I'll find you something to wear."

He closed the door to give her some privacy and went through her suitcase, searching for dry clothes. His family owned a goddamned underwear company, and she only had two bras? He fumbled through several pairs of thong panties. Shoving them aside, he swallowed and tried not to think about Alyssandra in underwear. Opting for pajamas instead, he pulled out black silk pajama bottoms and a lacy black top with thin straps. *Where are the Hello Kitty pajamas?* He grabbed the pants and retrieved one of his sweatshirts. If the roads were passable tomorrow, he'd buy her a thick, fluffy robe and flannel pajamas.

Grayson knocked on the door and waited. When she didn't answer, he opened it and found she hadn't moved. She seemed almost catatonic. With a tired sigh, he towel-dried her hair.

"Get dressed," he commanded.

When she made no move to help herself, he pulled her to her feet and unbuttoned her wet blouse. Realizing she wasn't wearing a bra, he stopped short of peeling off her wet shirt. She took over and tugged the shirt off. He saw a flash of her naked breasts before averting his gaze. She was a perfect B cup, his favorite size. He evened his breathing and waited, staring into the bedroom as she dressed behind him.

He had to get out of here. She was even more beautiful than he'd remembered from the Southern Unmentionables ad campaign. And definitely *not* a little girl now.

That photo shoot, the one he'd dreaded most, remained his favorite of all time. Once she'd relaxed, she'd revealed a sexy innocence that still haunted him. He didn't know what to think about the unbrotherly thoughts now permeating his mind.

"I'll be downstairs." He left and closed the door. God help him, they were about to be snowed in together.

Her teeth chattered so hard she feared they might crack. She couldn't seem to get warm, and it was an insidious cold, working from the inside out. Because of Josh's prank, she'd flunked this semester in college. Someone who'd supposedly cared about her thought it would be funny to make her think she'd had indiscriminate sex or been raped. Angrily, Lissy pulled on her pajama pants and Gray's sweatshirt and combed the tangles out of her wet hair.

The effort of getting dressed winded her. She returned to the bedroom, sat on the side of the bed, and covered her face. Logically, she knew she should be relieved. She hadn't been raped. She wasn't pregnant. Yet she still felt battered and emotionally empty—embarrassed to be such a naïve little girl, especially in front of a man she'd always admired. Taking deep breaths, she reached deep within and pulled herself together before slowly making her way downstairs.

Squatting in front of the fire, Gray poked it, and the muscles on his back flexed. His hair was still damp, but he'd changed into a dry pair of jeans. He stood and jumped when he saw her. Quickly he shrugged into a sweatshirt. His eyes held hers as he waited for her to speak.

"I'm sorry." She sank onto the couch next to the sleeping kitten. "I-I don't know why I acted so silly. I mean, I should be thankful. I'm not damaged goods after all. Just incredibly stupid."

"You're not stupid, nor are you — or would you have *ever* been — damaged goods. I expect better of you than this. Come, let's have some hot tea to warm up. My grandmother swears it fixes everything, although I think she adds a little something extra to hers."

She followed him to the kitchen and sank into the chair, feeling numb.

"Now, tell me what happened." He put on the kettle of water and stood, waiting for her to begin.

"Apparently nothing. I freaked out over a prank. Nice, huh? I flunked out of school, nearly got an ulcer from worry, stressed my parents, bothered you…all because some douchebag college boys thought it would be funny to make me think I'd done all of them."

Gray's lips thinned and his knuckles blanched, but his voice remained even when he spoke. "I'd call that emotional rape."

Lissy shrugged and shook her head, running a hand through her mop of hair. "It's okay. I'm glad I'm not pregnant. I'll never be put in that position again. I'll chalk this up to a learning experience. Don't trust anyone."

"That sounds a bit cynical for someone your age, but it may be a lesson well learned." The kettle whistled. "Tea?"

She nodded and accepted the cup and saucer from him. "Ya know, you could just use a mug. Less dishes." She dunked her teabag up and down, watching the tea swirl, much like her emotions.

Gray laughed. "My grandmother would be horrified that I'm using a teabag. Besides, I'll leave the dishes for you." He sat next to her and cupped her cheek, forcing her to look at him. "You're not a bother. And you will get through this. You're an incredibly resilient, smart young woman."

Looking into his face, she could almost believe it.

Grayson felt an overwhelming sadness. The innocence was gone from her crystal eyes. He'd always loved that about her, her sweet exuberance. A prank? A joke? *Sick bastards.*

They drank their tea in silence. She looked like a lost kitten.

"I'm sorry this has happened to you. While I'm thankful it wasn't an actual rape, I'm worried about you and the impact the experience is having, no matter what it was. It was wrong, Alyssandra. It was the worst kind of betrayal—a betrayal of your trust."

"Sort of like what Candie did to you?"

"In a way. Candie and I had grown apart," he admitted. "Our careers kept us on different coasts most of the time. In truth, I may have driven her away with my inattentiveness. But what happened to you was different—worse. My humiliation has been public, but I know I'll get over it. I have the life experiences to know that horrible things happen, but they always get better with time. You're young, and this could understandably be very damaging. It may well color your actions and thoughts regarding men in the future."

He paused, searching for words that might help. "Just know we aren't all immature jerks. And some immature jerks grow up to be semi-okay men—though others remain jerks forever. Be discriminating. You deserve the best."

She smiled, and he felt a light turn on inside him.

"Don't give up. I'm here for you if you ever need to talk."

"You're a very nice man, Gray. Thank you. I've always found it easy to talk to you. You don't treat me like a baby."

"No more tears, my brave girl. Let's decorate the tree. It will help to stay busy."

"You're right. Okay." She followed him into the living area, and he handed her the box of ornaments.

Opening them, she frowned. "Where are the hanger thingies?"

"The what?"

"The wire hangers. How will we hang them? Or are you going all Joan Crawford on me? 'No wire hangers!'"

Her attempt at a joke made him laugh. *She'll make it through this.*

"*Maman* always had everything ready for me and Frank to just decorate. I didn't know we needed 'hanger thingies.' I thought they came with them." He looked around, at a loss.

"What about you and Candie?"

"She hired a decorator. What do we do? Just leave the tree bare with lights?"

"No! We can't have a naked tree. Don't worry. I've got this." She scurried to the kitchen and came back with some gray wool. "I'll use this; do you have scissors or a knife?"

"Of course." He threw her his pocketknife.

"A handkerchief and a pocketknife — you're such an enigma, part gentleman, part good ol' country boy," Lissy teased as she cut pieces of the wool and fashioned hangers for the ornaments.

"My parents may have been French, but my stepmother and stepbrother are all-American. I'm the best of both worlds, bay-bee." His overdone American pronunciation and wink made her laugh. He vowed to make her laugh more over the next few days.

He returned to the kitchen to pour some wine and paused when *The National Intruder* caught his eye. As if accepting a punishment, he opened the rag and read the article with some surprise, anger, and ultimately, embarrassment. *That bitch.* He hadn't said one word to anyone about her betrayal, and yet she'd turned around and trashed him in the tabloid press.

He rubbed his hand over his face. *No, be fair.* She might not have said any of this. It wasn't like this was a reliable news source. He threw it back on the table, opened the wine, and poured two glasses. Sleet pelted the windows, and he sighed. It was going to be a long few days.

Walking back into the living area, he handed Lissy a glass, surreptitiously studying her appearance. Although her eyes remained slightly swollen, her color was better. She bit her plump lower lip as she meticulously tied hangers on the ornaments.

He picked up the sleeping kitten and put her on his lap, stretching his legs out on the coffee table. He stroked the cat and stared into the fire, trying to sort through his feelings. He *was* relieved to be done with Candie. Despite the embarrassment of the public breakup, it gave him a chance for new beginnings — to get out of this ennui that had been upon him for months.

Across the room, Alyssandra started decorating the tree. Looking over her shoulder at him, she smiled.

And he caught his breath.

Chapter Six

Lissy admired her pensive companion. His hair had dried all over the place, which did nothing to diminish his attractiveness. He stroked the kitten, staring into the fire as if lost in thought. She found herself irrationally jealous of a silly cat.

A log shifted in the fireplace, startling the kitten, which jumped out of Gray's lap to swat at her yarn. Daydreams interrupted, Lissy returned her concentration to the task at hand.

There was no way that article in *The National Intruder* was true.

Gray had always been one of the few adults to treat her as a person, not a kid. He was one of the most thoughtful men she'd ever known—certainly nothing like any of the boyfriends she'd ever had. Just look at the pearl earrings he'd given her for her eighteenth birthday—and for her high school graduation, he'd given her an engraved silver bracelet with a Thoreau quote: *Go confidently in the direction of your dreams.* She'd bet her last dollar he was a considerate lover.

"Gray?"

He didn't respond, his expression sad and haunted as he gazed at the fire. He must've read the article when he went into the kitchen.

"A penny for your thoughts," she offered as she finished tying the last hanging loop on a shiny red ornament.

"My thoughts would not be worth that much." He took a sip of wine, his brow furrowed. He grimaced when the kitten, now bored with the yarn, jumped back in his lap and bit his finger.

"We're a great pair." Lissy chuckled as she stood and hung an ornament on the tree. "We could form a club, the Lovelorn Losers."

He flinched, and she regretted her words. Her father always said she'd make a lousy witness on the stand because she didn't think before she spoke. She hung an ornament near the top of the tree.

"Just so you know, I don't believe that article. Not a word of it. She's either lying, or it was all fabricated." She turned back around, facing him.

He rested his cheek on one hand but made no comment as he watched her.

Lissy hung more of the ornaments. His continued silence and unwavering gaze made her feel awkward. "Shouldn't we have Christmas carols on or something?"

"Of course. Do you have any?"

Lissy nodded and retrieved her phone, plugging it into the sound system on the bookcase. She hit play and grinned as "Grandma Got Run Over by a Reindeer" began. Her heart lifted a bit when Grayson chuckled.

"Ah, yes, my personal favorite. I used to play it to annoy *Grandmère*. I'll be right back." Grayson put the kitten down and bounded upstairs. He returned with a camera and tripod. "We must have pictures; it is Christmas, after all."

"Noooo, I look dreadful. No makeup, swollen eyes — please don't, Gray." She switched the music to The Raveonettes' "Christmas Ghosts."

"Hush." He snapped several pictures in quick succession and laughed when she made a face. "Perfect. You can enclose that one in your cards next year."

"No one sends Christmas cards anymore. Did you get something for the top of the tree?" Alyssandra placed the last ornament and stood back to admire her work.

"No, but hold on." He went to the kitchen and returned with *The National Intruder*. "When I was a boy, I had an *au pair* who taught me origami. Let me find the instructions I need." He dug his phone out of his pocket and scrolled. Pulling off the front page with his ex's picture on it, he threw it in the fire. He then took the next page and began folding. When he was done, it was a paper angel.

"That's amazing. Can you make other things?" she asked as she cut another piece of yarn and attached it to the angel.

She tried to reach the top of the tree. "I can't reach. You do it."

"We'll do it together, and I'll set the camera up to take a picture of us. I can do a crane from memory, but that's about it. Supposedly if you make a thousand, your wish will come true."

"Really? Have you made a thousand?"

"Probably. I was a lonely child."

"The angel is perfect."

Gray stood behind her and murmured, "Indeed, she is."

She glanced over her shoulder, but his face was unreadable. When the camera was set up and she was ready, he hoisted her toward the tree. "Up you go; make a wish."

His strong hands on her waist sent warmth rushing through every nerve in her body.

Lissy tied the angel to the top of the tree just as the camera snapped the picture. Gray slowly lowered her to the floor. When her feet were once again on the ground, she turned to face him. His hands remained on her waist, and her hands came to rest on his firm chest.

The steady beating of his heart picked up as she smoothed his shirt. Forget peace on earth, or good health, or extreme wealth — she was suddenly very aware that he was a man, and she was a woman, and they were alone for a few days. Her Christmas wish was to feel those hands on her bare skin.

"Thank you. For everything." She lowered her eyes. "I-I can't think of anyone I'd rather spend Christmas with," she confessed softly, looking up.

Only the rims of his blue irises were visible, and he jumped back as if he'd been shocked. "I need to start the grill. You can finish up in here." Turning on his heels, he fled.

Grayson shivered in his coat. The wind was biting even under the cover of the back porch. His phone buzzed as he started the fire in the grill. It was Frank.

Well, isn't that just great timing? Is he Jiminy Cricket?

"Frank."

"Trip…man, she's brutal. What a bitch."

The grill flared, and he stepped back. *Why would Frank call Alyssandra that—wait, who the hell is he talking about?* "Who?"

"Candie. Haven't you seen the crap she's spewing on social media and to the tabloids?"

"No, and reception here is terrible," he lied. "She may or may not have said it. You know how that works. How's the family?"

"Wonderful, but we wish you'd joined us. Lissy won't be here, either. I don't know what the hell is going on with that girl. I hope she isn't headed down a bad road. She flunked every damn class last semester. Travis is worried it's drugs. Jess thinks it's some guy…"

Grayson glanced nervously at the back door. "I wouldn't worry too much. She's a smart young woman."

"I dunno, the kid's just not been herself lately. More unfocused than usual."

"Maybe if everyone would quit treating her like a child—"

The back door opened, and Alyssandra held up the platter of steaks. *Definitely not a kid.* He motioned for her to stay put, not wanting her to slip and fall.

"It's snowing!" she squealed, running to the railing.

Grayson put his fingers to his lips and pointed at the phone. *Okay, still a kid.*

"Well, well, well, you asshole. No wonder you didn't want to come here for the holidays. Having a repeat of the infamous double-D-twin Christmas?" Frank chuckled.

"No—not that it's any of your business. Look, I need to go. Please give my love to Jessica and the children; I'll call on Christmas, *au revoir.*" He hung up and took the steaks from Alyssandra. "Get back inside. Where is your coat?" He threw the steaks on the grill.

"I'll get my coat in a minute. Who was on the phone?"

"Frank."

"Everything okay at home?"

"Yes, yes, now get back inside. It's much too cold out here. Do you want pneumonia?"

"But it's snowing! It's so pretty!" She leaned over the rail and stuck her tongue out to catch a snowflake.

He glared at her. "Go back inside."

"Fine. You're so old and stuffy sometimes." She marched inside, slamming the door.

Ouch. Grayson sighed as he finished grilling. Perhaps it was best she thought of him as old and stuffy. It helped to keep things in their proper perspective.

"I'm so full. I can't remember when I've eaten this much. The steak was perfect." Lissy placed the last dish in the dishwasher and wiped the counters. She looked out the window where the dusk-to-dawn light illuminated the snow coming down. "Is this a blizzard?"

Gray laughed. "You're such a southern girl. In New York, this would be considered a light snowfall. However, in this remote area, without snowplows, we will indeed be snowed in for the time being." He didn't look too excited about the prospect.

"Tomorrow, I'm going to build a snowman. And I'm glad I bought the stuff to make snow cream."

"Just make sure the snow you use is white, not yellow." He pulled away from the doorframe. "You can watch television, if you like. I think I'll read."

"Okay." Lissy followed him, picking up the knitting needles and gray wool as she made herself comfortable in the overstuffed chair. Grayson put on his reading glasses—which made him look smart and sexy—and stretched out on the sofa. Noëlle settled on his flat stomach, purring loudly. Lissy's mind flashed to the redhead and the look of bliss on Grayson's face when he'd climaxed. Her mouth went dry, and she busied herself with starting the muffler.

"I've always wondered how you got the name Grayson if you're French."

"One of my Deschanelle ancestors fell in love with the English governess. Her surname was Grayson. Four months after their marriage, a son was born and named Grayson Olivier Deschanelle." He turned the page in his book, a thriller crime story.

"That sounds like a romance novel. Speaking of which, you're reading an actual book? I use an e-reader."

"I like the feel of a book."

She took a sip of her wine, looking around the cabin. "I really love this place; it's so cozy. If this were mine, I'd want to live here year-round. Of course with the two kids, it isn't big enough for Frank and Jessica."

The log walls, rock fireplace, and pine bookcases gave the place a masculine feeling. It had been Frank's home before he married her sister. Jessica had added her touch in the decorating. They still escaped up here when they could get a set of grandparents to watch their kids. She pulled the yarn away from Noëlle, who had changed her mind about sleeping and decided to play.

"Stop, silly cat." Leaning over, she scratched the kitten behind her ears.

"You don't seem like the type of girl to knit," Gray murmured.

"Really? Why not? I find it relaxing. My mother taught me how. I love to sew, too. I can't always find what I want in a store, so I just make it."

Glancing up, she blushed when she found him staring at her like a hungry wolf. Immediately he returned his attention to his book. *Did I just imagine that?* She resumed knitting with shaking hands. Daydreaming, she wondered what he'd do if she launched herself over the coffee table and kissed him.

"That takes talent — to visualize a pattern and make it work. Which makes me wonder why you're in nursing school?"

"Because my parents want me to get a job. Nurses always find jobs." She sighed. "I hate it. And it's one of the reasons they're so mad at me. I've changed majors four times and padded my schedule with art classes. They think my love of fashion is just a *hobby*."

Gray closed his book, giving her his full attention. She loved that about him, the way he *listened* to her, as if what she had to say was important.

He glanced at the fire. "My father thought photography was a waste of time, too. So I understand."

"How did you persuade him otherwise?"

"I proved to him that I had a good eye. And I learned as much about it as I could on my own. It helps that I had the finances from a trust fund to do so."

"I don't have any money. And my parents don't *listen* to me."

"It's all in the presentation, Alyssandra. You have to approach it with determination and passion."

She shifted when he said *passion*, watching him stroke Noëlle.

"You may be right. I've certainly made enough mistakes lately. It's time I go for what I want, come hell or high water. I want to experience life, not stand on the sidelines."

"Sounds like a plan." He resumed reading.

"Gray?"

He looked up from his book and raised his brow.

"What if there's something else I want to learn. Would you help me?"

"Photography? I can easily show you the basics."

"No, not photography. The art of making love."

He blinked but didn't say a word as his throat bobbled.

She shrugged and bit her lip, wondering what had possessed her to say that out loud, but forged ahead. "I've only been with immature *boys*. I want to make love with a *man*. I mean, we're adults. We've both been through a lot. There's not a whole lot to do here for however long the snow lasts. They say sex is a great stress reliever. No biggie." She smiled impishly. "Well, not that I'm referencing your size. From what I saw the other night, it's plenty big—"

"Good God, Alyssandra." He snapped the book closed and sat up, running a hand through his hair. "The things you say…Do you ever think before you speak?" He whipped off his glasses and rubbed his brow.

"It's just sex, Grayson."

"That statement proves how young and naïve you are. It is never 'just sex.' There are *always* strings attached. That point was brought home painfully with Candie…"

"You read the article."

"Yes, I read the article: I'm a heartless prick. A man who never gave her a damn thing, including an orgasm, which is a lie. Trust me—she isn't *that* good of an actress." He stood, pacing and gesturing. "And now *you* say you want casual sex. Didn't you learn your lesson with Josh?"

Hurt and humiliated, her vision blurred. She concentrated on her knitting until she was unable to see the needles and dropped a stitch. Angrily, she closed her eyes, feeling mortified.

Grayson paused and squatted in front of her chair, gripping the arms as he looked up at her. He sighed and hung his head.

"I'm sorry."

She glared at him and lifted her chin. "No need to apologize. You're right, of course. *I'm* the one who should be *sorry.* I wasn't thinking. What would a man like *you* want with a silly nitwit like *me?*" She lowered her gaze so he wouldn't see the tears starting again. "I think I'll go to bed. It's been a long day, my nerves are shot, and I'm a little drunk," she mumbled.

"That might be best."

She put the knitting in the bag. Her chest ached, and she felt a little dizzy.

He stood and moved out of her way.

"Do you want the bed?" she asked.

"No, I'll sleep down here."

Lissy nodded and ran up the stairs, not looking back.

Grayson sighed. Maybe Candie was right. After the way he'd just spoken to Alyssandra, *heartless prick* pretty much *was* an accurate description. She'd been through hell the last few weeks, and he'd purposefully hurt her feelings to make her back off. He should've handled the situation with care. She was still young, and he was well aware of her crush on him over the years. Perhaps she didn't realize the full ramifications of her suggestion.

She's not that young.

He threw another log on the fire and stroked the kitten weaving in and out of his feet. After moping for a half an hour and finishing his wine, he decided he might as well turn in for the night, too. Again he wished there was more than one shower in the cabin. A renovation adding another full bath downstairs would be his gift for Frank's birthday this year. He trudged up the stairs and knocked on the bedroom door.

"Come in."

Grayson cracked the door and found her curled on her side. "Are you okay?"

"I'm fine. Good night." There was a false cheerfulness in her voice.

"I'll be done in a few minutes. I need to shower and brush my teeth."

Lissy sat up and wrapped her arms around her knees. "If the roads are passable tomorrow, I'll be out of your way. Just forget my earlier suggestion; it must've been the wine talking. Thank you for your help, Gray. I really do appreciate it. And I'm sorry I bothered you. This won't happen again, I promise. I'll never be this pathetic, *ever again*."

"Alyssandra—"

She gave a self-deprecating laugh. "That's the second time I've thrown myself at you, isn't it? How awful it must be to have to put up with a silly little girl trying to seduce you. You'd think I would've learned my lesson the first time you told me you weren't interested." She pushed her hair behind her ear and hugged her knees tighter.

"*Mon Dieu*, Alyssandra, you were sixteen the first time, and we were in the middle of a photo shoot. Of course I turned you down! You're not silly or pathetic. I shouldn't have brushed you off the way I did just now. But the truth is, I'm much too old for you, my darling girl."

He sat on the side of the bed, his elbows resting on his knees as he rubbed his face and sighed.

"But you're not old. A-And I'm a woman."

"I'm not old, but I *am* too old for you. And it would never be 'just sex' with us. I care about you too damn much. Therein lies the problem. But trust me, *mon chaton*, it is taking every ounce of my self-restraint not take you up on your offer. You are a beautiful *young* woman. Some man, some day will be lucky to teach you what you want to know."

His confession hung suspended in the air for a few seconds before he catapulted off the bed. In trying to soothe her hurt feelings, maybe he'd said too much. But he couldn't stand the thought of her thinking she wasn't good enough, beautiful enough. Grabbing a clean pair of pajama pants, he hurried to the bathroom to shower and brush his teeth.

He tried not to think about Alyssandra's outrageous suggestion, but the memory of her gorgeous breasts had him taking things in hand…When he opened the door after brushing his teeth, he found her sitting with her head against the headboard, arms crossed, watching him with those expressive eyes.

"Good night." He hoped he didn't look guilty.

"Gray, you sleep here. I'm not sleepy after all."

He watched her hop off the bed and dig through her suitcase, pulling out the silky pajama top before dragging a pillow and quilt toward the door.

"You can have the bed—" he offered, still feeling like a heartless jerk.

She came and stood in front of him, the dim light from outside casting a shadow on her face. "Someday, Grayson Deschanelle, you're going to realize I'm an adult, capable of making my own decisions, whether they're right or wrong. And in my heart, I know this could never be wrong." She stood on her tiptoes and gave him a soft kiss on his cheek.

She was gone before he could respond. He let out the breath he'd been holding and collapsed on the bed.

Lissy picked up her knitting and put it down again, too wound up to sleep or concentrate on the muffler. Her heart was broken all over again. That had to be the reason it was pounding so hard. But the way Gray had looked at her…*Surely he feels this connection, too?*

She looked at the time and sighed. *Too bad it's too late to call Eddie. He'd put things in perspective and make me laugh in the process.*

She decided to do some yoga to relax. Just getting in the moment and breathing would help realign her emotions.

Not thinking.

Not feeling.

Simply being.

She meditated after she completed her poses and felt more grounded and at peace, refusing to give in to the self-pity or self-destructive thoughts anymore. One heartless prank would not define who she was as a person. Grayson's inability to see her as a woman would not negate her feelings. She stood and stretched one last time before settling on the couch to knit.

The muffler would either be a thank-you gift, a Christmas gift, or a goodbye gift. Whichever it was, it would be made with love and given with no strings attached.

Chapter
Seven

The next morning, Grayson crept downstairs, not wanting to wake Alyssandra. The fire had died down to glowing embers, leaving a chill in the air. He shoveled the ashes and added a log, trying to ignore the sleeping beauty on the couch. The quilt was on the floor, and she had one arm thrown over her eyes. Noëlle slept curled up at her neck. She'd changed into the thin silk pajama top, and it fell just under her breasts.

Against his better judgment, he allowed himself to stare at her another moment. Damn, how he wanted to photograph her — nude in black and white. The truth was, Alyssandra *was* just his type — if only she were older. Guilt spun him on his heels and marched him into the kitchen to start coffee. He stood leaning on the counter, gazing out the window as the coffee brewed, forbidden fantasies warring with his conscience.

A loud yawn pulled his attention from the winter wonderland outside. He glanced over his shoulder at the mussed, sexy woman in the doorway. She stretched and her top rose. He brushed past her to the living area and slammed out the front door to retrieve some more wood for the fire, hoping an ice-cold blast of wind would cool him down.

The snow continued to fall, and his heart sank, knowing they'd be stuck together for several more days. His resolve to treat her like a little sister was melting faster than a snowball in hell. Shivering, he picked up some wood and stomped back into the cabin.

"Good morning." Alyssandra held two cups of coffee.

He acknowledged her with a grunt and a scowl, making two trips to stack wood next to the fireplace. When he finished, she handed him a cup of coffee before curling up in the chair. He stood with one arm on the mantle, staring at the flames as he sipped the coffee. He avoided her eyes, afraid she'd read his thoughts.

"Did you sleep well?"

Grayson shook his head and winced as the kitten climbed his leg. Unsnagging the sharp claws, he handed her to Alyssandra. "You?"

"Like a baby."

And indeed, she looked refreshed. The circles were gone from under her eyes, her hair hung in a sexy mess down her back, and dammit, her nipples were hard and beckoning. He turned to hide his arousal.

"May I use your laptop? I want to send Mother and Daddy an email, and my phone battery is dead. I think my charger's in the car. I wish they'd get in this century and learn to text. It would be so much easier."

"It's on the desk. And so is my charger, if it will work." He threw himself on the couch and moved the pillow over his lap as he drank his coffee, ignoring the persistent kitten batting at him for attention. He'd always heard cats favored those who didn't like them. "*Stupide petit chat,*" he murmured with a smile as the kitten chewed on his shirt button.

Lissy sat at the computer and waited for it to boot up. "Your charger won't work on my phone. What's your password?"

Fuck. He closed his eyes and didn't answer, wishing he could reel back time sixty seconds.

"Gray?" Lissy waited.

"I'll do it." He got up and tried to block her from seeing, but being nosy, she peeked anyway.

Her mouth dropped open. "Wait, was that my name? With 1231 on the end? That's not real secure."

He ignored her, but the back of his neck was bright red.

She stared at the screen. Not only had he used her name and birthday as his password, his desktop picture was an outtake from the Southern Unmentionables ad campaign.

It was a black and white photograph of her wearing his shirt. She'd never returned it and still wore it to sleep in at home. One time she'd even snuck it in her purse when he was visiting Frank, found Gray's cologne, and sprayed it.

In the picture, she was looking over her shoulder at the camera and the shirt had slipped off a bit. It was beautiful photo, revealing nothing inappropriate yet promising so much in an innocent, yet provocative way. She'd never seen this picture, another had been used for marketing.

Her eyebrows lifted, and she met his gaze, which smoldered like the center of a lit match before he looked away, clearly unnerved. It gave her a sense of feminine power. Biting her lip to keep from crowing with satisfaction, she typed in her email server.

Gray returned to the sofa, shoved her persistent cat aside, picked up his book and reading glasses, and studiously ignored her. The cat curled back up on his lap once he'd settled. The chatty note from her mother helped take her mind off her simmering desire. In her reply, she gave her parents vague information about her past twenty-four hours and assured them she would talk to them in a few days, on Christmas.

Next she checked her social media, ignoring the hundreds of posts about what people were doing for the holidays. She read Eddie's lament on his lack of love life and the impossibility of getting an A in microbiology due to his bitchy professor. It took two minutes to dash off a quick reply to Jessica and laugh at the meme Travis had sent her. It only took two seconds to delete the twenty-three messages from Josh without reading them and then block him.

Frustrated, she turned off the computer and returned her attention to Gray. He hadn't turned a page in the last ten minutes. Such a stubborn man…He wanted her just as much as she wanted him.

"Want some breakfast?" she asked, taking his empty coffee cup. For a brief second, she thought she saw a glimmer of pain in his eyes.

"No, thank you."

Through the window, she admired the pristine blanket of snow. "I'm afraid you're stuck with me for a few days."

"Yes," he croaked.

She bit her lip to keep from laughing as she went to the kitchen. After a silent victory dance in front of the coffee pot, she returned with his steaming cup.

Picking up her knitting, she sat across from him in the overstuffed chair. "My parents seem to be having fun in London. I think Daddy feels guilty he didn't let me come with them. They canceled the Paris portion of the trip to do later with me. Mother complained that he's spending way too much money on me and the grandchildren."

"*Maman* and *Papa* are in Paris with my grandmother, *Grand-mère*, doing the same—spending too much on the grandchildren," he replied.

Only the crackling of the fire broke the silence.

"Most of my friends are married and have children, but I've never seen myself as a parent," he mused.

"Me, either. *Obviously.*" Lissy gave a self-deprecating laugh.

His gaze met hers.

Why, oh, why is he fighting this? "I can't take care of myself. How would I ever take care of a kid?"

Smiling, his eyes crinkled as he sipped his coffee. "You're quite *young*, Alyssandra. Now is not the time for you to be a mother. You need to figure out your life first."

"You act like you're a hundred years old."

"I feel it," he mumbled morosely.

"I'll have plenty of time to figure my life out working at the stupid bank. I'm supposed to learn how hard it is to make money to support myself this next semester, and then go back to school." She shrugged and picked up the stitch she'd dropped. "Of course, I'll be living at home, so it isn't as if I'll really be supporting myself. But I'm smart enough not to point that out to Daddy."

"Perhaps this will give you time to plead your case for what you really want to do."

"I don't think Daddy will agree to me working in the sex industry."

Coffee sloshed onto his shirt. "Christ, Alyssandra, how in the world has your father kept from killing you?" He slammed his now half-empty coffee cup on the table.

"I'm kidding. Geezus, that was too easy…" She laughed and jumped up to refill his cup. Returning, she sat beside him and grinned when he shifted so his leg didn't touch hers. Another three cups of coffee, and he'd be almost civil.

"You look like shit, Gray. You need some sleep, and all this caffeine isn't helping."

He glared at her for a moment and then nodded as he rubbed his eyes with the heel of his hand. "What the hell will we do all day, snowed in?" He groaned.

Lissy snickered. He jumped up and poked the fire until it was roaring.

She decided to cut him some slack. "I'm going to make a snowman and go for a run in the snow. Then I'll make us some snow cream."

Grayson plucked the kitten out of the Christmas tree. "Perfect."

For God's sake, please get dressed before I do something we'll both regret…

He stormed into the kitchen, angry with himself. What the hell had he been thinking letting her use his laptop? He'd changed the desktop photo in New York after Candie left him. The password had been Alyssandra's name and birthdate for years. It was the longest word he could think of and remember at the time. She must think he was some sort of creeper. *Fuck, maybe I am.*

He needed sleep. He needed more coffee. *He needed her…* No! He didn't *need* her. He *wanted* her. Big difference. And he was thirty-nine years old, not some horny teenager unable to control himself. Refilling his coffee, his mind drifted to the vision of her curled up asleep in bed.

Shit, if he ever got her in *his* bed, he'd likely end up dead of a heart attack.

Three hours later, Alyssandra jumped up and down as she placed one of Frank's baseball caps on the snowman. Grayson snapped a photo, capturing her delight. Her eyes sparkled, and her cheeks and nose were pink, matching her hat and muffler.

"He's perfect, Gray!"

Her infectious laughter eased some of the anxiety he'd been harboring, and he chuckled. "Is this really the first snowman you've ever made?"

"I'm a Southerner. We don't get much snow. The one time we actually had over one or two inches, I was sick with the flu, and Mother wouldn't let me out of the house." She dropped to the ground, moving her arms and legs to make a snow angel. "This is so much fun. I think I want to live someplace where it snows all the time."

Grayson continued snapping pictures. "It gets old when you have to shovel the shit."

Lissy laughed and sat up, her eyes wide. "Shhh, listen."

Grayson lowered the camera. The woods were still except for the occasional sound of an animal in the woods or a chunk of snow falling from a branch. "I don't hear anything."

"I know. Isn't it peaceful?" She looked up at him like a snow sprite, her face full of wonder.

His heart melted.

"I've never been so happy in my life."

The smile she gave him was unaffected and real. She was perhaps the most down to earth, sweetest girl he'd ever known.

He admitted, "Same here." He held out his hand. "Come, let's walk through the woods."

She grabbed his hand and jumped up. "What if we get lost?"

"Then I shall turn cannibalistic and eat you for supper. Survival of the fittest will be our motto. Ever hear of the Donner Party?"

"I might not object to being *eaten*," she purred. Giggling, she scampered ahead of him.

It took him a full thirty seconds to realize what he'd said to warrant that comeback. Furious, he stomped after her.

"I seriously doubt you've ever had to shovel snow in your life," she called. "You were born with a silver spoon in your mouth." She stooped, and before he could react, a snowball sailed toward him. Luckily, she was a poor shot.

Hanging his camera on a tree branch, he scooped up some snow, packing it well. "You've met *Papa*. Do you seriously think he didn't make me work?"

"Olivier is a lot of bark—not much bite, from what I've seen."

Grayson snorted and threw the snowball, hitting her square in the chest. "That's because *Papa* spoils you like he does his grandchildren. When he does bite, though, he holds on like a pit bull. If you don't believe me, ask Frank." He knew his smile betrayed his deep love for his father.

"I adore your father. You're right; he does spoil me. I have beautiful underwear because of him. And he always brings me perfume from Paris when he visits."

He frowned when she drew back to lob another icy missile at him. "Watch your aim. Don't hit my camera that's ten feet away from me," he teased.

Wrinkling her nose, she threw and hit his shoulder.

"Better."

"Gray?"

"Yes?"

"Are you rich? I mean…I know your family's company is successful, and you're in demand as a fashion photographer, but can you buy anything you want and not think about it?"

He chuckled, grabbing his camera from the branch. This girl kept him off kilter like no other woman. "What a rude question, *mon chaton*. And yes, I'm very rich. One might even say disgustingly rich. I am the last descendent of my mother's family. As a trust fund baby, I have a substantial inheritance."

"Cool. So I have the solution to Daddy's idea that I should get a job."

Grayson photographed her as she walked toward him. "And what would that be?"

"I could be your mistress." She stared at him through the camera lens, and his hand froze before clicking the shutter. A tortured breath hissed through his teeth, and she laughed. "I'm just joking!"

"You read too many romance novels." He wasn't completely convinced she was joking and headed toward the cabin, needing a stiff drink to counteract his hard dick.

"There's no such thing as too many romance novels." Lissy joined him as if she hadn't said anything out of the ordinary, and they walked silently through the woods. Grayson stopped to take an occasional photo.

"I want to take some pictures." Lissy pouted.

He snapped the picture, focusing on her lower lip.

"Use your phone."

"It's in the cabin. I'll be careful with your precious camera. Please?" She tilted her head and twirled a lock of her damp hair around her finger. When he didn't budge, she added, "Pretty please? With sugar on top?"

"Okay." Better to focus on photography than her outrageous suggestion. He handed her the camera and gave her a quick lesson on composition, setting it to automatic so she could point and shoot.

Arms crossed, he leaned against a tree as she played, taking pictures of God knows what. It didn't matter; he enjoyed watching her. Carefree and enthusiastic, she ran through the woods, squealing with pure, unadulterated joy. He even attempted a slight smile when she focused the camera on him. He hated having his picture taken.

"Stop." He held up his hand and pointed to his right. "Not me. Take a photo of the cardinal over there."

Lissy took a picture of the red bird before sneaking another shot of Gray. Devastatingly handsome in his jeans and coat, he looked like some Byronic hero against the snow. She zoomed in and caught a picture of just his enigmatic, ice blue eyes and long, dark lashes. The raw emotion in them took her breath away, and in spite of the cold snow, her cheeks felt hot.

She skipped over to where he stood and handed him the camera. "Can you take one of the two of us? Please? I don't know how to do a selfie with a camera; I don't think my arms are long enough."

He pulled her close and turned the camera to face them. "Ready?"

She nodded and smiled. After capturing the image, he showed it to her.

"Dammit, Gray, you made a face." She frowned and slapped his arm. "Do it again, please."

He laughed and took another, this time tickling her when he snapped the photo. Again, it was a silly picture. He snapped a series of quick photos before showing her again.

"Oh my God. These are horrible. We have to promise never to share them with anyone. Pinky swear."

He hooked his little finger with hers. "Agreed. Besides, we can't. Our families don't know you're in Tennessee, remember?"

"I know. Would it be so bad if they did?"

"Do you want to face the questions about why you're here?"

She shook her head. "You're right. I, um, wanted you to know that I appreciate everything you said after I found out I was the butt of a joke. It meant a lot to me."

"Part of your charm has always been your joy for life. Don't lose that, my darling girl." He brushed the outside of her cheek with the back of his fingers.

He'd called her that before. She didn't point it out, not wanting to spoil the moment. Instead she said, "Please, Gray, one serious photo, just for us. I want to remember today."

"Let me get the tripod. We'll take one with the snowman."

"I don't know how serious a photo with a snowman is, but okay." With wild abandon, she ran ahead, slipped, and ended up on her butt. She lay there giggling.

"I'm glad I switched to video," Gray teased. "If it were the Olympics, you'd receive a one from the French-American judge. Points taken off for your landing."

"You filmed that?" She narrowed her gaze and scraped up a quick snowball. He managed to duck, but the snowball hit the branch above him, raining snow down.

"Watch the camera!" A string of French expletives followed as he wiped his face and then the lens.

"Sorry!" She jumped back to her feet, dusting off her bottom. "That smarted. Snow isn't as fluffy as it appears."

He stormed toward the cabin and slipped on the slick step, nearly falling. This time a very American curse word came out. The murderous look he shot her when she snickered made her laugh that much harder.

A minute later he returned with the tripod, ignoring her excitement when a rabbit hopped by. At last the camera was ready.

She sidled close as they posed, and he stiffened.

When they'd finished, she looked through the ten photos. "Those are awful. Why won't you smile? Look at your face; you look constipated. One more. And this time pretend you like me."

"I'm not supposed to be in front of the camera. I'm not, nor have I ever been, photogenic. I have baby pictures and tabloid pictures to prove it."

"I bet you were an *enfant terrible*." Standing in front of him, she pulled his arms around her waist.

"So my grandmother says. My father wasn't around enough to know."

"I'm sorry."

He shrugged. "Let's get this over with."

"Okay." Mischievously, she wiggled her butt against him. His warm breath hissed in her ear. As soon as the shutter clicked, he stepped away as if she were contagious.

She looked at the photo and sighed. "Oh, Gray. You look so stiff and uncomfortable."

His face reddened. Now that she thought about it, maybe being *stiff* was what made him uncomfortable.

"Why won't you smile? Do it again," she begged.

Shaking his head, he readied the camera, grumbling, "You can take a hundred pictures of me, and maybe one will be halfway decent. One more and that's it. Ready?"

She nodded, spun around, and kissed him as the camera snapped the photo. His lips lingered on hers.

"No," he whispered.

"*Oui*," she replied.

Her heart raced, and her world spun as if on a merry-go-round. She held the lapels of his coat to keep from falling.

His hands wrapped into her hair, and he captured her mouth again. This time her lips curled with triumph.

He pulled her closer, deepening the kiss. It was a kiss of possession, almost punishing, and the most erotic thing she'd ever experienced.

It wouldn't surprise her if the snow was melting around them. His tongue explored her mouth, and she laced her fingers behind his neck, feeling intoxicated. Abruptly, Gray pushed her away, shaking his head. Their ragged breathing looked like wisps of smoke between them.

"Stop, Alyssandra. Please, for the love of God, just stop." He closed his eyes, pinching the bridge of his nose. "We can't do this."

Confused, Lissy stared at him, searching his face. The air between them hung thick with desire. *Not do this? How can we not?*

"I don't want to stop. I want you to make love to me. I refuse to deny what I'm feeling, and neither should you. In case you haven't noticed, I'm an adult, not a little girl."

"Fuck." He turned away, running a hand through his hair as he paced. His swearing cycled through various languages.

She covered her mouth, hiding her smile. "Gray, calm down. The roads are impassable, I'm rusty on my CPR, and you're *old*, remember?"

He stopped in front of her, glaring, his chest heaving as he tried to catch his breath. "That statement, Alyssandra, is *precisely* the problem. *I am much too old for you.*"

She crossed her arms in front of her chest, trying not to laugh. "Then by all means, carry on."

"If you don't stop, I swear to God I will turn you over my knee —"

She winked and purred, "I love it when you talk dirty, *mon amour.*"

To her utter surprise, he picked her up and threw her over his shoulder. She laughed the entire trek back to the cabin, bouncing upside down. Just before climbing the steps, he gave her bottom a sound *smack* that stung like hell...and turned her on like nobody's business.

Chapter
Eight

Grayson slammed the door, throwing his equipment on the end table. He turned, and Alyssandra slid down his body. Pinning her against the front door, he searched her face, looking for any hesitation, drinking in her magnificence like a man dying of thirst.

Am I dreaming? Hallucinating? Have I completely lost my mind?

Her lower lip quivered, but not from the cold, judging by the hungry look on her face. When she licked her lower lip, he groaned. His resolve to treat her like a younger sister crashed around them like an avalanche. Closing his eyes, he pressed his forehead to hers. She smelled of the woods and the sweet scent he'd come to associate with her alone. He wanted to devour every inch of her body, savoring her like a seven-course meal. A remnant of his conscience reminded him of her age, her vulnerability; he offered her one last chance to stop this.

"*Dis moi d'arrêter,*" he rasped hoarsely.

"What?" she whispered, gripping his coat.

"Tell me to stop, Alyssandra. For God's sake…"

"No." Standing on tiptoe, she trailed butterfly kisses across his jaw and whispered, "There is no stopping this, Grayson. This is what I want, what you want. It's kismet."

"No. It's insanity."

Her silver eyes appeared as serene as a still lake. "Perhaps it is, because I'm crazy for you."

"I make you no promises. Do you understand? I will not declare my love for you, nor will I get down on bended knee to ask you to marry me. I want you to have no doubts about this. I care for you, but I do not love you. This is sex only, no strings attached. When we return to the real world, we will never mention these few stolen days."

"I understand. Now it's my turn. I want to stay until after Christmas. Please?"

"Until the snow melts and you can get home."

"What if the snow melts tomorrow?"

"It won't."

"I want you for my birthday."

"I'm not much of a present, Alyssandra. And you will be home by your birthday, I promise. This is a terrible idea—" He moved to back away. *Stop, stop stop…*

She grabbed his lapels. "Until Friday, the twenty-eighth. Please?"

Her pupils dilated, and that full, pouty mouth tempted him beyond his limit.

"Think about it: this could be perfect. We're both going in knowing we're simply connecting on a physical level. Total honesty. Do you have any idea how wonderful that sounds to me after the crap Josh put me through?"

His last shard of self-restraint dissipated. "I do understand. I was with Candie Fontaine, remember?" He grinned at her, his hands moving down her waist to cup her firm, round ass. "Let me hear you say, 'This isn't a long-term relationship.'"

"Why?"

"I want to know you understand."

"Quit treating me like a child."

"You're only twenty!"

"You're hung up on this age thing. I'll be twenty-one in a few days. Look, I know I'm not that experienced, but you can teach me."

Grayson backed away and threw his hands up in frustration. "See? I knew this wouldn't work. You're already making it complicated. Never mind. We got caught in the minute—"

"Moment."

"What?"

"The phrase is *caught in the moment*. And if you believe that, you're in denial."

"I'm not in denial. I'm now being fully rational. This is a huge mistake. I'm going to start some coffee while you get out of those wet clothes. Go." *Save yourself, Alyssandra.*

Lissy crossed her arms.

Hell, I don't even sound convincing to myself. He hurried into the kitchen, putting distance between them.

"Yes, *sir,*" she hollered snidely, stomping upstairs. *Condescending, bossy asshole. How dare he treat me like I'm a child? He wants this as badly as I do.*

She tore off her clothes and hopped into a hot shower she didn't need. Her anger had heated her sufficiently. As she dried off, a wicked idea formed, and she laughed at her reflection in the mirror. After brushing her teeth, she ran her fingers through her damp hair one last time before skipping downstairs.

Standing in the kitchen with his back to her, Gray had removed his coat, wet socks, and shoes. He stood looking out the window, drinking a cup of coffee and shivering. She marched into the room.

"Coffee is ready," he said. "I'm going to shower—" He turned, and his mouth fell open. "*Merde.*" He slammed his coffee cup down so hard it sloshed onto the counter.

"You told me to get out of my wet clothes; I'm just being an obedient *little girl.*" She cocked her head to the side and grinned. Hands on her hips, she thrust her breasts out to their best advantage. Her nipples hardened as he continued to stare.

Just when she thought maybe this wasn't a good idea, she found herself pressed into his hard body, his hand tangled in her hair, the other cupping her bottom. His mouth slanted over hers, and there was nothing gentle in his kiss. It was one of barely controlled fury, and she thrilled in it. Tearing his lips from hers, he kissed her shoulder and nipped her neck with his teeth. His warm breath tickled as he murmured something in French. For all she knew, he could've been reciting the Ten Commandments. Whatever he said, it sounded sinfully delicious. She wrapped her legs around his waist and grasped his neck.

"There's no stopping this," she whispered, tugging his earlobe with her teeth and kissing across his strong, scruffy jaw.

"I'm afraid you're right," he replied, carrying her up the stairs to the bedroom. Gently placing her on the bed, he cupped her face in his hand. She moved to sit up, but he stilled her. "Let me enjoy the moment," he murmured, caressing her cheek. "You're even more beautiful than my wildest imaginations."

He pulled off his damp shirt, and Lissy smiled, enjoying the movement of his pecs as he tossed the shirt away. Reaching up, she trailed her index finger down the ripples of his abdomen, loving the hard ridges and mesmerized by the dark trail disappearing under his belt. His stomach contracted when she hit a ticklish spot. She sat up, following her fingers with her tongue.

"Back at ya, Gray." She fumbled with his belt and jeans, and the rest of his clothes joined his shirt on the floor. He stood naked before her, seemingly unembarrassed under her frank perusal. And why should he be? He was perfect. "You're gorgeous," she stammered.

"Hardly. You're beautiful, my darling girl." Gray smiled, pushing her into the pillow as he stretched his body over hers. He licked, nibbled, and kissed her as his hands roamed. His erection pressed against her, causing sensory overload. Her brain turned to mush, and she whimpered. He smiled into her neck.

"Is this real, Alyssandra? Or am I dreaming?" he whispered.

"Very real." She brushed his lips with her thumb.

"You have graced my nightmares and haunted my dreams...*Je t'adore, mon chaton.*" He stroked the hair off her forehead as he cupped her breast. He thumbed her nipple, and she arched her back as the current went straight from her breast to between her legs.

"So responsive," he murmured, taking the hardened peak in his mouth and tugging with his teeth.

"Dear God, Gray," she gasped, her hands in his hair as she moaned and moved underneath him.

He trailed his hand softly down her abdomen, and his lips soon followed. His blue eyes were so dilated she could barely see his irises.

"Do you know my favorite part of your body, Alyssandra?" he whispered.

"My smart mouth?"

He chuckled. "I have plans for that smart mouth, and as delightful as it is, no."

She shook her head as his hands and lips continued in their magical, hypnotically erotic descent.

"Right here, the curve of your hip. This dip from your hipbone to your abdomen." His lips followed his hand. "So incredibly perfect. I want to photograph it." He licked and nibbled, and she whimpered as her muscles quivered. Slowly he made his way lower, and she was convinced she would die before he ever got to the delicious spot that throbbed to be touched.

At last his tongue flicked over her clit, and she cried out, closing her eyes and bunching the duvet in a death grip. With expertise he circled and teased her until she careened into a mind-numbing orgasm. She panted; her lungs couldn't seem to get enough air in her frenzied state.

"Please, Gray," she whispered, reaching out to stroke his hair.

He gazed up at her with a wickedly seductive smile as he tasted his way back up her stomach. Once again, he lavished attention on her nipples as he inserted one, then two fingers inside her. Her eyes widened, and she moaned and writhed beneath him, exploding once more, crying out his name.

She peeked at him from under her lashes and found him smiling.

"Still with me, my darling?" He chuckled when all she could do was nod. He left for a moment, scrounging in his suitcase, and returned with a condom.

"May I?" she asked, reaching for the foil packet.

He rolled onto his back, his head resting on his hands as he smiled at her. "By all means. Use me and abuse me to your pleasure, Alyssandra."

"*Au contraire, Monsieur Deschanelle.* Your wish will be my command."

He laughed and stroked her hair. "I could get used to that."

"Payback can be a bitch," she warned, whisper-kissing along his chiseled jaw to the sweet spot on his neck that made him growl. She bit him lightly, and he hardened beneath her. She teased her way lower, biting his nipple. His hands fisted in her hair as she leisurely worked her way down the tempting trail to that which she sought. Grasping him in her hand, she rubbed her thumb across the head of his erection. Her gaze locked with his as she lowered her mouth, taking him deeper and deeper. He closed his eyes, stroking her hair as his hips bucked.

After a few minutes of her attention, he yanked her hair, whispering hoarsely. "Lissy, stop. You're killing me."

She paused and grinned at him, waggling her brows. "But what a way to go, huh?" Quickly, she unrolled the condom and sheathed him. Their laughter filled the room as he hauled her closer before flipping her over, pinning her with his body.

"If I'm going to die a happy man, I want to be deep inside you."

"You called me Lissy," she murmured softly. "Which I like, but I also like it when you call me Alyssandra. It rolls off your tongue—"

"Alyssandra," he barked, but his blue eyes twinkled.

"Yes?" She brushed the hair out of his eyes and licked the cleft in his chin.

"Do you want to talk or—?"

"Or. *Definitely* or." She lifted her hips to meet him as he plunged inside, forging their bodies into one. He hesitated a moment, allowing her time to adjust, kissing her and murmuring in French. He then began moving slowly, smiling when she moaned, needing more. She marveled at how right everything was in this moment. It was as if her soul had been an empty glass, and now it overflowed with passion, happiness, completeness—and something more. But now was not the time to analyze feelings. It was a time to experience being a woman.

His kiss deepened, becoming possessive. The French nothings he whispered in her ear and the warm hands skittering over her skin flared her passion into a raging inferno. Slamming deeper and harder, over and over, he teased her, bringing her close and backing off, chuckling when she slapped his arm with frustration.

"Something you want?"

She narrowed her eyes and dug her nails into his biceps. "Now."

"Patience is a virtue."

"I'm neither patient nor virtuous."

He threw his head back, laughing, and grabbed her hips, allowing him deeper access. Her eyes flew opened and widened.

"Look at me," he growled. The sound of their harsh breathing and slick bodies slapping against one another filled the air.

When she came, it was like the thrill of bungee jumping—falling with adrenaline pumping but feeling totally safe. With her legs wrapped tight around his waist, her inner muscles contracted around him. A few more hard strokes and he followed her over the precipice, shouting her name before collapsing on top of her.

Her heart raced to the point of pain, and she closed her eyes, gulping air.

When she could speak, she gasped, "I think I've died and gone to heaven." She kissed his forehead and wrapped her arms around him, wishing they could stay like this forever.

"*La petite mort,* a wonderful way to die," he agreed against her neck. He pushed up and peered down at her. "Lesson one complete. You made an A."

She laughed.

After disposing of the condom, he gathered her in his arms, pulling her close. His thumb made lazy circles on her back, lulling her toward sleep.

"Gray?"

"Hmm?"

"Thank you." She closed her eyes, sighed contentedly, and snuggled in to him. "It was better than just sex."

"I'm going to kill your cat." Spooning her back, Grayson handed Lissy the annoying, meowing kitten.

"Aw, don't do that. She's sweet. Besides, this is what you invited me for the first night I was here." She cuddled the kitten, and then turned her head and kissed his cheek.

"What?"

She rolled over and placed the now-purring kitten on the pillow next to him. "A *ménage à trois.* Two pussies and you."

"Not quite what I had in mind." His eyes crinkled with his smile. "Do you really like that sort of thing?"

"I will plead the fifth and go shower." He kissed her nose before getting up.

As he strode toward the bathroom, Lissy whistled her appreciation.

"What time is it? God, you have such a nice ass."

"*Merci.* It's two in the afternoon, and I'm starving. Go cook, or at least throw us together some sandwiches. And don't forget, you promised me snow cream."

"You're so bossy," she grumbled, climbing out of bed. Shrugging into one of his shirts, she scooped up the kitten and headed downstairs. The glowing embers of the fire roared back to life with the log she added. Under her breath she hummed happily and plugged in the Christmas tree lights. This all felt so homey, so comfortable.

She reminded herself it wasn't going to last.

Chapter
Nine

White Christmas played on the television as Lissy knit, and the soft light from the fire and Christmas tree added to the ambience. Luckily the power had remained on, but the roads were still impassible. The past three days had been the best of her life. They'd laughed, played in the snow, and Gray was giving her photography and cooking lessons. He'd also taught her the art of making love. College boys would never hold a candle to this man. No man ever would. With him, she was finding herself after being lost.

She'd completed the muffler and a beanie and now worked on a fun extra present she was knitting for Gray. Every so often, she stopped the kitten from playing with the yarn.

After dinner, Gray had stretched out on the couch to read. But his book lay untouched on his chest as he slept. She stopped knitting, drinking in every detail of the moment. It was unfortunate the snow would only last so long and her happiness would come to an end, unless she could convince him otherwise…

Shadows played across his handsome face. She loved the cleft in his chin and the sexy scruff on that impossibly stubborn, square jaw. She contemplated sneaking over to steal a kiss. Instead, she picked up her phone from the end table and took a picture.

Just a few days.

It would never be enough.

The rest of her life wouldn't be enough.

For all her talk of being okay with a fling, she was a liar. She wanted forever with him.

"Please tell me you're not taking pictures of me sleeping." His eyes remained closed, but his lips curved into a smile.

"*Moi?*"

"*Oui, toi.*"

"Okay, I admit it, but it's because I never want to forget how peaceful you look." She finished knitting the row, tucked it away, and turned off the television. "Do you want more snow cream?"

"No, thank you. I believe it sent me into a diabetic coma. Either that or this movie put me to sleep. I don't think any self-respecting soldier would break out in song and dance for his commander." He stretched, and the book tumbled to the floor. Noëlle jumped and took off running, climbing the tree.

"Hush, this is my favorite holiday movie. I love the songs, the clothes. It's fun." Lissy removed the nervous cat from the shaking tree and knelt beside the couch, cooing and petting her. She looked up and found Gray staring.

"The firelight on your face is beautiful. Someday…" He reached to pick up his book, but Lissy released the squirming cat and laced her fingers with his.

"Someday what?"

He stroked her hair, and she purred with contentment, averting her eyes from his, afraid he'd see the depth of her feelings, ruining what little time they had left.

"I want to—never mind." He wrapped her hair around his finger.

"Gray? Would you fulfill one of my fantasies, if I asked?" she blurted, looking back at him.

He rolled to his side, propping his head on his hand. Raising one eyebrow, his smile widened. "How kinky?"

Lissy blushed. "No, not that kind, Well…not yet."

"Pity. I rather hoped it involved those stilettos you wore when you were a teen," he murmured into her neck.

"But you made me take them off and put on flats. Right after you scrubbed my face."

"Because they were too provocative for your age. You were still in braces." He tugged her hair playfully.

"That's not fair. You photograph young models all the time. I'm pretty sure they wear sexy shoes."

"It's a job."

"Do you get turned on photographing them?"

"I'm *working*, Alyssandra."

"That's a non-answer. I bet you do. Did Candie ever get jealous?"

He didn't answer that either.

Laughing, she pretend-pouted and squealed when he hauled her to lie on top of him. She settled in like a smug housecat. He stroked her back as she gazed at the fire.

"I wanted you when I was teenager," she confessed softly.

"I know."

She turned and propped her chin on her folded hands and looked into his fathomless blue eyes. "And you wanted me," she stated matter-of-factly, holding his gaze, daring him to deny it.

She felt her power as a woman as she waited for his response. It was a heady feeling, especially after her disastrous previous relationships.

"Don't be ridiculous." His eyes shifted, and his brow furrowed.

She traced his lips with her finger. To be such a smart man, he sure was clueless. Couldn't he see this attraction between them was bigger than they were, cosmic by its very nature?

"I thought you hated me at times," she confessed.

"I never hated you. I was too old—"

"I suppose. You know, Juliet was only thirteen when she fell for Romeo."

"And you see how well that ended. Plus, Romeo was only a year or two older—"

Lissy placed her fingers over his mouth. "Gray, if I died right now, I would die happier than I've ever been in my life." She shook her head when he started to speak. "I know…I know…No strings attached, no long-term anything. This is enough."

She laid her head down so he wouldn't see the lie in her eyes. This *wasn't* enough. But it would have to be, because it was all he was willing to give. Perhaps someday she'd move on. But even if she did, she knew when she took her last breath, she'd remember her time here. He was the one who'd truly taught her to live.

"You never did tell me your fantasy." He continued stroking her hair and back.

"You never said what you wanted from me, either."

"I want to photograph you the way I see you — as a beautiful woman."

She smiled. "It makes me happy that you see me that way. Dance with me. That's my fantasy." She sat up and looked down at him.

"Something slow?" He smiled at her the way he did when he'd indulged her teenaged pouts at family gatherings.

Lissy shoved her hair out of her face and grinned. "Well, duh, you're old."

"Brat." He laughed as he gave her a kiss on her forehead. "Put on some music while I get my decrepit ass up."

Lissy plugged her phone into the sound system. The soft strains of Edith Piaf singing "La Vie En Rose" filled the cabin.

"Very nice. I suppose you think this is my kind of music?" His grimace turned to a smile as he pulled her close and began dancing.

"Sure. It's old, and it's French. I love this song. I don't know what it means, but it's beautiful."

She buried her nose in his chest. He smelled so good, like winter and fire. Tingles of desire zipped through her as they danced. *In this moment, he's mine. And life is perfect.*

As they moved, Gray softly translated the song for her.

She looked up. "I think that may be the most beautiful love song ever."

"Some say so. Hold on," he added after a moment. "I'll put on a real classic for you."

"I don't know how to waltz, Gray."

He clutched his chest as if mortally wounded, and she laughed.

"Very funny. Just how old do you think I am? This was *Papa's* favorite when I was growing up. My grandmother did not approve."

He plugged his phone into the sound system, and the sound of T. Rex's "Bang a Gong (Get it On)" filled the cabin. Grayson jumped on the coffee table. Lissy plopped on the couch, stunned by this side of him. Singing along, he slowly unbuttoned his shirt.

Damn. She ran to her purse, dug out a dollar, and tucked it in his waistband. He winked at her, and her heart raced like an Indy car.

He shrugged out of his shirt and threw it over her face. Grabbing her hand, he pulled her to the coffee table. He danced against her as he sang in her ear. A quick move and he was off the table and lifting her in the air before sliding her down his chest in a *Dirty Dancing* kind of way. When her feet hit the ground, he twirled her away from him and snapped her back close. With the expertise of a competitive dancer, he moved her around the room until she was breathless.

She gave up trying to keep up with him and bent over double, gasping for air. Kneeling in front of her, his hands skimmed her butt and down her thighs. With a quick jerk, he had her on the floor and stretched out on top of her, finishing with a searing kiss that left them both breathless and laughing.

"Now *that* is a classic, *mon chaton.*" He tapped her nose.

"Much better than a waltz. I can't breathe…"

"Are you okay?" He frowned.

She gulped air and closed her eyes, breathing deeply.

"Alyssandra?"

"I'm fine. I can't imagine your father dancing to that." She opened her eyes and cupped his cheek, resting her thumb in the cleft of his chin and giving him a quick, sweet kiss.

The fire crackled beside them, but it was nothing compared to the heat between them. Led Zeppelin's "I Can't Quit You Baby" wailed seductively through the cabin.

"You scared me. You get short of breath a lot…" He looked worried.

She smiled to reassure him. "You make my heart race, sexy man."

He stared into her eyes with a look of wistful resignation. "It's getting late." He rose and turned off the music.

In truth, her heart was still pounding, and she felt an odd sense of dread. "I'm not tired yet. I think I'll stay up a bit longer."

"Are you sure you're okay?" He sounded concerned but looked like a trapped animal. "I think you're still suffering from a type of panic attack. Promise me you'll get some help for this when you get home, if it continues."

"I'm fine, and I will." She smiled to reassure him, and he gave her a kiss before heading up the stairs.

She was far from fine. She was falling in love. Lissy stared at the fire as the clock on the mantel ticked away their remaining time.

The next morning, Grayson carefully eased out of bed so as not to awaken Alyssandra. It was Christmas Eve, and aside from the cat, he had relatively little to give her. The least he could do was prepare *Grand-mère*'s cheese soufflé for breakfast. Last night, as he'd stared at her, he'd seen so much more in her face than he wanted to acknowledge. She was falling in love.

And like a coward, he'd run.

He checked his phone for an update on the weather. It looked like they'd be here at least through Christmas. She was too inexperienced to drive on icy roads.

Inexperienced but a fast learner, in all things...

He stopped the thought from going any further and started the coffee. Thankfully, *Grand-mère* wouldn't be here to criticize the fact that he had no dry mustard for the soufflé. Giving Noëlle a saucer of milk and egg, he smiled as she lapped it up. When she was finished, she weaved in and out of his legs, chirping her gratitude. He'd miss this silly cat.

I'll miss more than the cat.

And that was the problem. He'd miss Alyssandra. Scrubbing his face, he berated himself for being weak. He shouldn't have let things progress like this.

This had to end. If the press got wind of this affair, Alyssandra would be hounded as his rebound from Candie Fontaine. The tabloids would shred her. If her world entangled with his, she'd lose her budding identity. Maybe he should call his friend Dylan, who'd been through something similar. But only ten years separated Dylan and his wife. Alyssandra was almost young enough to be his daughter.

Warm arms wrapped around his neck, and she kissed his cheek. "Good morning. Something smells delicious."

"*Soufflé au fromage.*"

"Sounds fancy." She refilled his coffee cup and poured herself one as well.

Gazing at her sleep-flushed face, bright eyes, and soft smile, his heart flip-flopped. *Why is this wrong?*

"We need to call our parents. It's Christmas Eve. What's the time difference between here and London and Paris?"

And there was the number-one reason. He was too old for her. Their families would never accept them as a couple.

"Five hours for London, six for Paris. One hour for Frank and Jessica."

"I bet the kids are out of control. I was always excited on Christmas Eve, weren't you? Mother would keep us busy baking, and sometimes Daddy would take us to the movie. Once Travis and Jessica started driving, they'd take me."

"Do you wish you'd gone home to be with them? When I was a boy, I remember Christmas Eve as being quiet. *Papa* would come home, and we'd attend mass. In the morning he'd watch me open presents and then go back to work. Things were better after he married *Maman.*"

Her gray eyes sparkled, and she bit her lip. "Go home? And miss this? Not at all. Do you?"

He didn't reply, checking on the soufflé instead. It looked perfect.

"Gray?"

"It might have been best," he admitted, placing the puffed perfection on the table with a sigh. "I'm a weak man—"

"Or I'm simply irresistible. And persistent," she interrupted. "I hate to think of you being a lonely little boy at Christmas. I will shower you with attention this year, to make up for the sad memories." She hugged him tight.

"Indeed, you are irresistible, my darling girl. That's the problem."

He sat, ready to serve, but she caught his hand. "I have no regrets. None. Please don't second-guess our decision. It's Christmas, a time for hope and believing. This thing between us? I think it qualifies as a miracle. At least in my book it does. We'll keep this secret and enjoy every minute, okay?"

He ran the back of his fingers across her cheek and leaned in to kiss her. She hummed in the back of her throat and teased his lips with her tongue.

Pulling away, he chuckled, serving her some breakfast. "Eat before it goes flat."

"Yum. Is this a family recipe?"

"It's my grandmother's, not that she ever personally cooked it, and it's lacking dry mustard. But it will do. I'm afraid our groceries are running out. But the weather said this morning the roads should clear by tomorrow afternoon or the next day."

"Perhaps we'll have to eat one another after all." She winked and smiled.

"You always say the damnedest things."

"And I have wonderful ideas," she countered.

"I can't argue with that."

Lissy tiptoed downstairs wearing Gray's shirt after a lovely lazy day of sex and naps. She laughed as Noëlle batted an ornament off the tree and proceeded to chase it all over the living room.

It was three in the afternoon here, so it would be eight in London. Lissy picked up her phone and dialed her mother.

"Merry Christmas."

"Lissy! Merry Christmas. Hold on, let me put you on speaker."

Lissy smiled as her mother fumbled with the phone and heard her father growl, "Give me the damn phone. There. Now it's on speaker, but it's hard to hear. We're walking to take pictures of London at night before church. Do you want to do that camera thing where you can see it, Alleycat?"

Lissy laughed at her father's use of her nickname. But no way she'd risk video chatting. "No, thanks. My hair's a mess, no makeup, and I can't talk but a minute. Merry Christmas. Are you and Mother having a good time?" She snitched a candy cane from the tree.

"Yes, yes, but I admit, it would've been better with you here. Your mother was right; I was a bit rough on you and too hasty canceling your trip. We'll come back with you. I promise."

Her eyes filled with tears. "I miss you, too, Daddy."

"Are you sure you don't want to go home and spend Christmas with Jessica and the kids? Which friends are you with? I hope you're having a good time. I miss you." Mother's voice was a combination of worry and suspicion.

"I'm fine and couldn't get home if I wanted to. It's snowing here and so beautiful! Not like the ice storms we get in Alabama—this is real snow." She glanced up, smiling as Gray approached, yawning. "Um, I wish I was there and love you both, but I need to go. Merry Christmas and have fun!"

"Send us pictures, dear. And call your sister tomorrow. Travis will be there, too. And wear a coat. You never wear a coat. And drive safe, we'll be home two days before your birthday. Of course your father has the usual party planned—"

"We'll be home by the time you finish this conversation," her father interrupted. "See you soon, Lissy. Merry Christmas."

"I love you. Bye." She hung up the phone, missing her parents more than she realized. She blinked the tears away.

"I should have insisted you go home for Christmas," Grayson commented, kissing her forehead. He'd put on a pair of worn jeans and a pale blue shirt, but she stopped him from buttoning it by kissing his chest.

"No, no. I'm fine. Besides, as fast as the weather moved in, I probably would've been stuck on the side of the road. You need to call your parents, too. It's Christmas Eve, after all."

Without thinking, she buttoned his shirt and straightened his collar. Glancing up, she found him staring at her, an unreadable expression on his face. "Did I do something wrong?"

He shook his head as if clearing a thought. "No, of course not. Go shower and get dressed."

"Why? Do I stink?"

"Not at all. You smell like sex and candy, sinfully decadent and delicious. However, I want to take pictures. It's Christmas Eve. And then I want to explore that lush body of yours from head to toe." He gave her butt a swat.

She scampered from the room. "Goodness…"

Grayson sat at the table and rubbed a hand over his face. When Alyssandra had straightened his collar, it had felt…wifely. And comfortable. His stepmother often did the same for his father. Honestly, this woman was fun, exciting, sweet, and sexy—the perfect girl. Life was going to be pretty damn boring when she left. The thought worried the hell out of him.

Just sex. No strings attached…

He fished his phone out of his pocket. Nothing would ground him more than talking to his father.

"Joyeux Noël, Papa."

He smiled as his father predictably fired off questions in his staccato French regarding Candie, wasting no time on generalities. Then *Papa* reminded him at least three times about the photo shoot in Paris after the holidays. After the brief conversation, his father wished him a *Joyeux Noël* and unceremoniously handed the phone to his stepmother.

"Merry Christmas. Sorry about that. You know your father is incapable of actually relaxing on vacation. He's also as concerned as I am about this business with Candie. What do you think about having a publicist handle this for you? Are you okay, son?"

He sighed. "I'm fine, *Maman*. And I don't need a publicist. It will disappear as soon as someone else piques their interest. Have you bought out the stores for the grandchildren?"

"Yes, of course. I always enjoy shopping in Paris." He heard her sigh and knew his attempt at diverting her attention hadn't worked. "You should've been with us. *Grand-mère* requests your presence, *soon.*"

Grayson chuckled. He could well imagine the old bat drumming her fingers, waiting to issue the invitation herself.

His stepmother continued, "Or you could still go visit Frank and the children. I don't like you being alone. I worry about you."

He chuckled when he heard his father muttering in the background that it was highly unlikely he was alone, and he'd better not see any scandals like a few years ago.

His father had not been pleased about the infamous twin incident.

"The roads are not good for traveling with the ice and snow. I will be with the family for New Year's and Grace's christening. I'm glad the family is okay with it being a private ceremony. Anyway, I'm fine; I just wanted to wish you both a Merry Christmas." He rolled his eyes as he listened to his stepmother's instruction to dress warmly.

"*Oui, Maman. Au revoir et joyeux Noël.*"

"Merry Christmas, Grayson. Here's your grandmother."

Grand-mère skipped the niceties about Christmas and commanded him to come home soon. He assured her he'd visit in a few weeks when he was in Paris for work.

He hung up the phone, and a feeling of unease settled about him. When the photos of him with the twins were splashed across tabloids and social media, his father had been furious, the resultant lecture blistering. In his father's eyes, he would forever be eighteen. *Papa* would probably have a stroke if he found out about Alyssandra. And *Grand-mère* would beat him with her cane. His grandfather had once had a torrid affair with a younger woman.

Even worse would be *her* family's reaction. Lissy's father and brother would probably kill him. He should end it now. But, dammit, she was like expensive champagne. One taste would never be enough.

Chapter
Ten

Christmas morning Lissy stretched and winced after their long, vigorous night of sex and exploration. Muscles she never knew existed were deliciously sore. She smiled, recalling his scowl when she'd told him she hoped he could keep up with her, considering his *advanced age*. His effort to prove her wrong had been worth it.

The last time they'd made love, mercy! Or rather, *merci!* They'd done things she'd only read about. Heat crept up her cheeks, and she bit her lip to keep from giggling and waking her inventive lover. Gray had put his sailing skills to work with some pretty fancy knotwork involving her robe tie.

Noëlle meowed and scratched pitifully outside the bedroom door—the same door Gray had fucked her against last night. Opening it, she picked up the kitten and climbed back into bed.

The cat padded back and forth between her and Gray—head butting and purring for attention.

He stirred without opening his eyes and murmured, "Just an hour, *mon chaton*. You have worn me out, just an hour for sleep, *s'il te plaît*."

Lissy nibbled his ear and whispered, "I know what you really want…"

His arm snaked out and grabbed her, pulling her close. "Again?" he groaned.

"Coffee," she purred in his ear, giving him a kiss on the cheek and a smack on his bare butt as she bounded out of bed. The kitten curled up on her pillow.

"*Oui, café.*"

"I'm going to shower and start breakfast. Rest up, old man." She laughed when he flipped her off before rolling over. He was snoring before she made it to the bathroom.

The tantalizing smell of coffee woke him. Or perhaps it was the gentle kiss on his cheek, or the nip of sharp teeth on his hand.

He opened one eye and glared at the kitten. "Your obnoxious cat bit me."

"It's a love nip. You don't get mad when I bite." She stroked his back and bit his neck playfully.

"Perhaps. I should impale you, *mon petit vampire.*" He rolled over and gave her a kiss. He raised his eyebrows when he spotted the tray of food on the nightstand. "Breakfast in bed?"

"*Joyeux Noël,* Gray."

Her smile widened as she waited for him to eat. She'd pulled her tangled curls into a ponytail and wore her robe. She had the glow of a woman who had been well-fucked.

"Yes, I actually cooked. Are you surprised?" She spread her hands over the food, a look of accomplishment on her face.

"Merry Christmas, Alyssandra." He looked at the breakfast and hid his trepidation behind a smile. "Thank you. You shouldn't have gone to all this trouble." *Really, you shouldn't have.* His stomach protested at the sight of the limp, greasy bacon.

"I wanted to spoil you." She sat gazing at him, waiting for him to eat. "*Bon appétit.*"

Spoiled *being the key word here.* Mentally crossing himself, he forked a rubbery egg and shoved it in his mouth with a bite of burned toast.

"Mmm, delicious," he lied, gulping down coffee.

"Really?"

Her relieved smile was like sunshine on a dreary day. Despite the effort it took to chew the eggs, he'd eat every damn bite to please her.

"Julia Child would be proud, if she were still living." He managed to swallow the last of the eggs and toast with coffee but eyed the bacon with dread.

"Would you like some more coffee?"

Oh, thank God. "Yes, please." He handed her his cup, and she ran downstairs to refill it. It was now or never. Moving quickly, he grabbed the bacon to dispose of it, but became entangled in the sheet and tripped. As if in slow motion, he watched with horror as Noëlle reached out, with claws bared, to swat at his cock. It was close, but he managed to move away just in time, swearing in two languages. He grabbed the bacon, flushed it, and made it back to bed just before Alyssandra returned.

"What's going on up here? It sounded like a herd of elephants."

He dodged the question with a kiss as he accepted the cup. "You're an angel. *Merci.*" Behind her back, he glared at the cat.

"Come downstairs. I have a present for you!" Her excitement was contagious as she shifted from foot to foot.

"May I shower first?"

She rolled her eyes. "Well, hurry. There are *presents* under the tree." The whine in her voice made him laugh.

"You can join me, if you'd like."

He wasn't a bit surprised when she followed him into the bathroom. Shimmying out of her robe, she joined him under the warm water. She grabbed the soap and began to wash his chest as he washed his hair.

"God, that feels good," he growled.

"You can't think about sex, Gray. Not when there are presents waiting to be opened."

He laughed. "But my present is right here." He kissed the top of her head and pulled her wet body close. He mentally added photographing her naked and wet to his must-do list. "Who came to see you last night, *le Père Noël* or *le Père Fouettard?*"

She continued to run her soft, soapy hands over him. "What's the difference?"

"*Le Père Noël* brings presents to good little girls. *Le Père Fouettard* brings spankings to naughty little girls."

"When I'm naughty, I'm very good, so which one do you think?" She grabbed him and stroked up and down.

He lifted her and pushed her against the wall of the shower as he kissed her neck. "Show me how naughty you can be, and we'll find out."

"But if I show you how naughty I can be, I'll never get to open my presents." She squealed as he hit a ticklish spot and slid to her knees. Her eyes sparkled as she took him in her mouth.

"Ahh, *I* must have been a very good boy."

"Come on, slow poke." Alyssandra grabbed his hand as she ran down the stairs.

"*Le Père Fouettard* definitely," Grayson muttered, giving her bottom a swat.

"Please, sir, may I have another?"

He shook his head and laughed. "No spankings for you, because then you'll whine when we end up back in bed."

"True!" She settled on the couch, grinning as she eyed the three presents under the tree with her name on them.

"I'm going to get a cup of coffee, and then my impatient little imp can open her presents."

"Hurry up. And after we open presents, I want to hear all about your sexy escapades of the past and where you learned to do all this stuff."

He returned from the kitchen with two cups of coffee, refusing to hand her one until she offered him a kiss. "I never kiss, nor fuck, and tell."

He stirred the fire to life and grabbed his camera. Moving the glaring cat out of his way, he grinned as Alyssandra bounced in her seat. The lights from the Christmas tree twinkled behind her and he enjoyed the play of shadows and light on her face.

"Now?"

She wore one of his button-down shirts and a pink silk thong, with her hair a riot of brown waves. Her beauty stole his breath.

Would he ever get enough of her? He wanted to know her every thought, study every nuance of her face, and hear every sound she could possibly make when he made love to her.

No woman had ever made him think about long-term commitment, yet he couldn't imagine being without this girl. He shoved the thought away. It wouldn't be fair. Maybe in another ten years, after she'd lived her life.

The need to photograph her was becoming an obsession — because he knew their time together would be coming to an end.

He took a sip of his coffee. "Don't you want to enjoy your coffee first?"

"No! You're so mean. I can't wait any longer." She dove off the couch, grabbed the presents, and placed them on the coffee table.

She laughed when she spied the present for Noëlle. "You even bought the cat—who you supposedly hate—a present?"

"No, but I knew you'd want her to have something. She's our baby."

"Our baby? Will I have to fight you for custody?" She tore the present open and laughed at the wadded-up paper ball he'd made. The kitten eagerly chased it around the cabin.

Lissy picked up the first present with her name on it, wrapped in Happy Birthday paper with colorful balloons.

"Happy Birthday? My birthday isn't until next week. The day before yours."

Grayson shrugged. "I had to use what I could find."

The color rose in her cheeks and her eyes widened as she withdrew the handwritten note—an IOU for an intimate photo shoot.

"You want to take pictures of *me?*"

"Yes." He paused as his gaze locked on hers. "*Nude.*"

"I-I'm just me. I mean, you've photographed models, stars…Naked?"

"You. In black and white. And yes, naked. Tastefully done, of course."

"I'd like that. A lot."

"Thank you. You have just given me *my* Christmas present." He wrapped a length of her silky brown hair around his finger and pulled her in close for a kiss.

"Gray?" she whispered.

"*Oui?*"

"Will you be in one of the photos with me?"

He chuckled, but the more he thought about it, the harder he laughed, until he realized she was serious. *Dead serious.*

"No, absolutely not. Open your next present." He motioned with his coffee cup.

Lissy grabbed a package wrapped in Happy Easter paper and shook it. She opened it and found another note with a password. "What's this?"

"Access to our photos from the past few days." He cupped her cheek in his hand. "As you will see, my dear, I am hardly photogenic."

"I happen to think you're the sexiest man alive. Thank you for this, Gray. I can't wait to see them." She gave him a kiss on the cheek. "Now may I open the last present?"

"Yes, impatient girl. Open it."

She carefully opened the present wrapped in actual Christmas paper and gasped. As if they were expensive jewels from Tiffany's, she admired the three twig ornaments: a tree, a snowflake, and a star.

"You made these for me?" Her eyes shimmered with tears.

"It isn't much, more like a joke."

"Not a joke. They are *everything.* You made them. For *me.* Thank you, Gray."

Pulling her onto his lap, he wrapped his arms around her waist. For a brief moment, he closed his eyes, inhaling the scent of her warm skin, the feel of her soft hair and sweet lips kissing his cheek. *This week won't be enough.*

"I wish we could stay here forever."

He nodded, but didn't say anything, not trusting his voice. They watched the fire for a few moments and then laughed as Noëlle tried to get her ball out from under the chair. Lissy retrieved the kitten's toy and handed him a gift, tied in a plastic bag with a gray yarn bow.

He unfolded the muffler and beanie she'd knit. "You do beautiful work, Alyssandra. And because you made it, it's even more special. Thank you." He wrapped it around her neck, using it to pull her closer for a kiss. He tucked the ends down her shirt and hugged her.

"What are you doing?"

"I want it to smell like you. This way, when I wear it, I'll think of you," he murmured, running his fingers through her silky hair. "And I have an interesting idea of what to do to you with this muffler."

"Ha! I'm sure you do. I confess, I did love it when you tied me up last night. I hope you *will* always think of me. I know I'll always think of you."

He pulled out the last cylinder-shaped knit piece and frowned. "A cock warmer?"

Lissy laughed. "No! Oh my God, it does look like it, doesn't it? It's a sweater for the jaguar on your car."

"Ah. Good. I was going to say, it would be a tight fit," he replied, lifting an eyebrow.

She shifted and straddled his lap, her forehead touching his. "This is the best Christmas *ever.*" Her voice sounded thick, and she gave him a knowing smile.

How could he think? All of his blood had pooled in his dick, now lodged against her thin, why-bother panty.

"See what you do to me?" He gripped her hips and rocked her. Her head fell back, exposing her long neck, and he kissed it, working his way down to that annoying button keeping her breasts hidden.

Her phone rang. They both groaned. "Don't move. I'll be right back." She ran and grabbed her phone from the desk.

"Merry Christmas, Jessica." Straddling his lap again, she grinned when he ran a hand up under her shirt, rubbing his thumb across her nipple. "No, I can't video chat right now. My friend isn't decent."

He snickered, and her hand slapped over his mouth.

"Did Santa come see Lee and Grace?" She smiled as she listened.

He assumed Jessica was recounting the children's Christmas. He'd hear about it soon enough when he spoke to Frank. He pinched her nipple and bit back his bark of laughter when she moaned out loud. She blushed, slapping his hand away and shaking her head.

"Huh? Oh, um, sorry. I wish you could try this cake I'm, uh, eating. It's delicious. You know how I love chocolate." She frowned and rolled her eyes. "Yes, for breakfast. You're not my mother."

Amused by her lie, he took her breast in his mouth. She smacked him again, harder this time, and glared.

"Sure, I'll say hi to Travis." She pinched him to stop. "Merry Christmas, Trav. Yes, I'm fine."

She blew her hair out of her face and her lips thinned as she listened.

Gray sucked her nipple into a tight peak and lightly twisted the other. A becoming blush worked its way from her neck to her cheeks, and her pupils dilated. Her dazed glare made him smile.

"I know, I know. But I don't want to work at your stupid bank. It's boring. I'd rather pick up trash on the side of the road or flip burgers. I'll talk to you later about it. Merry Christmas. I have to go. Give everyone my love. Bye." She hung up.

"I take it you have a job lined up at the bank when you get home?"

"My brother is bossy like my father. He wants me to be a bank teller." She rolled her eyes. "Why would I want to count other people's money?" She rode against him, her breasts bouncing in his face as she ground against his erection. "Oh, God, I need this..."

His dick throbbed to be inside her.

"Indeed. Counting one's own money is much more pleasurable." He wrapped his hand in her hair and pulled her mouth down to his. With his other hand he reached for the pink scrap of material... His phone rang.

"*Merde!*"

"Lemme guess, your brother?" Lissy laughed when he scowled and nodded.

He picked the phone off the end table.

"*Joyeux Noël*, Frank. Yes, yes, I'm having a very nice, quiet Christmas."

With an impish look, Lissy moved beside him and unzipped his jeans.

"And did *Père Noël*..." He choked and closed his eyes as she took him in his mouth, her hand stroking from base to tip, leaving him a blathering idiot.

"W-What? Um, er, gah..." *Shit, what did Frank just ask?* He gave up, unable to think.

He hung up and leaned back to enjoy his unexpected Christmas present. He'd call later and blame the weather for cutting them off.

"Hold it there, *mon chaton*. Look at the camera, not the squirrel. I don't want a big smile; I want the smile you give me just before I send you to heaven." His firm, no-nonsense voice made her shiver even more than the cold. No doubt about it, Gray in bossy mode was hot.

"Make love to the camera, my darling."

"I'd rather make love to you." She flashed him a hint of a smile, followed by a smoldering look.

"Are you an exhibitionist, Alyssandra?" he asked as he adjusted a camera setting.

Caught off guard, her mouth dropped. *How does he know I'm so turned on right now I want to pounce on him and rip his clothes off?* "W-What?"

"You heard the question."

"I'm glad we're alone," she hedged, too embarrassed to admit the truth.

One eyebrow rose as he waited.

"I don't know. Maybe? I do know I like you looking at me. It makes me feel sexy." Was that her voice, barely above a whisper? Louder, she blurted, "Can we hurry and go back inside? And do that thing with the hot wax and snow again?"

He chuckled. "Soon." His voice was full of promise as he shot another photo.

"You know, for someone who complained about me not having a coat on the other night, you haven't said much about it today."

"Poor baby. Photo shoots are work, not play. What's the phrase? Put your big girl panties on and just do it." He glanced around at the partially sunny sky and melting snow. An icy drop fell from a branch and hit her pebbled nipple.

Surprised, she squeaked. The shutter snapped, and she wondered if he'd somehow planned it.

"I'm not wearing any, you jerk."

He snickered, and the shutter snapped several times. "You're right. No panties. *Papa* would be disappointed."

"Are you disappointed?" she asked, giggling.

"Not at all. You're beautiful, Alyssandra. Your pink cheeks are quite appealing. And I plan to warm the other set with my hand later."

His heated stare elevated her temperature, not to mention her curiosity.

"Turn and look over your shoulder at me, *ma chérie*. That's it. Now throw the muffler over your shoulder. Besides, it isn't as cold today as it has been. With the snow melting, the roads will be clear by tomorrow."

"It isn't cold to *you*. You aren't the one out here butt-ass naked," she grumbled, doing as he'd instructed and looking at the camera flirtatiously. "But we don't need to leave tomorrow, do we?"

He hesitated. "Two more days at most. Then we need to return. We have the party at your parents' and the christening."

"Okay." She tried to hide her disappointment. Just two more days of heaven. How would she ever return to her mundane life?

"Neck, Alyssandra. Stretch your neck. Now part your lips and think of all the things you want me to do to you...Perfect. My favorite one, so far."

He draped his coat around her shoulders and pinched her bottom before lifting her into his arms. She cuddled into his warmth as he as carried her inside like a princess.

Standing her in front of the fire, he dropped a kiss to her forehead.

"You were perfect. The coffee is made. After I retrieve the camera, I promise I'll warm you better than this fire." His wicked smile and frank look of lust started the thaw process.

Will I ever get enough of him?

He returned a few moments later, stamping the snow on the doormat. His eyes flashed with desire as he closed the door. "Still cold?"

She shook her head no. "Gray..." Her voice trailed off, and he raised an eyebrow as he waited for her request. "Can we do one picture of us together? Please?"

"We did that the other day, with the snowman."

"We were dressed. That's not what I meant, and you know it."

"Don't be ridiculous." He frowned, clearly uncomfortable.

"You don't have to look at the camera. You can face me, just your back and incredible ass in the picture." She bit her lip, waiting for his answer as she peeled off his coat and muffler. Unbuttoning his shirt, she dropped a kiss to his chest and ran a nail across his nipple.

"Pretty please? With a blowjob on top?"

"How can I refuse that?" He laughed. "All right."

Muttering in French, he draped a sheet against the staircase for a backdrop and checked the lighting as she stood where they would be positioned. He adjusted the camera and took several test shots until he found the setting he wanted. With a sigh, he shrugged out of his shirt, kicked off his shoes and socks, and unzipped his pants. When he was finally naked, she drank him in, noting every detail. *How can so much raw sexuality be in one man?*

He lifted her into his arms, and his erection pressed against her. She squirmed, wanting more.

"You're in charge, Alyssandra. How do you want us?" His low, seductive voice and amused smile almost made her forget about the damn picture.

"Put me down and look at me." When he complied, Lissy placed her right hand on his shoulder and, standing on tiptoe, looked over his left shoulder directly into the camera. Her left hand gripped his ass possessively. She heard the low growl in his throat and smiled into his shoulder. The shutter snapped. Lissy gave him a quick kiss and ran to look at the photo.

She gasped and caught her breath. "Oh my gosh. I love it!"

"I'll be damned." Gray smiled at her. "You have a good grasp of composition, Alyssandra. The shadowing is almost perfect."

"It *is* perfect. Thank you. I want it poster size for my bedroom wall." She giggled at the horrified look on his face. "I'm kidding, Gray! You really are easy to tease. Is it the language barrier?"

"There is no language barrier. I speak English very well," he snapped, shrugging into his boxers and jeans.

"I'm sorry. It was a joke, yeesh." She rolled her eyes.

"I'm not amused. Your family—" He grabbed his ringing phone. "Hello? Yes, this is he." His color paled, and he sank into the chair as if he'd been hit. "When?" he croaked. He rubbed his brow. "How? Where is she?" His voice sounded strained.

Has something happened to his family? Her heart thumped unevenly.

"Yes, yes, of course. I will be there as soon as I can. The roads are clearing. I'll text you with my flight information." Disbelief remained on his face when he hung up.

"What is it, Gray? What's happened?"

"It's Candie. She needs me." Swiping his phone, he mumbled to himself in French.

Stunned speechless, Lissy stared at him. Surely she'd misheard. *Candie needs him? That bitch?*

"What? No! Gray, you *can't* go." She slammed her fist on the arm of the couch, shaking with anger and hurt.

Arctic blue eyes met hers, and the chasm between them split wide open.

"Why does your ex need you?" She didn't try to stop her petulant tears. "You promised me two more days."

"Candie's been admitted to hospital. Her manager said it's life threatening. She has no family. I don't know all the details. Now stop acting like a child." He brushed a kiss across her forehead and headed upstairs.

Lissy stared at his back but didn't follow. Instead, she channeled her anger into undecorating the tree. Thirty minutes later, he walked back downstairs with his suitcase. He'd showered and shaved. He glanced at the bare tree and box of ornaments.

"Be safe," she managed to say, carefully wrapping the lights around an empty paper towel roll.

"Alyssandra, I'm sorry. This is an unplanned emergency. But regardless, you knew this was all just a fantasy. Not the real world."

"Oh, yes. You've made it quite clear I'm too young for you and too stupid to know my own mind." She marched into the kitchen to get the stepstool and came back to take the angel off the tree.

"You don't have to do this. Frank has someone who comes in and cleans. She'll take down the tree…"

"Goodbye, Grayson." She refused to look at him, knowing she'd break down.

"Stay here until the roads are totally clear. You aren't used to driving on slush. Text me when you get home. My flight leaves in a few hours."

She didn't reply and didn't turn around, even though she could feel him staring at her.

He left quietly, closing the door behind him.

After he'd gone, she sank to the floor, still stunned that he'd left her to be with the woman who'd dumped him. Anger simmered and boiled down her hot cheeks as Noëlle begged to be petted.

A little while later, she wiped her tears and straightened her shoulders. He was a fool, but by God, she'd make him realize he was *her* fool…after she made him regret ever leaving her.

Chapter
Eleven

Grayson yawned as he sat vigil by Candie's bedside. It was just past midnight, and he'd been here for hours. Guilt weighed heavily on his heart. He'd tried without success to erase the memory of Alyssandra's stricken face when he'd said he was leaving.

He was the one who'd insisted their relationship would be just sex with no strings attached. Yet here he was, moping about leaving his current lover at the bedside of his ex.

What had he been thinking? He hadn't been, obviously. The past few days with Alyssandra had been like a dream, some kind of sexual fantasy bubble. His ego had been inflated by her attention, his body entranced by her exuberance, and he'd laughed and enjoyed their easy conversation. Being with Alyssandra had been like coming out of hibernation. After the boredom of a long, cold winter, she was sunshine and happiness.

Perhaps it was best that things had ended abruptly. He felt awful that he'd hurt her feelings, but they would heal, and she'd come to realize — as he did — that their worlds were too far apart to sustain a viable relationship, other than as family and friends.

With benefits?

Candie whimpered softly in her drug-induced sleep, bringing his thoughts back to her.

She'd slit her wrists after leaving a vague note that life had become unbearable and apologizing for hurting him. *On Christmas Day.* Why would she do something so desperate? Her actions compounded his growing guilt. He'd always struggled to be close to people. *Maman* attributed it to his lonely childhood.

Grayson gazed at his former lover. The hospital lights were not kind, nor flattering. She'd be unhappy if she knew this, and it would probably add to her depression. The questions ran through his mind on a loop. Why had she tried to kill herself? How unbearable could her privileged life be? Had she truly loved him? What about Antonio? Did they have a fight? Or was it her fear of aging? A combination of all these things?

He shouldn't have been so harsh with her on the phone just before Christmas. He shouldn't have ignored her texts and voicemails. But he was perplexed; after all, she was the one who'd left *him*, without warning. By nature a needy, somewhat narcissistic creature, she'd often complained he wasn't attentive enough. In truth, he'd never been fully vested in their relationship. It required little of him by design. He was ready to accept his part in driving her away and into the arms of Antonio. *Where is that bastard?*

Her restless stirring continued. Exhausted, he rubbed his face and leaned forward, smoothing the stray strand of enhanced blond hair from her face. She opened her eyes, blinked a few times, and stared at him for a moment, her dark eyes hooded and unfocused.

"You came."

"Of course."

"I knew you would." She turned on to her side, facing him. Her eyes now shone with excitement. "Is the press bad?"

"Don't worry about it. Concentrate on getting well."

Pouring her a glass of water, he hid his irritation. Her obsession with the press, her looks, and her age had always been a sore point between them. He believed all women were beautiful, no matter their age, size, or color, as long as they were confident and happy. Candie, on the other hand, had become increasingly harder on herself after her last film. She was a beautiful, thirty-six-year-old woman who insisted on playing twenty-something girls.

"Grayson! Did you make a statement? What are they saying?"

"Of course not. I have no idea what's being said. You know I don't read or watch that nonsense. I ignore them." *Who the hell cares what the press said? You slit your damn wrists.*

Instead of voicing his frustration, he tempered his tone and summoned his last ounce of patience. "Why, Candie? What could possibly have happened to make you do something so desperate?"

She sat up, and her voice rose. "You *have* to say something! Tell them you forgive me. Antonio's words won't carry the weight yours will, because in the fans' eyes, you were the one wronged." She kicked at the covers like a three-year-old having a tantrum.

"I *do* forgive you. While I wish you'd spoken to me first, I wasn't *wronged.* We were both responsible for not working at our relationship." He looked at her, puzzled, and wondered if he should call for a nurse as her agitation increased.

"Oh for fuck's sake, Grayson. Don't tell *me*; tell the *press.* You *have* to talk to them. I have to get the public to sympathize with me. My career is tanking because of those stupid photos with Antonio. They've made me out to be a fucking whore. A man in Hollywood can fuck anything and everything and it's okay; he's just a bad boy. A woman does it and she's labeled a slut. Damn double standard," she muttered. "I need a cigarette."

He was tired, and English *was* his second language. *I must've misunderstood.* "That may have been true a few years ago…You can't smoke in here. What do you mean I have to talk to them? I refuse to get involved in the media circus. Why do you even care what they say? If you want to be with Antonio, fine. You made it clear that was your choice."

He leaned back and rubbed his aching head. "It would have been nice if you'd told me you were leaving first. I thought we had an understanding. But that is the littlest of my concerns. For Christ's sake, you slit your wrists! You need some serious help. Trust me, nothing they write about you is bad enough to take your own life. Where *is* Antonio?"

She laughed. "Sometimes your English is so funny. The phrase is *least of my concerns.* You think I actually meant to kill myself? Don't be stupid. Antonio is back in Italy finishing up the picture. If you'll just make a public announcement about how you forgive me and love me, I'll go get a little work done, call it rehab, and come back looking rejuvenated, well-rested, and ready for my next movie. The public loves nothing more than a repentant sinner and a comeback story. Then we can vacation in Paris. Or Saint-Tropez. Even better, maybe we can have Antonio join us." The smile she flashed was as fake as her nails.

He stared at her for a full minute as everything suddenly went from soft to sharp focus. "This was a publicity stunt?"

"Of course it was, you idiot. I mean, I did cut my wrists, but I made sure someone found me in plenty of time. And I went across the street, not downtown. It really hurt like hell. I wasn't expecting quite that much pain." She presented her bandaged arms like they were a Golden Globe and an Oscar.

"You're fucking sicker than I realized." He stood up, disgusted. Had he ever really known her? "Goodbye, Candie."

"Wait! Where are you going? You can't leave me! I care about you. We can go back to the way we were. You have to help me, you bastard!"

He stormed out of the room, ignoring her desperate pleas to help salvage her career.

"Girrrrl! You look like Candie Fontaine in that last cheesy slasher pic. The one where she was a zombie." Eyes narrowed, Eddie grabbed Lissy's chin and turned her face side to side. "Positively haggard. Good thing I know exactly what you need. I have cheap wine, a chick flick, popcorn, and real butter—not that margarine shit." He pushed past her into her studio apartment, tossing a grocery bag and his backpack on the floor.

"Why don't you come in and make yourself at home, bitch?" Lissy slammed the door and jumped into his arms, wrapping her legs around his waist.

"Now this is more like it." His scruffy jaw burned her cheek, and his sculpted arms squeezed the breath out of her.

"Ow, okay, put me down," she whined, yet held on tighter.

She'd arrived at her apartment this afternoon, having stayed an extra night at the cabin, too scared to drive until the roads were completely clear.

Eddie Sanders was a six-foot-two blond god with sparkling blue eyes and a winning smile that turned heads. He'd been her best friend since he'd found her lost and near tears looking for her freshman English class.

On the long drive home, she'd broken down and finally called him. He'd had her pull over as she sobbed through the entire pathetic Christmas story until she was calm enough to drive.

"Don't start with me, Liss. I can't believe you didn't tell me about that douchebag Josh and his stupid friends. I could easily kick their asses. I deadlift three hundred and seventy pounds. But I'm *really* pissed that you're just now telling me about your hot and heavy fling with Grayson Deschanelle. Do you know how fuckin' jealous I am? That man is batting for the wrong team. Handsome as sin, French, and in the fashion industry — no way he should be hetero."

Lissy burst out laughing and crying at the same time. She was damn glad to see him.

Eddie held her, stroking her back as she pulled herself together. "If he didn't appreciate the fact that you're way better than that bitch Candie Fucktaine, you're better off without that French dumbass." She giggled, and he patted her on the butt. "Damn girl, you really do need the real butter. Your ass is gettin' scrawny."

He put her back on her feet, and she punched him, wiping her eyes on the sleeves of her red plaid flannel shirt. "Did you pull out an A in micro?"

"Barely. Last semester was a killer. I'm sorry I wasn't there for ya, Liss. Pre-med is tough, but honey, I can always take time for my best friend. You should've told me you were having problems with your classes. I could've helped."

She sighed and looked away, still embarrassed by her stupidity. "I was so confused. I moved around in a daze. I felt bad all the time. I didn't know if I was coming or going, and I was so ashamed…" Her voice cracked.

He grabbed her shoulders, his eyes full of concern. "So now what?"

"I'm going to finish packing up my stuff and go home. I have to work at Travis's stupid bank. It's supposed to teach me a lesson about the value of an education. Daddy said he's subletting my apartment."

"Who cares about where you're gonna live or work? I meant whatcha gonna do about that spunk-worthy hunk of man. If you don't want him, I'll take one for the team and do sloppy seconds."

Lissy shook her head and laughed, retrieving glasses for the wine. "We're done. He left me to be with Candie. What we had was sex only, no strings attached. He's a tag 'em and bag 'em kind of guy." Unscrewing the cap on the bottle of wine, she wrinkled her nose. "Damn, this really is some cheap shit, Eddie."

They sat on the futon, and Noëlle joined them.

He shrugged. "Nothing but the worst for us. Honey, sex with no strings attached never works unless you're a paid hooker. People have feelings. So, if Gray's truly an asswipe, you just need to forget about him and remember our deal. If neither of us has a spouse or significant other by the time we're thirty, we're shacking up together and raising a houseful of cats."

Eddie raised his glass and clinked Lissy's. The cat gave him a head butt in apparent agreement with their future plans.

"And then we'll have that turkey-baster baby." Lissy laughed as she petted the kitten, which walked back and forth between them, kneading and purring. "Good grief, can you imagine how awful a kid of ours would be?"

"Yeah, but that child would be damn good looking and know how to dress well." Eddie jumped up and put the popcorn in the microwave. "Start the movie, Liss. We can both lust after Richard Gere."

Lissy sighed. "*Pretty Woman* again? Good grief, Eddie. We've seen this six hundred times."

"And your point is?"

Lissy laughed. "True." She started the movie and threw back the contents of her wineglass.

Grayson checked the address and parked, happy to finally be here. He'd caught the red eye flight from New York, and finding Alyssandra gone from the cabin, had spent the night there before getting on the road to Alabama. Candie's stunt had led him to some serious introspection. The glaring differences between Alyssandra and Candie were like life and death. With Alyssandra, he'd found joy in simple things. He missed her and wished they could go back to the cabin and be alone.

But they couldn't—and even though he had no idea what would happen when he saw her again—he needed to explain how much she meant to him, and how much she'd helped him. So this morning he'd driven the rental car straight to her apartment.

It hadn't been easy finagling her whereabouts out of Frank. Spotting her car in the parking lot, he parked and let out a relieved breath. *She's here.* They needed to talk. *Correction*: he needed to apologize. He wondered for at least the tenth time if he should've phoned or sent her a text. He hadn't, afraid she'd refuse to see him.

Like a man walking the green mile, he ascended the steps to her apartment and knocked on the door. The day was overcast and cold, and the wind cut like an icy knife. The fog from his breath billowed as he waited. He knocked again and finally heard movement inside the apartment. The door cracked open. Noëlle attempted to dart out the door, and Grayson caught her. The cat nuzzled his neck, purring, and he smiled. At least someone was glad to see him.

"What do you want?" Alyssandra shoved her tousled hair from her face and grabbed the cat. In a man's button-down white shirt and bare feet, she looked sleepy and totally fuckable.

"May I come in?"

Her cold reserve cracked, and she glanced nervously behind her, biting her lower lip. "This isn't a good time."

Grayson shoved the door open, pushing her and Noëlle aside. The apartment was only one room with an adjoining bathroom—very tiny and very cluttered with packed and half-packed boxes everywhere. His eyes went to the bed, and his heart damn near stopped at the sight of a man's naked back. The chill he felt was no longer from the weather.

He raised an eyebrow, questioning. He didn't dare speak, afraid of what he'd say, all the while knowing he had no one to blame but himself. Taking a deep breath, he pulled his gaze back to Alyssandra, carefully keeping his face void of any emotion. However, there was no keeping the sarcasm out of his voice.

"Who's your *friend?*"

"Eddie. How's *Candie?*"

Touché. He shrugged. "Fine."

The man stirred, yawned, and rolled over on his side, propping his head on his hand. "Whoa...hul-lo." His eyes grew wide and twinkled with devilment. Waggling his eyebrows, he patted the bed and grinned. "Care to join us?"

Grayson shot him a withering go-to-hell look and stormed out the door, experiencing an uncomfortable sort of *déjà vu*. If he didn't leave, he'd end up in prison for murder.

As he jerked open the car door, movement from her doorway caught his eye. Lissy leaned against the doorjamb, petting her cat. She smiled and yelled, "What's the matter, Gray? It's just sex, no strings attached."

He peeled out, leaving a good inch of rubber on the road.

Lissy shut the door and giggled. "Oh, Eddie. I love you more now than ever."

He grinned at her. "I was serious. Damn, girl. He's even hotter in person. I could so hit that. Hell, I'd even do *you* to get to him."

"Eww, stop. You and I are not that kind of friends!" She laughed. "And yes, I know. He *is* the very essence of holy hotness, but Operation Make Gray Jealous is underway!" She giggled. "Did you see the look on his face?" The cat jumped from her arms onto the bed.

Eddie turned serious and looked at her as he played with Noëlle. "Yes, did you?"

She frowned. "What do you mean?"

"He was hurt, Liss. He looked like he'd been sucker punched. Is that what you wanted?"

"Yes…No…I don't know," she admitted softly. She ran a hand through her tangled hair. "I've thrown myself at him twice. And while I might have seduced him at the cabin, he still dumped me for his ex. Add this to my humiliation by Josh, and I'm done being taken advantage of. I've finally learned my lesson. I'm never going allow myself to be vulnerable again."

"I wouldn't cut my nose off to spite my face. You may be jumping to conclusions. What if he went to tell Candie they were over once and for all? He drove here to find *you*. Maybe he decided things weren't finished between you two. Men don't always express themselves clearly—trust me, I know. And English is his second or third language, so cut the guy some slack. If you ask me, love means allowing someone to see your vulnerability. And trusting that they'll protect it." Eddie scratched Noëlle behind the ears.

Mulling over what he'd said, Lissy picked up the garbage from last night.

"I don't care. He doesn't love me. He just wants to fuck me. That's not enough for me anymore."

"That didn't look like a man here for a quickie. And, Liss, if you don't care a thing about him, why have you slept in his shirt and cried yourself to sleep the past two nights?"

Chapter
Twelve

"*Merde!*" Grayson grunted as his nephew head-butted him in the groin. He tousled Lee's brown curls as the child crawled over his lap. A small elbow made contact with his ribs.

"Dadgumit, Trip! You can't be teaching Lee to swear in French, or any other language. Jessica will nail both of our asses, er, hides to the wall." Frank scooped Lee up into his arms. "This thing with Candie has really done a number on you. You look like hell. Or is it just turning forty? Mama's still mad you don't want a shindig to celebrate."

"You're the only one who calls me Trip. It's annoying. Hello." Gray stood and smirked, nodding toward the beautiful blonde standing behind Frank.

Frank turned and flinched when he saw his wife glaring. "Oh, shit, er, shoot. I mean, you look like *heck.*"

Jessica hugged Grayson. "He's right. You look like hell. Are you okay?" she whispered.

"It's been a rough few days." He took the baby Jessica handed him and smiled. "Grace. My favorite goddaughter and niece." The infant gave an ear-piercing howl and promptly spit up soured milk down his shirt. "I see you have your father's manners, *ma douce.*" He handed the baby back to Jessica.

"I'm so sorry!" Jessica bit her lip, probably to keep from laughing as she left the room.

Grayson shrugged and muttered, "I seem to have this effect on women lately."

Frank clasped him on the shoulder and motioned him to follow. "Losing your touch, old man?" He handed him a wet paper towel to mop up the mess.

Grayson shot him a dirty look. "Seems so."

He accepted the beer Frank handed him when he was done with the paper towel and watched as his stepbrother handed Lee a sippy cup of juice. Frank hadn't shaved, wore a faded pair of jeans and an old sweatshirt, and his hair was in need of a trim. But the look of pure, unadulterated happiness on his face left Grayson intensely jealous and unsettled.

"What are you dressing as for the party tonight?" Frank asked.

"I'm not."

"You have to. It's a costume party. Jess and her mother insist."

"What are *you* wearing?"

"Jess and I are going as Frank and Jessie James, get it? Mama and Pop are going to be Marie Antoinette and whatever king she hooked up with."

Grayson rolled his eyes. "Louis XVI. Your knowledge of French history is abominable—almost as bad as your taste in beer."

Frank frowned. "Yeah? Well, who was the thirty-third president of the United States? And this is my favorite beer. Plus, it was on sale."

"Truman, you moron."

"Shit. You always know the answer. Whatever—you have to wear a costume. It's the big family to-do. George always goes all-out for his youngest's birthday since it falls on New Year's Eve. She's bringing someone—hey, Jess, who is the date *du jour* Liss is bringing to the party? Josh?" Frank jumped as Lee flipped the lid off the cup and poured his drink on the floor. "Oh sh—er, crap, son!"

Grayson's jaw tightened at the mention of Josh's name, but Frank didn't see it as he scrambled to contain the juice.

Jessica rushed back in and frowned. "You can't watch Lee for three seconds?"

"Sorry, the little rascal's quick. What loser is Liss bringing to the party?"

Jessica moved Frank out of the way and cleaned the floor. "He isn't the loser; his name is Eddie, and he's pre-med. Josh was the loser—they broke up. Did you hear about this, Grayson? My sister flunked out of school after breaking up with some jerk." She shook her head. "Lissy's been uncharacteristically quiet about all of this. I'm afraid she's clinically depressed or something."

"Jess has been reading a lot of parenting books," Frank offered with a grimace behind her back.

Jessica stood and smacked him with the towel. Their son squealed with laughter.

"If she has a date with this Eddie guy, she must be doing okay," Grayson muttered as he gulped the rest of his beer, wishing it was something stronger.

He needed to get drunk—again. And this cheap beer wasn't going to do the trick. After finding Alyssandra with Dr. Feelgood, he'd returned to the cabin to mope. It was only at the insistence of his family that he'd returned to Pine Bluff for New Year's Eve, and of course, for Grace's christening.

Jessica frowned. "I suppose so. At least she's moving on—"

The doorbell rang, and Frank left to answer it with Lee in his arms.

"Um, Grayson? I'm really worried. Lissy looks terrible; she's lost weight and just seems distracted. Maybe you could talk some sense into her while you're here? You always were a good influence on her."

Grayson couldn't meet his sister-in-law's eyes and merely shrugged, relieved when he heard his father's booming voice. "Get ready, the grandparents are here to spoil your children rotten," he said.

He smiled when *Papa* entered the room with Lee on his broad shoulders.

"*Bonjour, Jessica et Grayson.*" His father smiled widely. "Where is my granddaughter?"

"Taking a much-needed nap," Jessica replied, giving him a hug and a kiss.

"*Papa, Maman.*" Grayson kissed his stepmother and tried to turn away, but she caught his cheek in her hand.

"Have you slept? Have you had a decent meal in the last week?" Her warm, brown eyes searched his face. He knew he looked terrible. He hadn't slept much in the past three days, but he didn't want to upset his family.

"I'm fine." He smiled, but she wasn't buying it.

She grabbed his arm and led him outside, shutting the door. Pulling away, she crossed her arms and looked him over from head to toe.

"You look positively exhausted. I'm worried about you, son."

"I'll be okay, *Maman*."

"Have you finally had your fill of the little lying bitch?" She tapped her perfectly manicured fingers, shivering slightly from the cold.

Caught off guard, Grayson blurted, "It was as much my fault—more so, actually. She's young—"

"Ha! Candie Fontaine may want the world to think she's *young*, but we all know better."

He rubbed his face, too tired for subterfuge. His mind was on Alyssandra, not Candie. "It is definitely over with Candie. No need to worry there."

"I know you cared about her, and I'm sorry you're in pain. But I can't say I'm sorry she's out of your life. She was a user and never good enough for you. I found her to be cold the few times I was around her. Probably because she has no heart." His stepmother pulled him into her arms and patted him on the back as she kissed his cheek. He hugged her, grateful for this woman who had loved him unconditionally since coming into his life.

"And she's a truly rotten actress," she added matter-of-factly.

He chuckled. "Thank you, *Maman*. I know and agree, on all counts. I'm leaving for Paris after the party and christening. Aside from work, a change of scenery, a nice Parisian girl to warm my bed, and some of *Grand-mère's* French cooking will help tremendously." He grinned and winked at her.

She snorted. "Please, your grandmother's never made anything more complicated than a very dry martini."

"True. But she takes the credit for Adele's skills as a chef."

"You don't need a *girl* to warm your bed. You need a *wife* to take care of you." His mother smacked his cheek lightly—one of the annoying habits she'd adopted from his father. "Let's go back inside. I'm cold and have grandchildren to spoil. I wish you'd get busy and provide us with some too. It's inconsiderate of you to make Frank do all the work."

"I don't think he minds at all," Grayson replied with a laugh.

His mother's eyes twinkled. "I'm sure he doesn't. I appreciate you letting us stay here with Frank and Jessica. It will give us more time with the children. You'll have fun at the Carltons."

Gray swallowed his frustration. The arrival of his parents bumped him from the guest room at Frank and Jessica's house. Since there wasn't a decent hotel close by, the Carltons had insisted he stay with them. There had been no graceful way to refuse, so now, he would be trapped in the same house as Alyssandra.

"Lissy, go upstairs and see if Grayson would like a sandwich. I know there'll be plenty of food at the party, but he may be hungry before then." Her mother pulled a plate of sandwiches from the fridge.

"Mother, Gray's a grown man. If he wants a friggin' sandwich, I'm sure he can come downstairs and get it himself."

"Don't be rude, especially in front of company." Patsy handed a sandwich to Eddie with a smile.

Lissy rolled her eyes. "He's not *company*; he's just *Eddie*." She'd convinced her family he'd moved out of the friend zone now that Josh wasn't in the picture.

"Thank you, ma'am. Gee, thanks, Liss." Eddie grinned and stuck out his tongue behind her mother's back.

So far he'd been on his best behavior, playing the part of her doting boyfriend. He looked very handsome in his pressed white shirt, maroon sweater, and khaki pants. Mother was smitten and probably mentally planning her wedding to the future Dr. Sanders.

Eddie accepted the glass of milk to go with his sandwich and flashed a smile that could melt the artic polar cap. "This is delicious, Mrs. Carlton. And you sure look pretty in green; it brings out your emerald eyes."

Beaming, her mother patted her hair. "Why thank you, Eddie."

Lissy gave him a quick kiss on the cheek. "You're such a brown-nosing suck-up," she hissed in his ear before trudging upstairs.

Why couldn't Jess have made Gray sleep on her back porch in the cold? It would've served him right. But *nooooo*, he was here, separated from her by only a connecting bathroom—the very same bathroom where he'd once scrubbed her face and given her a lesson on not falling for jerks who only wanted one thing. *What a fuckin' joke.*

She knocked lightly on the door and waited. No answer. *A smart girl would simply turn around, walk downstairs, and tell Mother he was sleeping.* But *this girl* is flunking out of college, she reminded herself as she slipped into his room, closing the door behind her.

He slept with one arm thrown over his eyes, the other rising and falling on his perfectly cut, bare abdomen. He hadn't removed his unbuttoned shirt—as if he'd collapsed, too tired to finish undressing. A part of her wanted to help him finish what he'd started, and she gripped the doorknob to keep herself in place.

Angrily, she marched to his bedside. *After the way he left me, why does he still affect me like this?*

He stirred, rolling to his side. She held her breath until his soft snoring resumed. Weariness marked his face, and his cheekbones seemed more prominent.

Sadly, she realized she loved him. Her heart ached for him, and she clutched her chest, willing the pain to subside. He wasn't a marrying man. He wasn't interested in long-term commitments. She knew this. He'd been very clear from the beginning.

But she'd lied to him—and worse, to herself. She didn't want casual, no-strings-attached sex. She wanted the happily ever after, or at the very least a committed relationship. And that might never happen with Grayson Deschanelle.

Had she simply been the flavor of the month? They'd only been together a few days, which in itself was depressing. *Even Candie Fontaine lasted two years.*

But he'd come to her apartment. Why? Was Eddie right and Gray did care for her? Should she ask him? A brave woman would. And she wanted to take charge of her life…

Pushing aside her fear of rejection, she sat beside him and ran her fingers through the gray at his temples. "Gray?"

He stirred and whispered, "*Mon chaton.*" He reached and pulled her to him, curling around her, spooning her back, not fully awake. Slipping his hand under her sweatshirt, his thumb grazed her nipple. His soft, sleepy growl of need gave her hope.

Lissy rolled over and cupped his face in her hand. "Wake up, Gray."

He stirred and stretched before opening his eyes. When he did, he looked haunted and vulnerable. "You're here. Am I dreaming?" Raspy from sleep, his voice held the seductive promise of what could be.

"Mother sent me up to ask if you want a sandwich."

He smiled and raised his eyebrows, his thumb brushing the underside of her breast.

"A sandwich? *Non. C'est toi que je veux.* Sorry. I mean all I want is *you*. Not a sandwich."

Lissy caught her breath for a moment. Was it just his exhaustion speaking?

"Do you want the sandwich or not?"

"No, thank you." He rubbed his eyes. "Just sleep."

Not me. "How's Candie?" She made every effort to keep the snark out of her voice.

"Fine. I'm not with Candie. I merely went to make sure she was okay after she slit her wrists."

"Selfish bitch," she mumbled harshly.

"What?" His voice sounded weary.

"I said she's a selfish bitch. Why would she put her family, friends, and loved ones through that?"

"Publicity." Grayson sounded defeated and rolled over. "And I totally agree with you."

"Publicity? It was a stunt? Who does that sort of thing? That's crazy. If you decide you want a sandwich, Mother said to come downstairs."

"Tell her thank you, but no."

Lissy sped out of the room before she offered him more than her condolences.

Chapter Thirteen

"**B**itch, I could steal those thigh-highs from you and not think twice about it." Eddie stroked her boots like he was petting Noëlle.

"I'd let you have them. They're killing my feet," Lissy grumbled, peering at her reflection in the hallway mirror.

She adjusted the wide, sweeping maroon Cavalier hat with two cat ears peeking out of the brim. The ostrich plume curled toward her face. Turning, she admired how the off-the-shoulder white blouse and maroon corset made her boobs almost voluptuous. But the best part of the costume had to be the long tail attached to the super-short brown shorts.

She shook her butt and giggled. "No wonder Noëlle loves to chase her tail. Daddy's gonna kill me when he sees half of my butt hanging out, but it'll be worth it. I'll die looking fabulous."

"True. You did a great job on our costumes." Eddie adjusted his Thor getup. "You look like a French sex kitten. Unless Gray is blind, you should definitely grab his attention." He winked at her.

"You look pretty fantastic yourself. And if I'm not mistaken, one of the waiters Mother hired has been drooling over you ever since he laid eyes on your biceps."

Eddie flexed his massive arms. "What, these lil ol' things? Of course I look fantastic, I'm *me*. Puh-lease. A waiter? I can do so much better—holy shit, was that him?" Eddie's head spun around so fast he probably got whiplash. His eyes widened when the handsome waiter with the nametag *Dante* winked as he strode by with a tray of hors d'oeuvres.

Lissy nodded and grinned.

"Uh, Liss? Just exactly how long do I have to play your hetero girl-toy?"

"Just a few more hours. Roll up your tongue and let's go out to the main tent."

Lissy grabbed his hand as they wormed their way through various fairy-tale characters, pimps, pirates, cowboys, and princesses. Scanning the crowd for Gray, she wondered if he'd changed his mind about attending. After two tail pulls, one inappropriate drunken offer—which Eddie handled with a warning growl—and several stops for small talk, they made it into the den area where one of the three bars had been set up for the party.

"Alyssandra!" Her father, dressed as Charlie Chaplin, hurried toward her with her mother, dressed as a flapper. "Where's the rest of your costume?" He scowled, ignoring her mother's nudge to be quiet.

Lissy shook her head. "I have on more than I wear at the beach. Daddy, this is Eddie Sanders. Eddie, this is my father, George Carlton. And of course, you've already met my mother, Patsy."

"And when have I ever approved of your or your sister's beachwear?" her father replied, turning his attention to Eddie and shaking hands. "So, Patsy tells me you're pre-med? How are your grades, son?"

"Straight A's, sir," Eddie replied.

"Very good. Have fun, you two." Daddy pointed at her. "And no drinking."

"It's my birthday, and I'm twenty-one," Lissy replied.

"Not until ten thirty tonight," her father called as he disappeared into the crowd.

"You need more clothes on. Did you forget your pants?" Her older brother, Travis, appeared at her side, dressed as a monk.

"Travis, this is Eddie. Eddie, this is my overprotective brother, Friar Fuckwad." Lissy frowned as she searched the crowd for Gray.

"Nice to meet you," Eddie replied, his gaze following the hot waiter even as he shook Travis's hand.

"Same here. Pre-med, right? Any relation to the Sanders that own—"

"Stop it, Travis. Did Mother already print the engagement announcement or something?"

"Probably. She's determined to get a big wedding out of one of us, and it sure as hell won't be me." He turned and stared appreciatively at a waitress walking by with an empty tray. "I think I'm thirsty. See ya around. Behave, Liss." Travis departed, leaving her and Eddie alone.

"Sorry, Eddie. Let's go to the bar out back. Daddy will never know. We deserve some liquid sustenance after all this family scrutiny."

In the backyard, a huge tent with two bars, a DJ, and a dance floor had been set up, and the air vibrated with the thunderous sound of disco music. She held Eddie's hand to keep from falling in the ridiculous six-inch heels. As they stepped into the tent, Jessica and Frank approached, dressed as a cowgirl and cowboy.

"Good grief, Lissy, has your father seen your costume? Or should I say, how little there is of your costume?" Frank asked with raised eyebrows.

Lissy cut her eyes to Eddie and laughed. "Yes, and so has Travis. How come no one is commenting that Jessica's about to spill out of her top?"

Jessica pulled her blouse up a bit. "Hi, you must be Eddie. I'm Lissy's sister, and this is my husband, Frank."

Eddie gave Jessica a quick kiss on the cheek and shook hands with Frank. Behind his back Jessica gave a thumbs up, fanning herself with a wink. Lissy rolled her eyes.

Geezus, maybe Eddie's playing the role of boyfriend too brilliantly. Her family would have them engaged before midnight.

Marie Antoinette and King Louis XVI walked over to join them.

"Lissy, you look beautiful, *ma belle.*" Olivier Deschanelle kissed her on both cheeks. She'd always loved Frank's and Gray's parents. Gray was very much like his father—although his father's accent was much more pronounced, and Olivier's hair was completely white.

She hugged Gray's stepmother, Lynn. "You two look fabulous! Did you get the costumes in Paris?"

"Yes. How did you know we were in Paris?" Lynn asked, and then answered her own question. "Of course, Jessica must've told you. We spent Christmas there. It was beautiful, but I'm glad to be home."

Lissy swallowed nervously and moved on to introductions. "Lynn and Olivier Deschanelle, this is Eddie Sanders. Eddie, the Deschanelles are Gray's and Frank's parents." She refused to look at Jessica, knowing she'd slipped about Paris. Wrapping an arm around Eddie's waist, she exchanged pleasantries and small talk with everyone.

Movement from across the room caught her eye, and she plastered on a wide smile and sidled closer to Eddie. She assumed Gray was staring at her, but it was hard to tell behind his Ray-Bans. He wore a dark suit, and she wondered what his costume was supposed to be. He spoke to the waitress with the skimpy top and enhanced boobs, who laughed and nodded at whatever brilliant thing he'd just said in her ear. She then had the gall to smooth a hand down his lapel, which didn't need straightening.

Lissy clenched her fists, wishing she could wipe the smile off the woman's face.

No one was dancing yet, and Lissy decided it was time to get this party started.

"Come on and dance with me," she demanded, dragging Eddie toward the dance floor. The DJ had just started Flo-Rida's "Low."

Lissy gave Eddie an inviting smile as she danced, showing off her best assets. When he gave her butt a swat and pulled her tail, she laughed. Damn, the boy could move, and he was fun to dance with. She cut him a sexy look and a wink as he pulled her close, dirty dancing with her.

On a spin, Lissy caught a glimpse of her brother's horrified face. She stepped up her game a notch, dancing down Eddie's leg. Eddie hauled her up and did a bump and grind. For a few moments she and Eddie were the center of attention, but soon other couples joined them on the dance floor.

The song ended, and the DJ threw on another club song.

"We're about to have some company. Do I let him cut in or beat his ass?" Eddie asked in her ear.

Before she could give an answer, Gray stepped in and expertly took over as her dance partner. She still couldn't see his eyes behind the dark glasses. She danced closer, enjoying the feel of his hands on her hips as they moved to the music.

He grinned at her as the suggestive chorus started. "No *Dirty Dancing* moves with the family watching," he said, keeping space between them.

"Wouldn't dream of it. Besides, you think you're old. So maybe you're more like Danny Kaye?"

He laughed. "I'm not *that* old."

Her heart pounded, and a faint sheen of sweat coated her skin. She really didn't feel like dancing at all, but kept up the pretense of having a good time.

As the song ended, Gray whispered in her ear, *"Le chat botté."*

"W-What?" She pulled away, suddenly aware of several family members watching them.

"Puss in boots." He pulled his glasses down and winked at her. "*My* puss in boots."

Shocked, she sputtered, "My boyfriend's here!"

Feeling lightheaded, she walked outside to get a breath of fresh air and regroup.

Eddie found her sucking in air like a drowning victim. "Are you okay?"

She nodded, as she inhaled. "Just cooling off for a minute." She attempted a smile as the tightness in her chest eased.

"Okay. Well, if you don't mind, I'll be inside at the bar, drinking a diet soda. I promise to be totally sober when I drive home, but a certain waiter with a sexy Italian accent is getting drinks at this particular bar…"

"Go. You've played the part long enough." Lissy waved him away.

Eddie gave her a kiss on her forehead and left.

Chapter
Fourteen

Grayson stood at the bar, nursing his drink, when Eddie walked over and ordered a Diet Coke. The kid glared at him with an intensity meant to intimidate. Luckily, only *Grand-mère* scared him. Grayson raised his drink in silent toast.

"Just so you know, I'm gay." Eddie sucked down the soda with an irritating slurp on the straw.

Grayson's lips curled. Taking off his sunglasses, he stuffed them in his pocket. "I know."

"You do? Shit, I thought I was pretty damn convincing." Eddie frowned, his eyes following the waiter.

"You were. I may be the only one who knows. Aside from Alyssandra…and Dante over there." Grayson nodded toward the waiter, who was now glaring at him.

"When did you figure it out?"

"When you were dancing with her and watching him."

"Well, shit." Eddie clunked the glass down on the bar. "Busted." He chuckled.

A grin split Eddie's face. "I like you, Deschanelle. But don't hurt her. *I mean it.* I will kick your ass all the way back to New York City if you do. Understand?"

"Totally."

Grayson admired his loyalty.

"She's outside. Go get her, tiger. I've got someone who needs to experience Eddie Sanders." He turned his attention to the waiter.

Grayson began easing his way through the crowd, but was stopped by Dylan McAthie.

"Grayson! Hey, man. How's everything going?"

Friends for years, Grayson shook Dylan's hand and nodded to his wife, Jennifer. He'd been their wedding photographer and had worked with him on a number of projects. They'd also raised hell together many times.

"The jumpsuit's a little flashy for you, Dylan."

"I'm Elvis; Jen's Priscilla. I figure since the tabloids always say I'm hangin' with him, I'll just *be* him."

Grayson chuckled and kissed Jennifer's fingers. "Beautiful as always, Mrs. McAthie."

Her cheeks flushed. "Thank you. That accent always gets me. How are you?" She looked over at her husband. "You need a sexy French accent, Dylan."

"The only French words I know are the dirty phrases Grayson taught me."

"That would work," she replied as she turned to talk to Jessica.

"Buy you a drink?" Grayson asked Dylan.

"That accent doesn't work on me, bud."

Grayson laughed as they walked to the bar and ordered.

"So what's up? I heard about you and Candie. The cashier at the local grocery store stays up on all the trash gossip. I figure about ninety-five percent of it's bullshit, but something happened. You okay?"

"It's over between us, and yes, I'm fine. She's the past." Grayson swirled his drink, hesitating. "May I ask you something?"

"Sure."

"I know you and Jennifer had a difficult time when you first got together…"

"We did," Dylan agreed.

"Was it the age difference?"

"Somewhat. She's ten years younger. But shared experiences and kids have evened things out. Why? Is there a younger woman in your life? Or more than one?" Dylan nudged his arm and laughed.

Grayson grimaced. *That damn twin incident again.* Maybe talking to Dylan wasn't such a great idea.

"No twins. But she is younger than I am."

"Just remember the rule."

"What rule?" Grayson asked.

"Half plus seven."

He frowned. *What's Dylan talking about?* "I don't understand."

"Don't date anyone under half your age plus seven."

"Who made this rule?"

"I dunno; it's just a rule. Who is it?" Dylan asked, tipping back his beer.

Thankfully, Jennifer returned to ask Dylan something and Grayson snuck away. According to the rule, Lissy was too young for him. Even Dylan would think so.

He sighed.

The past few days without her, he'd gone through the motions of living. She'd become an obsession, and it probably made him a creeper, but he couldn't stay away. He needed to talk to her. To explain, apologize, and hopefully work something out between them.

He stepped outside and found her alone by the covered pool. The sound of laughter and dance music drifted from inside the house and the tent, but thankfully they were alone. Lying on a lounge chair, wrapped in a beach towel, she shivered. Her pale face looked almost ghostly in the dim light.

"Alyssandra?" He sat beside her, brushing a strand of hair from her face.

"Where's your waitress? Or did you come out here to ask me to join you in a threesome?" Her eyes remained closed.

"What are you talking about?" He shrugged out of his jacket and tucked it around her.

"I saw you flirting with her." Her eyes opened and glared at him.

"Interesting. I didn't realize simply requesting a scotch neat was an American way of flirting. I'll have to remember that." Smiling, he glanced around, confirmed they were alone, and kissed her soft lips.

"Stop it. My boyfriend will kick your ass," she said. "And why aren't you in a costume?"

"Ah, the same boyfriend who wanted both of us at your apartment? You seem to be fascinated with *ménage à trois*. Is this something you'd like to explore? And I *am* in a costume. I'm a secret service agent."

"That's lame, and you know it."

"Should I go ask your boyfriend if he's ready to join us?"

Her outraged gasp made him smile.

He shrugged. "I've never done this with another male; it could be interesting, watching you as we both—"

She attempted unsuccessfully to push him away. "Stop it!"

Grayson laughed. "Don't worry. I believe Eddie is seeking pleasure elsewhere with the handsome Italian waiter. What is it with my ex-girlfriend and your new boyfriend and these Italians?"

"I'm gonna kick his ass," she grumbled. "When did you find out he's gay?" Her hand trembled against her chest, and she was breathing through her mouth.

"When you two were dancing, he kept looking at Dante." Gray eyed her sharply, not liking the bluish tint to her lips. "Are you unwell?"

"My heart's racing. It always does it when I'm near you," she admitted, her cheeks flushing bright against her alarming pallor. "Or maybe it's because I'm still angry with you."

"Deservedly. Will you forgive me?"

"I don't know. I'm confused. You left me to go back to Candie. But then you came to see me…And now you're back. I think maybe I'm supposed to hate you."

"You probably should." Surely it was the strange lighting by the pool that had her appearing so fragile. He took her cold fingers and kissed them. "But you don't?"

"Nope. Disappointed? It would've been your out."

"Quite the opposite." He smiled. "Let's enjoy the party tonight and talk tomorrow. We'll slip away somewhere."

"You broke my heart," she whispered, her eyes shiny. "Why didn't you tell me what had happened? I would've understood. But you just up and left me, saying Candie needed you without explaining what the emergency was. I had to read about it on social media."

"And I'll forever regret doing so, my darling. Please forgive me. I didn't elaborate because I didn't know all the details. But I should've handled things differently. I think I was scared."

"Of Candie dying?"

"No, of my growing affection for you."

"You could've called."

"I thought you deserved an in-person apology. I went to your apartment…"

"We're both fools." She sighed. "Now what? Where do we go from here?"

"To be honest, I don't know. Come, it's your birthday; let's celebrate and talk later. I like your costume. Did you make it?"

"Okay, let's go. And yes, I did." She stood and offered him his coat, some of the color returning to her face.

"It's wonderful."

"Gray? Will we really talk? Or is this going to be just sex? With no strings attached?"

"I think sex would be awkward in your parents' home. We'll talk, and then see about new beginnings."

"At the risk of throwing myself at you again, I want you to know I'm okay with sex-only if it means having you in my life. I think we're good for each other."

Picking up her hat, he placed it on her head and shrugged back into his jacket. "Alyssandra, I'm not sure I'm cut out for what you're seeking. I'm forty years old, and I've never had a relationship that lasted more than a few months until Candie—and you saw how well that turned out. I don't make promises I can't keep. But let's discuss this later. It's your birthday. You need to have fun."

"Do you want me?" she asked.

"I do. Do you want me?"

"I have since I was fifteen."

He frowned.

"I'm just stating the truth."

"I have something for you," he replied.

Curiosity flickered in her eyes. "You don't have to buy sex with me."

"I would never do so. You mean a great deal to me. Happy birthday, Alyssandra." He pulled the blue box with a white ribbon out of his pocket.

"You bought me a present?"

"I shorted you at Christmas."

She bit her lip. "Oh, your package is pretty big," she quipped.

He chuckled. "*Merci.*"

Her hands shook as she took the gift. Opening it, she gasped, removing the necklace with a single pearl on a platinum chain. "It's beautiful, but I don't think I should accept it. It's too much."

"I would give you anything you want. *Joyeux anniversaire.*" He took the necklace from her hands and fastened it, nuzzling her neck when he was done. The pulse visible at the base of her neck pounded.

She turned and shook her head, opening her mouth to say something, but then closed it.

"What were you going to say?"

"You'd give me anything except agreeing to openly date me."

He hesitated. "I'd do anything to protect you," he stressed.

Instantly, her eyes shuttered, and she turned away.

He caught hold of her hand. "I'm sorry."

She shot a look back at him. "About?"

"Not being what you want…"

"I want *you* for my birthday, Gray. And I want to be *your* birthday present. There's nothing wrong with us being together. These mixed signals of yours are confusing."

"It's complicated, but I'll try to do better. That's why we need to talk." He looked around, relieved they were still alone.

"I promise I'll keep quiet." She moved closer, copped a feel, and gave him a quick kiss.

He smirked. "Uh-huh."

"I meant about *us*. But I can be quiet when we make love, too."

"Maybe if I gag you."

"Okay." She shot him a sly smile and winked.

"Yuck." Lissy wrinkled her nose.

"Gross," Jessica agreed.

"My eyes!" Travis bellowed.

Frank and Gray nodded as they watched their parents dancing to Marvin Gaye's "Sexual Healing."

"Jessica, I'm begging. I know Daddy said no drinking for me. But don't you think *this* warrants a drink?"

"I have to say yes. I mean, I know they had to have had sex — we're all here — but still…Besides, you're legally twenty-one. Happy birthday."

The waitress Travis had been eyeing all evening came by with a tray of champagne.

Lissy's mouth dropped when her mother grabbed her father's butt. *How much has she had to drink?*

"This is downright disturbing." Travis downed his glass, frowning at the dance floor.

"Daddy might say the same thing about you chasing after that waitress. I think she's married, Travis. Don't you ever learn?" Jessica hissed. "Where's Eddie, Lissy?"

Lissy squirmed. "He had to leave. He's got MCATs to study for."

"With your poor grammar, you should be studying as well. He *has* MCATs, not 'he's got.'"

"I'm not in school, and you're not my teacher." Lissy threw back her champagne and stomped off to get another one, feeling out of sorts and tired.

Leaning toward the bartender, she felt someone tug her tail as the DJ announced one last slow song before the fireworks.

Turning, Gray grabbed her hand, tugging her to the dance floor. He pulled her close, but not too close.

"This is so corny," she grumbled, enjoying the feel of his arm around her waist. He wrapped her right hand in his, holding it against his chest.

"Indeed. I like being corny with you. Pretend we're Danny Kaye and the blonde with the ponytail in that Christmas movie you love."

She grinned. "Vera-Ellen. And that's *White Christmas*. The costumes are so beautiful." She was nearly as tall as he was in the ridiculous boots. "Careful, Gray. People might think you actually *like* me."

He chuckled. "I do like you, Alyssandra. Very much. I'm just not sure I'm good for you."

Lissy leaned back and looked at him. There was no mistaking the desire simmering in those beautiful blue eyes. She glanced around nervously to see if anyone else noticed.

"I like you, too." She leaned in and whispered, "I especially like you when you're naked. And I think you're very good."

"Ditto. I wish we could turn back time and be at the cabin."

Fireworks exploded over the lake in a riot of color and sound. Her father always insisted on a huge display with no expense spared. Lissy turned after a particularly brilliant starburst to look at Gray. He wasn't watching the fireworks at all.

Her breath caught in her throat at the raw need on his face, illuminated by the burst of light. Something tugged on her behind, and she laughed when she realized Gray was pulling her tail and moving slowly toward the woods. She glanced around, but all attention was focused on the wondrous display in the sky. She tucked her hand in Gray's and followed him into the trees.

He stopped suddenly and backed her against a huge oak. She shivered in anticipation of his kiss. Shrugging out of his jacket, he wrapped it around her shoulders, yanking her to him by the lapels.

"Shhhh," he whispered against her lips.

His hands roamed down her body, and she gasped with pleasure. "Gray?" All rational thoughts fled when he pulled down her peasant top, exposing her breasts. He massaged her nipples into hard pebbles as his mouth sought hers.

"*Oui?*"

"Someone could catch us…"

"Isn't that part of the thrill?" he murmured as one hand moved under the waistband of her minuscule shorts, finding her already embarrassingly wet for him. One, then two fingers slipped into her. His mouth latched on to her breast and her knees weakened. When she moaned, he silenced her with kisses and worked her into a quivering frenzy. It felt so wrong and so right all at the same time. She exploded, and a million pieces of self-preservation were scattered forever with that orgasm. He silenced her with a hand over her mouth and smiled against her ear.

She looked around, feeling nervous. Her family was less than a hundred yards away. The appreciative sounds of the partygoers rose to the sky as the fireworks continued. It took her a few seconds to realize Gray was rolling on a condom and without thinking, she tugged off the bottom of her costume, anxious to feel him inside of her.

"I love the boots," he whispered raggedly.

His lifted her in his arms, shoved her back against the tree, and entered her swiftly, stilling for a moment. Lissy wrapped her legs more tightly around his waist, urging him to move, wanting him deeper. The possibility of being caught fueled her need.

Gray pounded into her furiously, silencing her orgasm with another mind-numbing kiss. A few strokes later, he followed her over the edge, clenching his teeth, his breath sawing with the exertion. It had been quick and savage, almost animalistic—and it was by far the most intense orgasm of her life. He held her tight for a moment as they regained their breath.

The chill in the air made her that much colder as her sweat evaporated. The smell of sex hung heavy between them.

"Damn, Gray. That was some birthday present." Lissy clung to his damp neck, glad for his support—there was no way she could stand on her own at the moment.

She felt his lips curve into a smile, and he nodded, still breathing harshly.

"Don't have a heart attack on me. My father will kill you," she joked.

"True," he chuckled.

"If I were to die right now, I'd die happy," she blurted. A strange feeling of apprehension made her shiver.

"At age twenty-one? That's hardly likely, my darling girl." He kissed the tip of her nose and pulled out.

She felt disconnected, as if drowning in an uncharted sea as he stood her on her own shaky legs. Toeing the earth with his shoe, he disposed of the condom and zipped his pants before silently helping her dress.

The finale of the fireworks started, and they edged back toward the party.

"Wow. Did you see that chrysanthemum? Daddy knows they're my favorite. That was amazing."

Gray chuckled. "*Wow* is an understatement. That show in the sky has nothing on what just occurred."

They made it back as the last firework fizzled and the crowd began to softly sing "Auld Lang Syne."

"That was some display."

Lissy jumped and reluctantly met her sister's stony gaze. Under the dock lights, Jessica looked a lot like her mother with her lips thinned and arms crossed in front of her chest. Lissy nodded and swallowed as Jessica shot a speculative look between her and Gray.

Then Frank joined them, staggering just a bit. "Happy New Year, and happy birthday, Trip," he slurred, raising his drink and grinning. "Fuckin' forty. Glad it's you and not me."

He patted Jessica on the butt, making her squeal. Obviously she'd be the one driving home.

"Thank you. *Bonne année.* The fireworks were spectacular. Your father outdid himself this year."

Lissy was in awe at how calm, cool, and collected Gray sounded. After the best orgasm of her life, she didn't think she could string three coherent words together.

"Cold?" Jessica asked, pointedly staring.

Lissy realized she was still wrapped in Gray's coat and curled her toes inside the uncomfortable boots to keep from fidgeting.

"Y-Yes. Gray was nice enough to let me borrow his jacket."

"Well, hell, Liss, you're only half-dressed. No wonder you're cold," Frank chided, not really paying attention to her. He stumbled, and Jessica caught him. With a wide grin, he gave his wife a sloppy kiss on the cheek. "Ready to go home, sexy mama?"

Seeing her brother-in-law drunk would've been amusing under different circumstances. Thankfully, it kept him from noticing her guilt.

"Only if I'm driving, Frank." Jessica's narrowed gaze zeroed in on Gray before returning to Lissy.

"Of course you are, sugar. You're my desired driver."

"Don't you mean *designated?*" Jessica smiled, her attention diverted back to her husband.

"That too." He gave her a leer.

She laughed. "Let's go. Good night, Lissy. And happy birthday to both of you." She pulled a twig out of Lissy's hair. "We'll talk tomorrow after dinner, okay?"

Lissy shrugged, not feeling nearly as confident as she pretended. Jessica turned to walk away with Frank, who smacked her on the butt again, making her shriek and laugh.

Lissy shot Gray a look. "She knows."

"She suspects." He took her hand, guiding her toward the house. "We'll be fine. *Bonne année et bonne santé,* Alyssandra." He gave her a kiss on both cheeks.

"Happy New Year's birthday, Gray, and good night." She shrugged out of his jacket and handed it back to him as Travis walked over.

"'Night, Liss. Hope you had a good birthday. See ya tomorrow at dinner." Travis gave her a salute and wave.

Her parents were next, each one giving her a birthday kiss and wishing her Happy New Year. She chalked it up to the amount of alcohol consumed that no one but Jessica seemed to discern she'd just been fucked to hell and back.

Beyond exhausted, she dragged herself upstairs. Shedding the costume, she took a quick shower and brushed her teeth. Her eyes were bright, her lips still slightly puffy, and her cheeks pink from more than the cold night air. Pulling on her pajamas, she glanced at the bathroom door that led to her sister's old room, where Gray was staying. She briefly considered slipping in, but decided it was too risky. Exhausted, she crawled into bed.

Underneath the bathroom door, she could see the light flick on, and the shower started. With a frustrated sigh, she rolled over, trying not to think about Gray naked and wet. Or how much she wanted his arms around her. Or how she needed him to tell her everything was going to be okay. Or how she loved a man who was conflicted about relationships in general, and more so about theirs.

The bathroom door opened, and Lissy sat up. Wearing a pair of navy pajama pants, with his hair still damp from his shower, Gray put a finger to his lips and locked her bedroom door before joining her.

"Set your alarm for four. I'll go back to my room then."

She did as he asked. "Gray—"

"Shh. Neither of us would be able to sleep apart." He pulled her close, his arm wrapped firmly around her waist. His hand slipped under her pajama top to cup her breast as he kissed the back of her neck.

"I should hate you, but I don't."

"I know, and I'm glad."

Lissy smiled when almost immediately his soft snore ruffled her hair.

"Happy birthday, my love," she whispered.

Chapter
Fifteen

Chilled, Grayson reached over to pull Lissy closer but found only a pillow. He was back in his own bed, alone. He cracked one eye and looked for the bedside clock. It was seven in the morning. He rolled over and stared at the ceiling, guilt settling firmly on his conscience with the light of day—and not just any day. His fortieth birthday.

He categorized the reasons a serious relationship with Lissy wouldn't work: the age difference, the relentless press coverage, he didn't *want* a committed relationship, she *needed* to figure out what she wanted to do with her life, and he lived nine hundred miles away in New York City, when he wasn't in Paris. *Just sex. No strings attached.* Honestly, a part of him was embarrassed by his infatuation with her. What was wrong with him? He wasn't some randy, hormonal teenager, yet he was acting like one. He couldn't seem to get enough of her.

The bathroom door opened slowly. Seeing him awake, Alyssandra's face lit up with a wide smile. She hurried over, leaned in, and kissed him, compounding his guilt.

"Happy birthday. I came to see if you'd like me to bring you a cup of coffee," she whispered.

"You're not my wife." His tone sounded sharper than he'd intended, and he instantly wished he could hit replay and erase the hurt in her eyes.

This really had nothing to do with her; it was him having the problem.

She straightened and glared at him. "No, because if I were, you'd be sleeping on the couch."

He sat up and rubbed his face. "I'm sorry. I didn't mean that the way it sounded. I meant you don't have to wait on me. I can get my own coffee." He grabbed her hand and pulled her to the bed.

She refused to look at him, and he cupped her cheek in his hand.

"I'm sorry. I really didn't mean it the way it sounded." *Or did I?*

"We need to lay out some ground rules, Gray. But not until after you've had your pot of coffee."

"I agree, on both counts." He brushed the hair out of her pale face. "Lissy, are you okay? After our tryst in the woods?"

"You called me Lissy." She grinned and rubbed his cheek with the back of her fingers. "It was fuckin' amazing. And *tryst* sounds like something a grandpa would say. You're *only* forty."

He pinched her nipple in response. "Brat."

Her blush spread down to her chest, and her nipples hardened beneath the silky pajama top. She pushed him back on the bed and kissed him passionately, her tongue exploring his mouth as she trapped his hands in hers. Pulling away, she smiled into his ear and whispered, "But my parents will be waking up any minute now, so I'll go…before you *have* to marry me in an old-fashioned shotgun wedding."

She sprang out of bed and left the room with Noëlle scampering behind her.

He wondered if that sort of thing still happened in this small town.

Lissy was pouring a cup of coffee when she heard Gray on the stairs. Putting on a brave smile, she tucked her growing love for him into a special place in the back of her mind where she would revisit it later. She was not yet ready to withstand the potential disappointment this relationship held. And on the flip side, she didn't dare hope, yet. She handed him the coffee and busied herself wiping the counters.

"That's good, thank you." He drank appreciatively but paused, searching her face. "You're pale. I'm worried about you."

"I told you, I'm fine. Just a little tired." She smiled, but truthfully, she didn't feel well. She was sore from last evening's adventures, but something else was going on. She felt generally out of sorts. She attributed it to dreading the confrontation she was sure to have with Jessica later today—and the talk with Gray.

His eyebrows drew together, as if he didn't buy her story, but he put the empty coffee cup on the counter and nodded. She could hear her parents coming downstairs, talking about last night's party.

"I'm going for my run before the start of the festivities today."

He brushed the back of his fingers across her cheek before he left, and she had no time to dwell on it as her parents joined her. Like Gray, her father wasn't a morning person, and he sank into a chair as Mother poured their coffee. Everyone would soon arrive for a typical Southern New Year's celebration of family, food, and football. Her parents were in their element; they loved entertaining, especially when it came to their children and grandchildren.

"Are you okay, baby?" Her mother's eyes narrowed.

Lissy made a conscious effort *not* to roll her eyes. *Do I look that bad?* "I'm okay, just tired. It was a great party last night. Thank you." She gave her mother what she hoped passed for a reassuring smile. "And thank you for the book on the crown jewels from London and the money for my birthday."

"You're welcome. Your father and I thought it was a fun party, too." Her mother turned toward the cabinets and dove into preparing the huge brunch for the family. Within moments she was barking orders like a drill sergeant as Lissy hustled to help.

"Did you enjoy the fireworks?" Her father scanned the headline news on his tablet, sipping coffee. Lissy was thankful it held his attention; it kept him from seeing her hot face.

"Yes, Daddy, it was the best ever."

"Is Gray awake yet?"

Why is he asking me? Does he know? Frozen for a moment, she forced herself to let out the breath she'd been holding. Her father continued to peruse the news. It was just a question.

"He went for a run; you just missed him. If you can spare me for a few minutes, Mother, I'll shower and get dressed."

She fled the room before her parents could ask her anything else.

The run helped clear Grayson's head until the shuffle on his phone switched to a song Alyssandra had downloaded while they were at the cabin. *Sonofabitch.*

He pushed himself to run harder, faster. Thankfully the next two days would be busy, filled with family functions — today the New Year's celebration, and tomorrow Grace's christening. He'd promised her they'd talk, but he wondered if they'd actually have any alone time to do so. And then he'd leave for Paris.

"Fuck!" He bent over, hands on his knees, his heart racing. He gasped for breath as he hit the runner's wall — just as he realized Paris without her held no appeal. *Fuck, fuck, fuck.* Images of Alyssandra popped in his brain like a slideshow.

The way her gray eyes had sparkled with excitement as she'd played in the snow.

The way she bit her lip when knitting.

The sweet smile on her face as she played with that ridiculous cat.

The god-awful breakfast she'd cooked and been so proud of.

And the smoldering look she'd given him in those thigh-high fuck-me boots. Goddammit, he wanted more than just sex. Grayson scrubbed a hand over his face. For reasons he still couldn't completely parse out, he wanted Alyssandra like no other woman. There would be a myriad of problems if he pursued this path. Would they be insurmountable? There was only one way to know, and he had just two damn days to figure out how to do it.

The noise at the brunch table reached a deafening level as the children cried and screamed and the adults talked and laughed about the party last night. However, Gray remained quiet, only speaking when spoken to.

Frank slapped him on the back. "What's the matter, old man? Can't hold your liquor like you used to now that you're forty?"

Gray laughed, but Lissy could tell it was forced. He'd appeared uncomfortable all day with the attention given to his birthday, complete with a red velvet cake her mother had made with "four" and "zero" candles. Frank's ribbing hadn't helped. Nor had the gag gifts their families had given him.

He'd also gone overboard in ignoring her, and she wasn't the only one noticing it. Jessica watched them like a cat with two crickets. She was obviously itching to get her alone, using excuses to go to the kitchen and asking Lissy to help. Lissy avoided her by playing the role of sullen youngest child, trusting her mother to jump in to save face in front of company. She had to find a way to escape before Jessica nailed her to the wall with her endless questions.

"Mother?"

"Yes?"

"I'm going to go get the last few boxes from my apartment after brunch. Is that okay? Eddie will be moving in as soon as I'm out."

Her mother frowned. "Lissy, we have guests, and it's New Year's Day."

"Yes, but the christening is tomorrow, and then I have to start *work*." She finger-quoted the word and shot her brother a drop-dead look for good measure.

Busy talking sports with Frank, Olivier, and her father, Travis missed her dig.

"I'll ride with you," Jessica offered as she took the squalling Grace from Lynn.

Crap. I should've thought the plan through. The last thing she needed was time alone in a car with her nosy sister. "There wouldn't be room for all the boxes with the car seat. And you can't leave her; she's breastfeeding." Lissy gestured toward the baby, now sucking her pacifier.

"Frank can feed her. I have some breastmilk already pumped at home—"

"I'll go," Gray interrupted as he wiped his mouth with his napkin. "I can help you carry the boxes."

His eyes carried some unreadable emotion.

"That would be wonderful. You can keep her in line and not let her dawdle," her mother replied with a bright smile. "If you see Eddie, tell him I wish he could've come for brunch today. He's such a nice boy. He's always welcome here. I'm thrilled he'll be subletting your apartment. Everything worked out perfectly."

"Leave the boy alone. He needs to study. Especially if he's going to support Lissy in the manner to which she'd like to become accustomed, since she doesn't feel the need to excel on her own," her father interjected.

Lissy huffed. "Sure, if I see him." *He's probably passed out at the waiter's place.*

Thank God her parents remained clueless. Lissy nearly lost it when Gray winked at her across the table. Her poor mother was in for a rude awakening when Eddie ended up being a bridesman instead of the groom...if she ever got married.

"Thanks, Gray. Let's go ahead and go." She looked over at Jessica and stuck out her tongue. "Have fun doing the dishes, Jess."

This was better than she could've planned. Together, she and Gray could come up with a plausible scenario to placate her sister's inquisitiveness. Seriously, Jessica should have been an FBI agent instead of a teacher. And they'd have time to talk. *But did she really want to? What if this ended up being goodbye for good?*

Lissy grabbed her coat, hat, and muffler. After thanking her mother for the cake, Gray met her at the car wearing his long black coat and the muffler she'd made him for Christmas.

"I'll drive your car," he suggested. "It's bigger than the rental."

Feeling suddenly exhausted, she didn't argue and handed him her keys. She wondered if she was coming down with something.

She leaned her head against the window, wishing she felt better and wondering what Gray was thinking about. "Thank you for coming with me. I didn't want Jessica bombarding me with questions."

"I know."

"What should I say to her?"

"Nothing. It isn't any of her damn business. Take a lesson from the royal family: never complain and never explain. We need to discuss how we're going to do this."

"We're doing this?"

"I hope so," he replied. "I mean, you want to, don't you? You said you didn't hate me."

She smiled, her joy easing the heaviness she felt. "Not much," she teased. "Yes, I want to. That's enough for me right now, the knowledge that you care for me. But honestly, after the late night,

I'm exhausted. Can we put off the logistics just a bit? Maybe talk when we get there or on the way back?"

He glanced over at her and frowned. "You do look tired. Rest, my darling."

She closed her eyes, letting the motion of the car soothe her, only to wake up with a start when Gray called her name.

"What?"

"Alyssandra, we're close. Do I go with the GPS?"

"Already?"

"You slept for over an hour."

Yawning, she sat up straighter and pointed. "No, turn here. We'll take the shortcut down Frat Row to the apart—" Lissy froze when she saw Josh meandering down the sidewalk. She wished they'd driven Gray's rental car instead of hers. The jerk saw her car and flipped her off. Lissy ducked her head, staring in to her lap.

"Who the hell was that?" Gray craned his neck to get a better look.

"Nobody. Just keep going. Keep your eyes on the road," she croaked, more shaken than she'd realized.

Gray pulled over and parked. "Is that who I think it is?" He tore off his seatbelt.

"Just let it go, Gray. I don't care. Josh is an asshole."

"Oh, fuck no." Gray shot out of the car, running after Josh.

Lissy wasn't far behind. Gray grabbed Josh and threw him against a car. Lissy tried to intervene, tugging on Gray's arm.

"Gray, he isn't worth it."

Pinned to the car, Josh appeared too frightened to offer resistance. And no wonder, Gray's anger was a marvel to behold.

"You little punk! Give me one goddamn reason why I shouldn't castrate you and feed you your own balls for dinner."

"Who the hell are you?" Josh asked.

"Stop, Gray. Let him go. We have a lot to do and not much time to do it in."

With a sneer, he released Josh and stepped away, wiping his hands as if they were filthy.

Josh straightened his jacket and glared at Gray then at Lissy. "For crissake, Liss. How many times do I have to tell you it was a fucking *joke?* No harm was done; keep your old man away from me, or I'll press charges."

Lissy shook her head and stepped back. Gray sent Josh sailing across the hood of the car he'd just been pinned against. She grabbed his arm.

"Come on. We need to go."

Tugging him, she convinced him to get back in her car. They buckled their seatbelts, and her heart raced as if she'd been the one in the altercation.

"You didn't have to do that," she said after a moment. "But I'm kinda glad you did."

"He deserved it," Gray replied, shaking his hand. "But damn, that hurt."

Chapter
Sixteen

They parked at the apartment and loaded the remaining boxes into her car. Their task complete, Lissy looked up at Gray as he shut the trunk.

"Gray?" An undeniable awareness sparked between them as their eyes locked.

Without saying a word, he led her back into the apartment. He'd barely closed the door before they were peeling off their coats. His cool fingers cupped her hot cheeks as he kissed her. Kicking off his shoes, he maneuvered her to the bed. His hands traced her body, sending shivers of anticipation through her.

"I can't stay away from you," he whispered, his lips following his hands.

"Then don't." She brushed his cheek with the backs of her fingers. "Kiss me like there's no tomorrow."

"We need to talk—"

They did, but she didn't have the words to describe what she felt for him. Instead she'd let her lips, hands, and body do so. But one thing first…

Lissy flipped over on top of him, brushing her fingers through his hair. "I hate to leave you, but I must." She sighed melodramatically and kissed the cleft in his chin and his cheek.

"What?" He gripped her wrist.

"I have to pee." She giggled. "And get a condom. Don't start without me."

"I won't. It isn't as much fun," he replied with a laugh. "Hurry back." He grabbed her knit hat off her head and twirled it on his finger.

"Oh! Your hand! Hold on." Lissy crawled off the bed and brought him a frozen mixed drink in a pouch. "This is all I have, but it might help with the swelling."

"You drink this? It looks awful."

"It is. That's why I still have it." She wrapped it in a paper towel and held it to his hand. "Be right back."

Finished in the bathroom, she gazed at herself in the mirror. She hadn't had that much to drink yesterday, but she really felt like crap. Growing up she'd always been a curvy girl. Not anymore. She looked like a wraith from a spook house: pale with dark circles under her eyes. What could Grayson possibly find attractive about her? She groaned and leaned forward. *Is that a zit forming on my chin?* Great. She grabbed a condom from the cabinet and sighed, realizing she didn't really feel like having sex. All she wanted was sleep. But would it upset Gray? How she wished she had someone besides Eddie to confide in. With this man, she felt way out of her league. She cracked open the door and found him waiting.

He frowned as she came out of the bathroom. "You don't look well."

She crawled up next to him and admitted, "Honestly, I don't feel that great."

"Alyssandra, I think maybe things have progressed too fast. Perhaps this physical exhaustion is due to the emotional pendulum we've been on. I don't want to ruin things with you. You're young, and you've been through a lot lately. I think maybe you need time to find yourself…"

Lissy looked up at him and cupped his cheek in her hand. "I *have* found myself. I found myself in your arms, and I want to stay there, in whatever way works. You're leaving for Paris soon; I want our last few days to be perfect. Plus, it's your birthday. I didn't get you anything…" She fumbled with the condom, but he stopped her from opening it.

"Any day with you is a gift. What time do we need to be home?"

"Sixish."

Grayson glanced at his watch and smiled. He found his phone, setting the alarm.

"What are you doing?"

"We'll catch a quick nap."

"Just sleep?"

"Just sleep. Sweet dreams, my darling."

It was no wonder she loved him. At times, he was exceptionally considerate. He pulled his long coat over them for a blanket.

"I'll keep you safe and warm."

"Always?"

"Always."

"Alyssandra." Grayson kissed her hand, attempting to wake her gently. "How do you feel?"

"Better," she responded, not fully awake. She snuggled closer.

He chuckled. "We have to go. We're going to be late as it is."

Startled into motion, Lissy sat up, shoving her hair out of her eyes. "What? I thought you set an alarm. What time is it?"

"Almost five. I must have turned it off," he admitted sheepishly, looking around with a yawn.

She scrambled off the bed, shoving her feet into her shoes. "Oh my God. We have to go. What do we do? What do we say?" In her haste, she'd slipped her shoes on the wrong feet and hopped around on one foot, switching them.

"We could tell the truth—we fell asleep."

"Oh sure, like anyone ever believes the truth. I'm toast when I get home. If Mother doesn't kill me, Jessica will." Lissy shrugged into her coat, pulled on her muffler and hat, and grabbed her purse.

She waited for him to follow her out of the apartment. "Hurry up and give me the keys."

"I'll drive." Grayson followed her down to the driver's side of her car.

"No, it's my car. Give me the damn keys." She held out her hand with a look that was a bit scary.

He dropped them in her hands. "You still look dead sleepy."

"Dead sleepy? Oh, you mean dead tired. *Dead* is what I'm going to be when I get home. Just shut up and get in the car. I've got this. It isn't my first time being late for a family function." Lissy pulled out before he could close the door.

He pressed his lips together tightly to keep from criticizing. He may have botched the phrase, but she still looked terrible, despite their nap. Now would be the perfect time to discuss their future — though with her driving, they might not have one. He swore softly in French and closed his eyes as she passed another car before cutting the poor bastard off.

"Alyssandra!"

"Yes?" She glanced at him. He pointed at the road, flinching as she once again swerved.

"Pull over. I'll drive."

"No, that would be a waste of precious time. That would be crazy. We're late enough." She grinned. "Wait, I *am* crazy. The doc at that clinic told me so."

"As bat shit," Gray agreed with a smile.

"Totally. It's why you love me." She laughed and hit the gas pedal a little harder.

Grayson swallowed his fear, unsure which was more unnerving, her driving or the thought of loving her.

"I'm sorry we're late," Lissy apologized as they came in the front door of her parents' house.

"Grayson, you were supposed to keep Lissy from getting distracted," her mother chided.

Gray shrugged. "You know how she is; what could I do? I tried, but I failed. Your daughter has the organizational skills of a gnat on crack. Plus, part of it is my fault. I wanted to see the campus." He went to the bar and poured a stiff scotch, downed it, and poured some more. Lissy wanted to smack him, but his excuse was working. She turned when Jessica grabbed her hand.

"I need you to help me; we'll be right back, Mother," Jessica said.

Reluctantly, Lissy followed her upstairs. Jessica slammed the bedroom door shut.

"Ow, your claws scratched me." Lissy rubbed her hand and glared at her older sister, praying offense truly was the best defense.

"What's going on?" Jessica crossed her arms.

"I love your pink blouse. Is that new? I'd like to borrow it to make a pattern." Maybe deflection would work. Lissy tossed her coat on the bed.

"Come on, Lissy. I love Grayson—you know I do—but he's much too old for you. Not to mention he has a reputation for being a little on the wild side. There was that time with some twins—"

"Oh for heaven's sake. Would you stop?"

Jessica's hands moved to her hips. She looked a lot like Mother, except her hair was blond.

She raised an eyebrow and frowned. "Then explain what took you so long."

"I don't feel well," Lissy replied. And it was the truth.

Jessica's look switched from suspicion to worry. "Do you have a fever?" She put her hand on her forehead, now in mom mode.

Lissy made a strategic decision to go with a half-truth. "No, I just feel out of sorts. I think I'm overly tired from packing all week, the party, and then the drive to and from school today."

"But what about last night? I saw you coming out of the woods with him." Jessica scrutinized her like a police detective.

"We just went to get a different view of the fireworks. No biggie." Lissy shrugged but didn't quite meet her sister's eyes.

"Liss—he just came out of his one and only long-term relationship, and it lasted, what, two years, if that? I know you've adored him since you were a teenager. But if this is what I suspect, I'm afraid you're headed for heartbreak. I don't want you to be his rebound."

"Don't be silly. There's *no* relationship between us. He still thinks I'm a kid." This time, Lissy looked directly into her sister's eyes. Unfortunately, that was also partially true.

To get her emotions in check, she grabbed her coat and hung it up. Swallowing the lump in her throat, she smiled and faced her sister. "Let's go eat some peas and greens for luck and money."

"Do you want to lie down? I'll tell Mother you're not feeling well."

"Nah, I'll sleep when I'm dead."

Alyssandra and his mother were helping with the dishes, his nephew was asleep on the couch, and the rest of the family was watching a ballgame in the den. Grayson seized the chance to escape upstairs. He opened the door to his room and found Jessica nursing Grace, cooing softly to the baby. She didn't hear him enter, and Grayson quietly picked up his camera and shot a picture.

At the sound of the shutter releasing, Jessica looked up and blushed. She pulled the blanket up to cover herself and Grace. "I didn't hear you come in. I'm afraid it's habit to come back to my old room. I wanted some peace and quiet to feed Grace."

"I apologize. I shouldn't have taken the picture without your permission, but you and Grace looked so perfect, I did it without thinking. In Europe, there isn't such a big deal made about nursing children. It's natural and beautiful. Would you like to see the picture?"

When she nodded, he pulled it up on the camera.

"Oh! I do like it. I'd love to have a copy for Frank."

"I think he would like that very much. Again, I'm sorry for the intrusion. I am the guest here; this is still your room." He politely turned away as Jessica moved the baby to adjust her clothing.

She laughed softly. "You don't need to leave. I'm decent." She held the baby to her shoulder, patting her back. "Please. Sit and talk to me. I hope my family didn't go too overboard for your birthday. I told Frank the AARP application and cane were too much."

"It was fine." Grayson sat on the edge of the bed. *This must be what it felt like to face the Spanish Inquisition.*

"What happened to your hand?"

"I hit the doorframe moving a box." The lie fell easily. *Is this my future? Lying?*

"I'm worried about Lissy."

Having played cards for years with *Grand-mère*, he remained calm and unruffled under Jessica's intense perusal. She continued to pat Grace's back and was rewarded with a small burp.

"She wasn't feeling well today," he conceded.

"I'm not talking about just today. She hasn't been herself for quite some time. She may not have been an A student, but to flunk all of her courses? She's lost a lot of weight and isn't sleeping. Do you have any idea what's going on with her? Has she said anything to you?"

He ran a hand over the design in the duvet, taking a moment before answering. "I think you should ask her, not me."

"I have." She stood with Grace in her arms, facing him. "Grayson, I love you. But Lissy is my sister. She's young and confused about where her life is going at the moment. You're a lot older and more mature. Just be careful with her feelings. That's all I'm asking."

Grayson looked up and nodded. She leaned over, kissed his cheek, and left without another word.

Chapter
Seventeen

Lissy took two more Advil and crawled into bed, tired of being tired. A knock on her door surprised her. "Come in."

Mother entered with a mug of tea. "Are you okay?" she asked, sitting on the edge of the bed. "Lissy, I'm sorry about Christmas. There will be other trips. Is this what the problem's been? You just aren't yourself."

"I'm fine. Maybe this is a bug or something that has me feeling icky. Flunking out of school was my fault; Daddy has every right to be mad. I, uh, let the thing with Josh get to me. I'll do better, I promise."

"Did you get your flu shot?"

Just as Jessica had done, her mother felt her forehead.

"Yes, I got one at school."

"No fever. You're probably just run down or still heartbroken. As for Josh, no boy is worth this much anguish. But look on the bright side!"

"The bright side?"

"You have Eddie. He's such a nice, well-mannered young man—with drive and ambition."

Guilt washed over her, and she buried her face in her pillow. "Yes, Eddie's a great guy. But don't push things, Mother."

She laughed. "That's what your father said, too. Look, I know you're disappointed about your father's decision to keep you out of school this next semester. I tried to talk to him, but he's standing firm. Just do your sentence at the bank and apply for the next semester. Sometimes a break is needed to reassess. Think of it as a chance to figure out what you want to do with your life."

"Mother, nursing isn't for me."

"Neither was teaching, social work, or library science."

"I know Daddy wants me to major in something where I 'can make a living,' but I really want to go into fashion design. I think I can make a living that way."

Mother sighed. "That will be a hard sell to your father."

"I'll never live up to my perfect older siblings," she grumbled.

"Lissy, your brother and sister are hardly perfect. Do you think I color my hair just because of you?" Her mother kissed her forehead. "You'll be fine. Have you considered talking to Grayson's father? Maybe show him some of the lovely things you've sewn. Your father respects him, and he's in the business. I'm sure he'd give you some good advice."

"And you'll talk to Daddy?"

"And I'll talk to your father. I love you."

"Love you too." She squeezed her mother's hand before she slipped out the door.

Sometime later, the bed dipped, and Lissy stirred and looked at the clock. It was midnight. A freshly shaven face nuzzled and kissed her neck. She rolled over. Lying on his side, with his head propped on his hand, Gray gazed at her, his face unreadable in the dim light from the cracked bathroom door.

"Hi," she whispered, leaning up to kiss him.

"Hi," he whispered in return. His hair was damp, and he smelled of soap and toothpaste.

"I didn't think you'd come."

"Why not?"

"I don't know. I think I'm just having a pity party." She turned her face into the hand stroking her hair and kissed it.

"I don't understand, Alyssandra."

"I'm going to miss you terribly when you leave. And I feel on edge, like I'm barely hanging on…"

He moved to his back, placing his hands behind his head as he stared at the ceiling. "I'll miss you, too. But I'm afraid things are going to get worse before they get better. Perhaps being apart will be best. For a while, anyway."

"But you'll come back, right?"

"Alyssandra, I'm in uncharted waters here. I don't like subterfuge; I like things straight up. And yet I find my life has become complicated—especially now with Candie's stunt. *Papa* made me look at some of the coverage, and he's insisting I hire a publicist. Candie's being ridiculous with her melodrama. If the press got wind of our relationship, it would affect more than us. We have our families to consider, too. I care deeply about you and don't want to hurt you, but I don't know that we can do this right now. I think your exhaustion is at least partly due to the secrecy of our relationship. It's stressful."

"Why is it so wrong for us to be together? Just because you're older? Are you saying I don't know what I want or need?"

"No. I'm saying I'm not sure what *I* want or need."

"But you care for me."

"I do. You're all I think about lately."

"I know you want me. Surely you need me, just a little?"

"Yes. And that's what terrifies me." He rolled over. "Go to sleep, my darling girl. We'll figure this out. I'm not leaving yet." He kissed her softly on the lips and pulled her close, his arm around her waist.

Yet… She bit her lip to keep from crying. The simple word stabbed like a knife.

An hour later, Lissy sat up and clutched her chest, her heart pounding with such force she found it difficult to breathe. *Did I have a nightmare?* If so, she couldn't remember it. Panic gripped her like a portent of death. These anxiety attacks had grown both more frequent and more intense. Quietly, so she wouldn't disturb Gray, she staggered to the bathroom, needing light to offset her terror. Sucking in a deep breath, she held it. Sometimes that would slow her heart, but not this time. Feeling sick and dizzy, she fell to her knees in front of the toilet and threw up. She sank to the floor.

"Alyssandra?" At the door, Gray rubbed his face, his hair a tousled mess. He squatted beside her.

"Sorry I woke you up. Go back to bed." She panted like a dog in August, praying her heart would slow down.

His brow creased as he helped her to her feet. "What's wrong?" He kissed her brow and cupped her cheeks, gazing at her.

"I'm not pregnant," she snapped.

"I didn't think that." He felt her forehead. "No fever. But something is wrong with you."

Lissy closed her eyes and held her breath again. Her heart did a quick beat and a thump and slowed, leaving her feeling weak.

"Quit. Everyone and their uncle has checked me for a damn fever. I'm okay. It must've been a bad dream. Go back to bed."

She pulled herself together and brushed her teeth under Gray's intense stare.

"You need to go to the doctor."

"I'm fine. They'll just tell me I'm crazy, remember?"

"I insist."

His high-handed manner didn't help her crankiness. Tired and in no mood to argue, she pushed past him to get back to bed. She felt as if she'd run a marathon.

"Leave me alone."

He followed her and whispered, "Alyssandra, if you don't go to the doctor, I'm going to tell your parents you're ill."

Furious, she turned back and snapped, "Fine. And I'll tell them you're fucking their daughter." She clapped her hand over her mouth. *Why did I say that?*

He swore softly in French and walked away.

"Wait, Gray. I'm sorry, I didn't mean it." She scrambled to the end of the bed, but he never looked back, quietly shutting both bathroom doors between their rooms.

Lissy waited a minute to catch her breath and then made her way to his room. She found him staring out the window. She rubbed his back, and he flinched.

Tears spilled down her cheeks. "Please, Gray. Please forgive me."

"Good night, Alyssandra. You asked to be left alone. Now I'm asking you to leave me alone. Go to bed. Your bed, not mine. We both have a lot to think about." His voice sounded strained.

Wiping the tears from her face, she stared at him for a moment before leaving. This time, she was sure her heart was breaking.

After Alyssandra left, Grayson continued to stare out the window, wondering how his life had gotten so out of control. Her words had angered him in a way he didn't think possible. Part of him wanted to apologize and tell her he was afraid he was falling in love. *Afraid* being the key word. It made him want to run like hell. This wasn't going to work. She was young and impetuous. What had he been thinking?

If their relationship got out, it would not only disrupt their families, it would likely make the tabloids. He'd never liked being in the limelight. That's why he was *behind* the camera.

He lay down, but his bed was cold and empty, a fitting analogy for his life.

A few hours later, he gave up trying to sleep. An early morning run might help burn off some frustration. Changing quickly, he grabbed his phone and sprinted out the front door. This wouldn't be a quick run. He needed time to sort through his feelings and fears.

Three hours later, he returned, pausing just inside when he heard Alyssandra's parents in the kitchen.

"I wish you'd put down your tablet and *listen* to me. Something is wrong with Lissy. She doesn't look well and isn't acting like herself." Patsy sounded concerned.

"She needs to get over that idiot college boy, grow up, and settle down," George commented.

Feeling only mildly guilty, Grayson eavesdropped, hoping his name wouldn't be mentioned.

"I don't think Josh is the problem. They broke up, remember? You met Eddie. She seems to be crazy about him. I think it's something else."

"I can't keep up with her social life. Apparently neither can she. That's why she flunked a semester. You worry too much, my dear. A few months working for her brother ought to put her on the right track. Travis won't cut her any slack just because she's his sister."

Patsy moved away, muttering, the conversation over. Relieved, Grayson released the breath he'd been holding. They didn't suspect the real reason for her distress. He entered the kitchen and nodded to George, who continued to peruse his tablet. Patsy leaned against the counter sipping her coffee. A furrow creased her brow.

"*Bonjour.*"

"Good morning." She poured his coffee and handed it to him with a warm smile.

"Thank you."

"Morning, Grayson." George motioned for him to sit.

He froze when he heard Alyssandra coming down the stairs. She entered the room wearing her bathrobe, her hair pulled up in a messy ponytail, dark purple smudges under her eyes. George put his tablet down and Patsy looked at him, silently nodding toward their daughter.

George scowled. "You look like hell, Alleycat."

Alyssandra poured herself a cup of coffee. Grayson watched as she studiously ignored his presence.

"Gee, thanks, Daddy."

"Did you sleep at all last night?" Her mother rubbed her back and kissed her pale cheek. "I still think you're coming down with something."

Alyssandra ignored the question about sleep, instead shooting Grayson a death glare before turning away. "What time is the christening?"

"The ceremony is at ten. I don't know why they didn't want to do this during church on Sunday."

"I'm afraid that's my fault," he said. "The issue with Candie — I'm sorry."

Patsy quickly apologized. "Oh, no! I didn't mean to make you uncomfortable. It will be nice just having family there. After the service we'll go to the country club for lunch. Olivier and Lynn have to fly back to New York late this afternoon. When will you be leaving, Grayson?"

"Tomorrow morning I fly to Paris." Staring at Lissy, he frowned. George was right. Alyssandra looked dreadful. He decided to push it, come hell or high water. "I agree with your father, Alyssandra.

You don't look well. Perhaps you need to see a doctor? You wouldn't want to pass anything along to Grace."

She glared at him. "I'm fine! Would y'all just *stop*. It's insomnia, that's all."

"Tomorrow why don't you schedule an appointment with Dr. Bradley? It can't hurt to have a checkup," Patsy offered.

"He's a freakin' pediatrician, Mother. I'm not twelve! Besides, I have to go to *work* tomorrow, remember? I'm sure my new boss would frown on me taking off the first day. You know what an ass Travis can be."

"Lissy, don't talk like that. If you're sick, Travis—"

"Geezus, get off my case." Lissy poured another cup of coffee and slammed the pot back on the burner. She grabbed a granola bar. "I'm going to go get my hair done. I'll meet y'all at the church." She stormed out of the room.

"Do something, George," Patsy snapped.

"What do you want me to do? Take her out back and switch her?"

"Maybe if you hadn't spoiled her all those years and then cracked down when she's vulnerable. She had a broken heart! And for your information, she'd make a lousy nurse!" Patsy stormed out of the room.

George shook his head. "What in the world does Lissy being a lousy nurse have to do with the current situation? Most of the time I have no clue. Women. Can't live with 'em, can't live without 'em."

Grayson raised his coffee cup. "No truer words were ever spoken."

Jessica's green eyes narrowed, and her mouth flattened. "Really?" she hissed.

Compared to the tongue-lashing she'd received from her mother when she walked into the church, this was nothing. Lissy sighed. She wasn't late—as a matter of fact, she was early. But that hadn't impressed her family one bit. Not when they saw her hair.

On a whim, she'd had her hairdresser add small colored streaks of purple, green, pink, and blue. They were discreetly hidden tiny clip-ins, but her family didn't know it. They didn't understand her fashion sense. They never had. Her black dress needed the pop of color. She'd added pink stilettos for Gray's sake.

By God, she was determined he'd see what he was going to be missing. In a rapid pass through the stages of grief regarding their relationship, she'd gone from despair, to anger, and now revenge. Lissy wasn't sure if revenge was an actual stage of grief, but it described her current thoughts on the matter. He'd never actually said so, but she *knew* the man had a thing for high heels.

The families posed for various pictures after the christening. Her father loved pictures and made Gray take what seemed like hundreds. Gray then turned the camera over to her to get some photos of him with the family and Grace. She took the pictures and even managed to sneak one of Gray holding Grace up in the air, the baby grinning down at him as he smiled widely. She loved it, one of the few pictures where the man didn't smirk.

This morning at the hairdresser's, in a fit of anger, she'd deleted all of the pictures from the cabin she'd downloaded on her phone, and now she regretted it. But then again, maybe it was for the best. She'd dwell on them, possibly become homicidal, and end up in prison for the death of Grayson Deschanelle. And who'd want to wear an ugly, baggy orange jumpsuit for life?

A clearing throat snapped her out of her daydream. Gray gestured for the camera. She slapped it into his hand and nearly jumped at the almost electrical connection between them. It wouldn't have surprised her one bit if it melted in his hand. His intense eyes held hers for a moment before he looked at the pictures she'd taken and nodded his approval.

"Very nice. You have talent. Now, you hold Grace."

Lissy took the baby and glanced nervously at her niece. She wasn't a natural with kids like Jessica. However, Grace grabbed her finger and cooed and Lissy smiled, entranced. Her eyes filled with tears, which she blinked away as she kissed the baby's sweet forehead.

She looked up at Gray. "How do you want me?"

For one brief, unguarded second, heat smoldered in his gaze. He looked so damn elegant in his black suit, crisp white shirt, and patterned tie.

"You know what to do," he said. "Just look at the camera and smile."

She did as he instructed and then turned to hand the baby off to a grandparent.

"No, wait! We need one of both godparents with Grace." Frank took the camera from Gray and motioned him to stand next to her. "Smile, you two."

Lissy had no doubt Gray was giving his typical smirk, and she was fairly certain her smile looked more like a grimace. Frank handed the camera back to Gray, who frowned and shook his head when he previewed the picture. They posed for one more.

"I like your hair, *mon chaton*. It matches the circles under your eyes," Gray whispered.

Lissy stepped closer and dug her heel into the top of his foot as she smiled for yet another picture.

"Thank you. Now it can match your sore foot," she retorted as she handed the baby to Frank.

She snickered as Gray muttered a few choice French words, causing his father to shoot him a warning glare.

"Oops, sorry. These heels make me clumsy." She tossed her hair and walked away to speak to his parents.

As she exchanged quiet small talk with Olivier about fashion design, Lissy cast a surreptitious glance at Gray.

Squatting eye-level with Lee, he nodded, giving their jabbering nephew his full attention. He caught her peeking at him and gave her a smile. Lissy's heart flip-flopped in her chest. She sighed. This rift between them was her fault. Her threat to tell her parents had been a shot below the belt—and just because he'd expressed concern about her health. Truth be told, she was worried, too. These panic attacks were taking over her life.

She giggled when Gray's father knelt, flipped up the hem of her dress, and then had her turn as he examined the fit as if she were a mannequin. Lynn fussed at him to quit working and enjoy the day as her mother praised her sewing skills.

After Olivier expressed interest in seeing some of her sketches, she turned and spoke to Travis, assuring him she'd dress appropriately for work tomorrow. When he pointed at her hair, she argued there was nothing in the employee handbook about hair color. But she said it in jest, too excited by Olivier's promise to talk with her further very soon.

The bank didn't seem so bad at the moment. Her evenings without having to study would give her time to work on her clothes. This glimmer of hope made her future almost bearable. She could feel Gray staring at her. She gave him a brief smile, which he returned.

Then her father announced it was time to move to the country club for lunch, and the two families headed to the cars.

"Lissy, you ride with Grayson. Lynn and Olivier will ride with us so we can discuss plans for Lee's birthday party. It will be the next time all of us get together." Her mother smiled and waved as she brushed past.

As they stepped out of the church, someone ran forward with a huge camera, snapping away.

Gray took her elbow and steered her to the car, instructing her through tight lips, "Get in and do not look at the photographer. Ignore him."

"Yo! Grayson! Have you heard from Candie? Is she recuperating? Will you take her back? She's begging," the man yelled, clicking away.

Ignoring the question, Gray walked around to the driver's side without acknowledging him.

"Who was that?"

"An annoying bloodsucker." Gray peeled out of the parking lot. "Which way? Do not look back."

"Turn left at the stop sign." She tried to peer into the side mirror. "Was that paparazzi?"

"Yes." Glancing in the rearview mirror, he laughed and eased up on the gas. "Okay, you can look back."

She turned around and laughed. Both of their fathers were berating the man. Daddy had his finger in his chest while Olivier gestured wildly.

"Alyssandra, I never want you bothered by them. But for a while, I'll be plagued by them because of Candie. She's been unrelenting with her so-called *leaks* to the press."

"That's crazy. Just tell them she's a psycho attention whore."

He laughed. "While that's true, it's best to ignore them. It will die down soon. Maybe I should ask Dylan to do something stupid. He's used to making the front page."

She giggled. "Gray, I'm sorry about last night. I didn't feel well. I'm not going to say anything to my parents. That was horribly childish and nasty of me to threaten you. Look, we've had fun. And we're family; we're going to have to see each other on holidays, even if you don't want to."

"It isn't that I don't want to."

Her hand shook as she pushed the blue strand of hair behind her ear. "Well, if you're in town and I'm in town, maybe we can hook up or something." She peeked at his stony face and looked away. "Just sex, of course. No strings attached."

"Is that what you want?" he asked softly.

"Yep." She dug her nails into her hand.

"Are you sure?"

What the hell? Is this some sort of trick? If she proclaimed her love, he'd run back to New York so fast her head would spin. It was a struggle, but she managed to keep her voice casual.

"You're the best fuck I've ever had, so yeah, it'd be great if we can figure out how to get around our families. But if you're not interested, fine. I'm not begging." She stared out the side window.

"I like it when you beg." He paused to look both ways at a stop sign. "The best ever, huh?"

Putting on a sunny smile, she looked at him. "Well, so far. But I'm young. I have plenty of time to experiment and see. Of course, that's if I ever get out of this hick town to find someone."

His lips curled. "No matter what our relationship is or becomes, no more threats, Alyssandra. You're better than that. You're a woman, not a spoiled brat."

"I promise."

"Well, in that case, I might need to visit my niece and nephew for Groundhog's Day. That's a pretty big holiday, isn't it?"

Lissy bit her lip but snickered. "Very big."

"And Easter, birthdays, Bastille Day, Memorial Day, as well as the usual Thanksgiving and Christmas." He paused and added, "However, I won't make it for national Bat Appreciation Day. I'll need to spend that with *Grand-mère*."

She laughed. *It isn't over. He still wants me.* "That's not nice. Is she that bad?"

"Scary as hell. I saw you talking to *Papa*. He was examining you like a runway model. I confess to being a little jealous…"

"Ah, well, I do have a penchant for older men…" She giggled. "He said my sewing and fitting was impeccable, and he wants me to send him some of my sketches. He said we could video chat about it. Your dad's so cool, Daddy always screws up live streaming."

Gray smiled. "Your eyes light up when you talk about fashion. Go after your dream, Alyssandra."

By the time they reached the country club, the tension between them had dissipated.

Chapter
Eighteen

Grayson glanced over at Alyssandra as her head lolled against the window. It had been enjoyable, but there was an undercurrent of sadness during lunch at the country club. Plans were well underway for Lee's birthday party, and *Papa* had even given Alyssandra a homework assignment to complete before then as the families said their goodbyes.

Riding home, she'd fallen asleep almost immediately. Gray pulled on his lip, concerned. It wasn't normal for someone to sleep this much.

He parked, and she stirred.

"Sorry, I must've dozed off." Her sleepy smile, husky voice, tousled hair, and those damn heels switched his dick to an instant hard-on.

He shifted uncomfortably in the seat and threw the car in reverse.

"Where are we going?" She sat up, seeming more awake now.

"You tell me. Where do you go parking around here?"

"Parking?"

He nodded and waited for directions.

"As in making out, heavy petting, fogged windows?" Her brows knit together.

"Sounds about right."

"In the daylight?"

"We don't do anything by the book, so why should we make out by the rules?"

"Turn here. What will we tell my parents when we arrive late?" She directed him for several miles until they turned onto an old abandoned road. It led to a spectacular view of the lake. Gray parked the car, shrugged out of his coat, and shifted his seat back and down.

"You're showing me around Pine Bluff. Be kind to me, Alyssandra."

"Be kind to you? And FYI, the tour of Pine Bluff would take all of five minutes. This will need to be a quickie."

"This is my first time." His voice was soft, his smile seductive as he brushed her lower lip with his thumb.

"First time for what, exactly?" She swallowed.

"To go parking."

"Are you kidding me? Didn't you go to high school in the States?"

"Yes, but I never went parking."

"You never made out or had sex in a car?"

"No. That's what cheap motels were for. It's up to you to make sure I have a pleasant experience. In fifteen minutes or less."

He gave her the fakest innocent look she'd ever seen.

"How could you get a room if you were just a kid?"

"I dated older women." He laughed. "See? You're my first and only on so many levels."

"I like the sound of that." She tossed her coat in the back seat.

Grayson hauled her to straddle his lap, her back to the steering wheel. The windows fogged almost immediately. "Shut up and kiss me."

She kissed him as if there was no tomorrow.

He ran a hand up her stocking-clad leg. "You're killing me. Thigh-high stockings and heels?"

"You like?" she asked, nipping his lower lip.

"Very much," he replied. His mouth ravaged hers as his hand crept up her leg. He grunted and stilled at the insistent tapping at his fogged window.

"*Merde!*" Gray grabbed his jacket and placed it over his face.

Lissy giggled and cracked the window an inch. "Uh, hi, Dylan."

Dylan McAthie peered at her. She'd forgotten this road was on the edge of his property. Beside him, his daughter was attempting to look into the car.

"What are you doing, Lissy? I saw the out-of-county tag and wondered if someone was having car trouble. You okay?"

"No, no car trouble. Thanks, Dylan." She bit her lip to keep from laughing.

Understanding dawned, and he smiled. "In my day we did that sort of thing at night. Behave and be safe. Hey, I hear you're moving back for a bit. Interested in babysitting?"

"Uh, sure."

"Great. I'll have Jen give ya a call. See ya around, Grayson, you rule-breaker, you." Dylan laughed and took his daughter's hand as they walked away.

From underneath his jacket, Gray swore.

Lissy rolled up the window and looked down at Gray. "Rule-breaker?"

"Half plus seven. It's a guy thing—don't worry about it." He chuckled. "Now I remember why I never went parking."

"This was a first for me, too."

"Parking?" he asked doubtfully.

"No. Getting caught." She curled up on his chest and stroked his firm jaw. "Gray?"

"Yes?"

"Just hold me."

He kissed the top of her head and wrapped his arms around her waist. "What made you decide to put the colored streaks in your hair?"

Lissy shrugged. "Just because."

"I like it."

She repositioned herself to look at his face, accidentally elbowing his solar plexus. He grunted.

"You do?"

"Yes. It suits you. Wild and crazy."

"I suppose the operative word there is *crazy*." Lissy smirked as she ran a finger round and round one of the buttons on his dress shirt.

"It is."

She laughed. "They're just clip-ons." Turning serious, she asked, "If you could freeze one moment from this past week, which would it be?"

"You in the snow."

"The naked pictures? Perv." She hid her self-satisfied smile in his neck.

"No, the look of pure, unadulterated joy on your face as you played in the snow." He stroked her hair and smiled. "And you?" he asked, softly.

She nestled back under his chin and smiled. "Right now."

"Why now?"

"Because you're still here."

Lissy smiled and nodded every so often during the after-dinner conversation with her family. But her heart wasn't in it. The pain had returned to her chest. Gray would be gone tomorrow.

He'd promised her that tonight, when they were alone, they'd talk about their future. The fact he was planning a future was enough. They'd figure out how to make this work.

She looked over to see him absentmindedly stroking Noëlle in his lap. He and her father were talking politics. They might as well be speaking in French for all she understood.

Her mother entered the room dressed for a party. She frowned. "Lissy? You still don't look like you feel well, and you have a big day tomorrow with your new job. Go to bed early tonight."

Gray stood, much to Noëlle's disgruntlement, and helped her mother with her coat.

"Why can't we just call and say we aren't going? We've had a busy week," her father grumbled as he stood and shook Gray's hand.

"They're *your* business associates," her mother retorted with a laugh. "And you were all excited about it two weeks ago when *you* told me to accept the invitation." She turned to Gray. "We'll see you in the morning before you leave for the airport. You're welcome here anytime, Grayson."

"Thank you." He smiled and gave her a kiss on both cheeks.

Lissy kissed her mother and father good night and watched them leave. She and Gray remained still, listening as the car pulled out of the driveway.

Glancing up at Gray she asked, "Do you want a drink for our talk?"

"No, thank you."

"May I plead my case first?"

He smiled. "You're not on trial, but of course. Ladies first."

"How archaic." She took a deep breath. "I don't need you."

His brow furrowed, but he didn't interrupt.

"But I want you. I think we're good together, like ice cream and hot fudge. I know there's an age difference, and some might think you're a creeper, but I don't care what others think."

"A creeper?" he teased, chucking her under the chin. "Am I the hot fudge?"

"Okay, a perv. But you're *my* perv, and I kinda saw you as the ice cream. Cool on the exterior but melt-in-your-mouth delicious."

"Alyssandra, this is no joking matter. You say you don't care what people say, but that's not true. You care a great deal about your parents and their opinions, as do I."

"I do but they'll come around. Am I not worth fighting for? Is what we have just about the...*physical?*"

"No. Give me some credit. Alyssandra, I care for you because of your sense of humor, your passion for life, your exuberance. Yes, you're beautiful, but it's that *je ne sais quoi* that shines from within you."

"Th-That's good, then, right? I mean, what's the problem?"

"While I care deeply for you, and perhaps I'm even falling in love with you, I have no desire to get married."

"That's fine. It's just a piece of paper."

"You say that now, but what if you want children?"

"You don't have to be married to have kids. Next argument."

"I want to be with you, but we need to be discreet."

She lifted her chin. "I don't want to be your dirty little secret. I'm worth more than that."

"You're *not* my dirty little secret. Paparazzi are brutal, and I want to protect you and our families from the aftermath of Candie's publicity stunt. I will do anything in my power to keep you safe." He kissed her tenderly. "*Mon chaton*, you are my life and my heart. I want to give *us* time before the world finds out we're a couple."

"I get that. I do. And I agree. So we're doing this?" She pointed at him and back at herself.

"Discreetly. For now."

"You really think you might love me?"

"I always have. But my feelings have grown deeper since Christmas. That time together opened my eyes, and I no longer see you as a little girl. You're an intelligent, funny, sweet woman. I can't imagine life without you. You brighten my day with your smiles, and your kindness soothes my soul. I think we have a beautiful future ahead of us. But you're young. You have dreams and aspirations. I never want to hold you back. If you want to pursue them, I'll be here waiting for you. I want you to continue to grow as your own person."

She stared up into his eyes, her arms wrapped around his neck. "I've always been crazy in love with you. And I see no reason why I can't be my own person *with* you. You make me want to be a better person. I feel like I'm dreaming, and I'm scared I'll wake up and this will all be gone. So until the Candie mess dies down, we're a secret couple, right?" She grinned. "Or are you scared of my father and brother? Travis does have a mean right hook."

"It's not a dream. And we need to think carefully about how we will inform our families. I do anticipate some resistance, mainly because of the age difference, don't you?"

"I suppose so. But, Gray, they'll come around. As long as we're both happy. Our parents love us."

"I hope so. Come, let's go upstairs and spend our last few hours alone doing more than talking. You're still wearing the garter belt and stockings with those heels, yes?" He turned out the light and took her hand, leading her upstairs.

She laughed. "You have a thing for high heels, don't you?"

He pinned her against the wall on the staircase. "I do. Especially with sexy lingerie."

She smiled into his kiss. "Perv."

"Are you complaining?" He unzipped her dress, pulled it over her head, and stood back, his ragged breathing fanning her cheek. The moonlight slanting through the windows in the foyer illuminated her, but his face remained shadowed. She could feel the energy zapping between them in her racing heart. His eyes traced over her black, sheer demi-bra and panties and the thigh-high stockings and heels.

"Don't move." He ran upstairs two at a time and came back with his camera and the long strand of fake pearls from her dresser.

She was shocked when he grabbed her by the back of the head, his hand tangled in her hair, pulling her face up to his. He kissed her mercilessly, biting her lower lip as he pinched her nipples. Unsnapping her bra, he dropped it, smiled, and stepped back. In his professional manner, he instructed her how to pose as he draped the pearls. Still under the influence of his kiss, she did as she was told. Whenever he watched her, either through the lens or not, it turned her on. He had correctly pinned her as an exhibitionist, but only for him.

"You are my muse. You inspire me, my darling. Arms above your head, crossed at the wrist, legs crossed with one foot slightly in front of the other. Perfect. Now look down at the floor. Tilt your head slightly. Perfect." He took several shots before putting the camera down on the staircase.

Lissy caught her breath, her heart hammering as he took her wrists and kept them pinned above her head as he kissed her.

"Dear God, what you do to me, Alyssandra."

Taking the pearls, he dragged them across her hard, aching nipples before tying her wrists with them. She whimpered, wanting him so badly she couldn't seem to catch her breath. He squeezed her wrists, still above her head.

"Keep them there. Don't move them, understand?"

"Yes," she whispered.

Kneeling before her, he slipped her panties off and parted her legs.

"I must taste you. But don't move unless I tell you."

She whimpered at the sensation of his warm mouth on her clit. His tongue swirled, his lips sucked, and his teeth brushed across her, pushing her closer to the edge. Just when she thought she'd fall to pieces, he stopped and inserted his fingers, crooking them to hit the magic spot as he pumped in and out. When he again sucked gently on her clit, she screamed and dropped her wrists to his neck, positive her quivering legs couldn't hold her up. He stood and unwrapped her wrists, and she jumped into his arms.

"Please, Gray, fuck me."

Gray smacked her ass. "I told you not to move. We need to gather our things."

The stinging intensified her pleasure.

"Oh God, Gray…"

He put her down, and she grabbed her clothes and the pearls. Laughing, they ran toward her bedroom. She collapsed on her bed, struggling to catch her breath as Gray took the camera to his room.

Returning, he smiled down at her as he unbuttoned his shirt. "I want to make love to you. Slowly. Tenderly. I will worship you, Alyssandra, with my body and take you to heaven."

Lissy nodded, her heart still pounding. Shakily, she kicked off her shoes, and peeled down her stockings.

"Tsk, tsk," Grayson teased as he kicked back on the bed. "I was hoping for a slow, seductive striptease, *mon chaton.*"

"Oh. I can't think…" Weak and nauseated, she picked up Gray's shirt and shrugged into it, feeling cold and clammy. Something was terribly wrong.

"I'll be right back." Her voice sounded far away, even to her own ears. She made her way toward the bathroom, but the walls seemed to close in around her, as if she were in a tunnel. Fear squeezed her chest relentlessly. "Gray?"

He was by her side in a minute.

"I'm really sick, please…" She sank to the floor and gave in to her pain.

Crumpling in front of him, Lissy clutched her chest. Terrified, he fell to his knees, attempting to check her pulse. Grayson whipped his phone out of his pocket and called 9-1-1. He gave terse instructions as to where the ambulance was needed, frantically pushing his fear aside as he concentrated on the operator's questions.

"Yes, she has a pulse, but I can't count it, it's too fast and faint. *Oui*, I mean, yes, she is breathing. No, she's unconscious. No, I can't stay on the phone. I must call her parents." He hung up and realized he didn't have their number. Instead he dialed Frank, trying to keep the panic in his voice controlled so as not to frighten her.

"Hey, Trip," Frank said as he picked up.

"Find George and Patsy and meet us at hospital. It's Alyssandra. Hurry!" He hung up and took her in his arms, hurrying down the stairs to wait for the ambulance. He could hear sirens in the distance. Her body was limp.

"Alyssandra, help is on the way." He couldn't contain his panic. She was too cold, too clammy, and her lips had a blue tint. "Dammit, what's wrong?"

He dropped to the floor and checked her pulse. "Alyssandra! *Ne me quitte pas!*"

Not finding a heartbeat, he started CPR. Moments later, the paramedics entered the foyer and took over the chest compressions. The seriousness of the situation washed over him when they placed the paddles on her chest.

"Everyone clear!" the EMT shouted just before the paddles sent a current of electricity through her body.

She convulsed horrifically, and Grayson closed his eyes, propping himself against the wall.

Chapter
Nineteen

Grayson sat in the corner of the crowded waiting room, his face buried in his hands. Over and over, like a mantra, he repeated to himself, *She can't die; she can't die.*

"Grayson!"

He raised his stinging eyes and dashed tears away as Jessica rushed toward him, crying.

"Dear God, no." She sank to chair beside him. "Is she gone?" The hysteria in her voice snapped him out of his own grief and guilt.

"No! At least I don't think so. Nobody will tell me anything. They had to shock her heart. I heard them say they think it's a drug overdose. She doesn't do drugs. She's only twenty-one years old, and she's dying. Please, Jessica, go find out for me…" His voice cracked.

Jessica ran to the desk, gesticulating wildly. When she returned, her eyes were bright with tears. "They're still working with her and will send someone to speak to the family soon. Travis is on the way, and Mother and Daddy will be here as soon as they can. Frank will come when the babysitter arrives. What happened?"

"She said she didn't feel well. She clutched her chest and collapsed. She was breathing, but her pulse was so weak and fast I couldn't count it. Then she lost consciousness, and I was doing CPR when the ambulance arrived…I can't lose her—"

"I don't understand. They think it was drugs? Travis has wondered, but I didn't see any signs." Jessica pulled a tissue out of her purse and dabbed at her eyes.

"No. I don't believe it's drugs. That's what they kept asking me. She doesn't even drink much." He rubbed his eyes. "I think she's been ill for a while…" He looked away and sighed. "She came to see me before Christmas, at your cabin. We were snowed in together, but I didn't realize she was sick."

"To see *you?* Why? Are you…together? I mean, I suspected, but I didn't really want to believe it."

He looked at the floor, not meeting her gaze. "Just since Christmas, I swear." He looked up when he heard her tapping a text on her phone.

"I'm texting Frank to stop by the house and get Mother and Daddy's medications and stuff for Lissy. I don't know how long we'll be here. We'll talk about *you* and Lissy later."

He nodded.

Travis and the Carltons arrived at the same time. Patsy's eyes were red-rimmed, and George looked shell-shocked. Jessica told them what little she knew. Thankfully no one thought to question him and his part in all of this. They waited restlessly until a doctor came and ushered them into a private consultation room. He was grateful when Jessica took his hand, signaling that he could come along.

"I'm Dr. Patel, the cardiologist on call. Your daughter is one lucky girl. She had an arrhythmia—an irregular heart rhythm—and this evening it became a dangerous one. We've ruled out an overdose." He held up a hand when Grayson and Patsy started to object. "It's routine to assume a diagnosis of overdose with someone her age and with the presenting symptoms. We've been able to get her heart back into a normal sinus rhythm, and we have her on a medication that will hopefully keep it that way.

"I've called in a specialist to review her case, and together we'll decide the best course of action. Tentatively, at this point in time, we think she has Wolff-Parkinson-White Syndrome, which, while serious, can be dealt with by medication or a catheter ablation—a surgical procedure. Once treated, she should be able to live a relatively normal life. She'll be transferred to the cardiac care unit as soon as a bed is ready. Any questions? We'll know more tomorrow after more tests are run."

"When can we see her?" Patsy asked, clutching her husband's hand.

"She's asking for her parents and her boyfriend, Gray. Parents first, then boyfriend."

All eyes turned and focused on him, but Jessica squeezed his hand in support. He hung his head, staring at the floor as he struggled to keep his emotions in check.

Jessica and Travis stayed in the waiting room with him as their parents went to check on Alyssandra. Beside him, his sister-in-law drummed her fingers on the arm of the chair, watching uneasily as Travis paced. She sent a quick text to Frank, reporting the doctor's findings.

Gray cracked his neck and shrugged the tension from his shoulders, waiting for the well-deserved explosion from Alyssandra's brother. Face flushed, Travis stopped in front of his chair, clenching and unclenching his fists. Grayson resolved not to put up a fight; he deserved whatever Travis had to dish out.

"Travis, why don't you take a walk outside? Get some fresh air," Jessica suggested, placing a hand over his fist.

Travis pointed at him. "I have a lot of questions—"

"I know; we all do. But not *here*," she insisted.

With an exasperated sigh, Travis stormed outside.

"Thank you," Grayson murmured.

Jessica patted his arm. "He's upset."

"I would be, too," Grayson acknowledged.

"The last thing we need is a brawl in the ER waiting room. You two can duke it out later, at home."

Frank sprinted into the ER, and she bolted from her seat, throwing herself into his arms.

"Hey now, sugar, everything's gonna be okay. I got your text; the news sounds good, right?" He held her tightly and kissed her forehead. "Look, there's your dad. He's motioning for you. Go see your sister."

She darted to her father.

Grayson stared at the ugly tile floor.

"You're in some deep shit, Trip. Jess filled me in. Watch out for Travis's right hook."

"Noted."

"Be prepared; here comes her father," Frank warned.

Looking up, he watched as George shuffled toward them.

"She's resting quietly. Patsy and Jessica are with her." Removing his glasses, he wiped tears from his eyes. With a groan, he sank into the chair next to Grayson.

Travis came back in and glared at Grayson before squatting down in front of his father's chair. "Is she okay, Dad?"

George nodded. "You can go see her when Jessica comes out. I doubt you'll get your mother to leave."

"Speaking of which, I brought stuff y'all might need." Frank handed his father-in-law a duffle bag. "Your evening medications are in there, and your pipe and tobacco. If you sneak around to the side of the hospital, you might be able to catch a smoke. I also brought clothes and toiletries for the women and Lissy's phone and charger."

"I always knew you were a good son-in-law," George joked. He stood and took the pipe and tobacco. "Travis, come with me. You can be my wingman."

Even Grayson chuckled at that.

"Dad, you're going for an illicit smoke, not to pick up women. I'll be your lookout," Travis clarified.

"*Wingman* wasn't the right word?" George shook his head. "I can't keep up with the lingo."

"Come on." Travis placed a hand on his father's shoulder and guided him outside.

Frank turned to him. "What the fuck were you thinking, Trip? The news about Lissy was bad enough but to hear you and she had hooked up..." Frank rubbed his brow. "Dammit. She's just a kid. Not to mention my sister-in-law."

Grayson swallowed nervously and looked away, not wanting to have this discussion. Not now. Not here. "I know."

"She was with you at the cabin? Do Mama and Pop know?"

"I can't do this now. I'll explain everything later." His head pounded.

He needed to see Alyssandra, talk to her, and make sure she was all right. Dammit, he wanted to hold her and never let go. The sight of her body convulsing as the paramedic zapped her heart played in his memory on constant repeat.

They looked up when Jessica came back.

"Grayson, she wants to see you."

He nodded and shot out of the chair, pacing impatiently before being buzzed behind the steel double door. He ran to the cubicle the nurse pointed out but froze when he saw her. His heart seized, and he wondered if they might need to shock him as well.

"She's been asking for you," Patsy commented.

He pulled his gaze from Lissy's still, pale figure and met the narrowed, questioning face of her mother.

Patsy turned her attention back to Lissy. She straightened the covers and leaned over the bed, kissing her daughter on the forehead. "Grayson is here. I'm going to go check on your father. I'll be back." She walked out without looking at him.

He kissed Alyssandra's lips and stroked her cheek softly. "Alyssandra."

"What?" she murmured with a tired smile, not opening her eyes.

"This has been the longest damn day of my life." He pressed a kiss to her palm and held it to his face.

"Just call me Sleeping Beauty." She opened her heavy lids and smiled, her thumb stroking his cheek. "You need to shave."

"*La Belle au bois dormant.*" Perching on the side of her bed, he stared at the heart monitor as the line beeped rhythmically and steadily across the small screen. "You need to sleep, my darling. I just wanted to make sure you were okay."

"I'm fine." She wiped his tears away. "Don't, Gray. I'm okay. Matter of fact, I'm tripping on some good drugs. Get it? Tripping, Trip." She gave him a crooked smile. "That name fits you. I see at least two of you—where's the third?"

Gray chuckled and kissed her hand. "I hate that nickname. Enjoy it, Alyssandra. Because when you get out of here, I'm going to beat your sweet ass for not going to the doctor sooner."

"You lay one hand on my sister and I'll *kick your ass.*" Travis stood at the door, glaring.

"Please, don't upset your sister. We'll talk later."

"I'm okay, you two. Don't fight." She smiled and appeared to be attempting to focus her eyes. "I'm not crazy, and I'm not pregnant. All is good. Hey, Trav? I might not pass my drug test tomorrow. And I may be a little late to count your money, but I really don't care…" Lissy's eyes fluttered closed.

"*Pregnant?*" Travis hissed. He turned and grabbed Grayson by the elbow, propelling him back toward the waiting room.

Patsy and George hurried past them to be with Lissy. Grayson shrugged out of his grasp.

"Outside now!" Travis snarled.

He nodded but was happy to see Frank and Jessica follow. Frank might be mad at him, but he was his brother and would have his back if needed.

"Why is my sister relieved to *not* be pregnant?" Travis punctuated his words with his index finger into Grayson's chest.

Frank intervened and Travis pulled away, pacing. Grayson didn't blame him one damn bit.

"Alyssandra thought she was pregnant—"

Travis drew back his fist.

Grayson shook his head. "Not by me. She came to me for help."

"Who? Who the hell did she think—wait, Eddie? I'll kill that doctor-wannabe prick."

"No, not Eddie. And if she wants you to know, she'll tell you. She went to a women's center, and she wasn't pregnant. They told her the symptoms were caused by anxiety. Looking back *now*, it was probably this heart rhythm irregularity."

"Josh." Jessica's green eyes widened as she put two and two together. "About the time she started failing school, she told me she and Josh broke up…"

"Okay. So Josh's ass is the one to kick, and you're *not* in a relationship with Lissy." Travis's eyes narrowed, glinting like silver bullets. "Or are you?"

Grayson looked away. "I'm not discussing my relationship with Alyssandra."

"Oh, hell yes, you are, you sonofabitch. You've been a guest in my parents' home and seducing my kid sister?"

Grayson shoved his hands in his pockets and silently stared at him, neither denying nor confirming anything.

Frank intervened. "Whoa, now. Let's wait and discuss this some other place and some other time. All that matters right now is Liss getting better. Everyone's keyed up and tired." He pulled him away as Jessica tugged on Travis's hand to go back into the ER.

"I don't envy you, Trip. I dealt with Travis as a protective brother when Jess and I first got together. But I'm *your* brother, and I've got your back."

"Thank you." He ran a hand through his hair, trying to collect his scattered thoughts.

"I know you don't want to talk about this. But tell me one thing. This wasn't just a hit-and-run rebound deal, was it? I mean, you wouldn't do that to Liss, would you?" Frank eyed him anxiously.

"No. I don't know what this is. We were in the process of trying to figure it out —" He stopped when he spotted Jessica running toward them. His stomach sank.

"She's having another episode," she cried before tearing back into the building.

His heart exploded, and he broke down and wept.

The next morning, George walked with Grayson around the hospital parking lot as the sun rose. "They seem to think it's probably going to be best to do the operation instead trying the medications to control these episodes." George puffed on his pipe.

Grayson nodded, blinking his bleary eyes. Patsy remained in the CCU waiting area. Frank, Jessica, and Travis had gone home.

"I like you, Grayson." Her father stopped and looked up at him. "I don't know that I necessarily like you with my daughter, but…" He shrugged and took a few more puffs on the pipe.

Grayson knew the lawyer was weighing his words carefully.

"Lissy's always been headstrong, the child who marched to her own tune, no matter what. She was our surprise baby, and a welcome one, but it's been difficult keeping up with her," George admitted. "Travis and Jessica were far from perfect, and Lord knows they tested us. But Lissy has gone beyond testing and pushed the boundaries. According to her mother, I've spoiled her." He shrugged. "Maybe some of this is my fault."

George resumed walking, and Grayson silently kept pace. How was he supposed to assure her father of his good intentions when they weren't good at all? Or at least they hadn't started out that way…

"It's as if my daughter's been lost, and I don't know how to guide her anymore. Like learning all this new-fangled stuff like GPS. Give me an old-fashioned road map, and I'll find my way. If you're part of the reason she's wandering into dangerous territory, I'm asking you to leave her alone. You're nineteen years older than she is, so you need to be the one to use your head, and not your heart or your hormones." He turned and faced Gray. His pipe smoke circled them like a smoke signal.

Grayson shoved his hands in his pockets, taking a moment to search for what to say. He'd expected anger, not cautious acceptance.

"You've been in the unsavory side of the press lately," George added. "I don't like it."

"Nor do I. And I want to shield Alyssandra from it as much as possible. I understand your reservations, especially with the age difference. I've fought my attraction to Alyssandra, but this pull between us—it defies words or reason. However, I can assure you, I am not why she was lost. We've only been together since Christmas, and we're still exploring where this relationship will go. I promise I've been as honest as I can with her. We both know the age difference is a factor, as is the distance between us."

"Agreed," George said.

"She needs to find herself as a person," Grayson continued. "And yet, I can honestly say, she is more focused than most girls her age. Her passion for life, her wit, and her kindness make her special. I will never stand in the way of her dreams and aspirations. Did you know she's quite talented in fashion design? I've seen her sketches."

George paused. "No. I mean, she's always doodled and liked to sew. She got that from her mother…" He sighed. "Perhaps I haven't paid as much attention as I should have."

"She'll find her way. I have confidence in her."

"Good." George nodded. "It's my dream that she finish college, somewhere. Anything you can do to encourage her to go back to school would be appreciated. She hasn't got a lick of sense about money except how to spend it—I know she shouldn't work at a bank. This is just a lesson." George chuckled. "Don't tell her mother I said this, but she's right. I don't think Lissy's cut out to be a nurse. Maybe she *can* do something with this sewing business."

A man with a camera approached and Grayson scowled. "We need to go back inside."

George looked over, surprised. "What are they doing here?"

"I'm afraid Candie has amped up her ridiculousness." He steered George to the nearest entrance, ignoring the paparazzi.

Once inside, Grayson sighed. "I apologize for this intrusion." He motioned toward the door. "Just ignore them. As for Alyssandra, I care for your daughter deeply—more deeply than I have even shared with her. Her health is everyone's main concern at this time. With your permission, I'd like hold off on this discussion until after she and I have had time to figure things out."

George nodded. "I don't like this aspect of your past. As for your feelings for Lissy, fair enough. But if you break her heart, you'll answer to me. And don't expect her mother to be as understanding. Especially with this press involved. Watch out for Travis's right hook, too."

Chapter
Twenty

"Gray?" Lissy struggled to open her eyes. Every part of her felt heavy as she fought the effects of all the drugs she'd been given.

"He's in the waiting room," her mother answered.

Lissy smiled at her mom. "You should go home. You look tired."

Dark circles marred her mother's beautiful face, and her bobbed brown hair was mussed from sleeping in a chair. She wore a pink sweatshirt and jeans, but still had on her pearls from last night. Lissy smiled. No one could rock pearls with a sweatshirt like her mother.

"I'm not leaving until I'm sure you're okay. You're my baby."

"I'm not a baby, but I'm glad you're my mother."

"They need to keep you on whatever medication you're on," her mother teased. "Usually you're wishing I wasn't." She wiped her eyes with a tissue.

"Please don't cry. I'm fine. And we may have our differences, but I love you. How long have I been here?"

"Not quite twenty-four hours."

"I hope Travis isn't too pissed I missed work. He should've just let me start next Monday, anyway…" She squeezed her mom's hand. "Mother?"

"Yes?"

She changed her mind; she couldn't put a voice to her fears about dying and didn't want to burden her mother further. Instead she said, "Why don't you go home? Gray can stay with me awhile."

Her mother sighed, and the crease between her brows deepened. "I don't know what to think about of all this...you and Grayson."

"I need to see him. Please? Just for a few hours. You can go home and get a nap and come back."

"You won't stop until I give in, will you?"

"No."

"I don't approve. He's much too old for you."

Lissy took her mother's hand. "I think I love him..."

"Don't be ridiculous. You're too young. You've always had a crush on him —"

"Didn't you tell me that the first time Daddy kissed you, you knew he was the one for you?"

"Yes, but —"

"Love can't be confined or even defined. Love is love, Mother. It's what you and Daddy taught us."

"That's not fair." Her mother gave her a sad, worried smile. "We'll discuss this later." She leaned over and kissed her forehead, brushing the hair from her face. "And when you're better, we're going to have a talk about that hair stunt. I'm glad you didn't really dye your hair to look like a unicorn on drugs."

Lissy laughed and hesitated a second. "Would you bring my birth control pills back with you?" Her mother sighed, but she nodded as she left the room.

Lissy sat up and let the dizziness pass before grabbing her IV pole to go to the bathroom.

"Are you supposed to be out of bed, *mon chaton?*" Gray grabbed her arm to steady her.

"I didn't hear you come in. I gotta pee. Badly. I've had, like, a gazillion liters of this IV stuff pumped into me. I want a shower, too."

"Wait for the nurse."

"I can't wait; I'm going to bust." Lissy continued toward the bathroom with Gray holding her arm and guiding the IV pole. "Okay, you can step outside now."

"Not a chance. I'll turn my back, but I'm staying right here. And no shower—not without a nurse present."

"Okay. But you have to step out for a few minutes. Leave the door cracked, but you can't be in here. This is too embarrassing. I'll yell when I'm done. Please, Gray, I'm dying. Just go."

"I've watched you vomit," he protested.

"Just go!"

He finally stepped out, and she nearly cried with relief. She called him when she'd finished and he returned to watch her, yawning in the mirror as she brushed her teeth.

"Why does every embarrassing thing that has ever happened to me involve you?" she asked.

"I have no clue."

His hair was unkempt, his eyes swollen and red-rimmed. The blue sweatshirt didn't go at all with his dark dress pants. She grinned at him in the mirror.

"What?" Gray rubbed his eyes and scratched his scruffy jaw.

"You look so un-put-together—very unlike the normal debonair Grayson Deschanelle."

"I grabbed the first shirt I could find as they loaded you into the ambulance." He grabbed the IV pole and helped her back to bed. "I like your current outfit. Easy access," he teased. He kissed the back of her neck and swatted her butt as she climbed in.

"This thing is hideous. Why can't they make hospital gowns in pretty prints? I think I'll design some. I don't remember much about last night, but I'm sorry if I scared you." Exhausted, she settled back in bed with a relieved sigh.

"I never want to go through anything like that again." He placed a gentle kiss on her forehead.

Grabbing his hand, she tugged him toward her. "You look dog-tired. Come lie down with me."

"I don't think that's appropriate."

She smirked and scooted over. "Since when are we appropriate? It isn't like we're gonna do anything." Looking into his eyes, she saw her fear reflected there. "Please? I-I'm scared."

Instead, he pulled his chair close and laid his head down next to hers. Lissy moved his hand to her heart and held it there.

"*Tu es ma raison de vivre,*" he whispered.

"What does that mean?"

"You are my reason for living, if we're being literal."

"Stop staring. I'm sure I look dreadful." She kissed his rough jaw, cupping his cheek in her hand.

"You're here. That's all that matters…" His eyes filled with tears.

Lissy stroked his hair. "I'm okay. You can feel my heart beating—watch it on the monitor or listen to the steady beeps. Go to sleep, Gray. Now that you're here, I'll be fine."

In a matter of seconds, soft snores whispered in her ear. *He must be really tired*—no way he could be comfortable. But she wouldn't wake him for the world. Lissy smiled. Nothing could go wrong with him by her side.

She looked up when the nurse came in to check on her. A middle-aged woman in blue-flowered scrubs, she frowned upon spotting Grayson. Lissy put her finger to her lips and begged with her eyes not to disturb him. The nurse shook her head but smiled as she checked the monitors and IV.

Lissy mouthed a silent *thank you*.

The nurse winked and left, closing the door.

Lissy slowly surfaced back into consciousness, blinking as she remembered she was in the hospital. Gray was not here; instead her brother sat by her bedside.

"Hey, you." Dressed in a navy suit with a red tie, Travis was the epitome of a successful banker.

"What time is it?"

"Supper time. You missed work," he teased. "I came by to check on you before heading home. How are you feeling?"

"Okay. Where's Gray?" She looked around the room.

Air hissed between his teeth. "Frank took him home to get a shower and pick up his rental car. Mother will be back in a minute; she went home for a few. Jessica's home with the kids, and Dad will be here later."

"Who sent the flowers?" A huge bouquet of spring flowers sat on the built-in dresser across from the bed.

"The Deschanelles. Do you need anything?"

"No." She caught hold of his hand. "Don't blame Gray."

Travis stared back without saying anything for a moment, and then nodded. "I blame him, but I won't hurt him, okay?" She nodded and he added, "Until he hurts you. Then all bets are off."

Lissy grinned. "You've always been way overprotective."

"That's what older brothers do. It's preparation for when we have daughters." He pinched her nose lightly. "I gotta run. Love you."

He gave his mother a quick kiss on the cheek when she walked in as he waved goodbye.

"When is Gray coming back?"

"Soon. He left about thirty minutes ago." Her mother's sage-colored blouse enhanced her green eyes, but makeup couldn't conceal the circles of worry. Lissy braced for a blistering lecture, praying her illness might prevent it from happening now, but knowing it would come sooner or later. Mother handed her the birth control pills. "Obviously you need these."

Lissy blushed, but having been raised by a lawyer, she refused to answer on the grounds that anything she said would be used against her. She took the pill with a sip of water.

Her mother crossed her arms in front of her chest. "How long has this been going on?"

Okay, so much for illness stalling the lecture.

"Christmas."

"This Christmas?"

"Yes."

Her mother blew out a breath. "I like Grayson, but he's too old for you. What about that nice Eddie?"

Lissy rolled her eyes. "Eddie's my best friend. And he's gay."

"I knew it was too good to be true," Mother muttered.

The door opened, and the nurse had a wheelchair. "Last test today before your cardiac ablation tomorrow." She smiled as she moved Lissy's IV bag to the pole on the wheelchair.

The heart rate monitor began beeping rapidly.

"Are you sure I have to do this?"

She was scared. She'd never even been in a hospital except to visit people before last night.

"Your doctor thinks so. The medication isn't holding off the arrhythmias. The cardiac ablation has a high success rate. The surgery has minimal risks. I'm sure you'll breeze through this."

Despite the nurse's reassurance, her breathing stuttered like a dying fan. Grabbing her phone, she sent a quick text before getting in the wheelchair.

I need you.

"Bitch, don't you know I have to study? The things you do to get attention…Oh, hi, Mrs. Carlton." Eddie's ears reddened when he saw her mother knitting in the corner of the hospital room. "Thanks for letting me sublet Lissy's apartment. It's a lot closer to campus."

"Hello, Eddie, and you're welcome." Her mother smiled but still looked sad.

"You should've stayed home and studied. Sorry I texted you. I'll be okay." Lissy kissed his cheek and hugged him best as she could, truly glad he was here. He wore jeans and a University of Alabama sweatshirt, which surprisingly, made her miss school.

"I lied. I needed my best friend," she admitted.

"Stop, Liss, you're gonna muss my hair. I brought you a present." He handed her a Super Soaker squirt gun. "If the nurses or docs piss you off, get 'em." Lissy laughed as he sat on the bed and began his mindless chatter.

It was just what she needed—something to prevent her from thinking about her future. Or if she even had one.

Chapter
Twenty-One

Grayson didn't know how Lissy had pulled it off, but he was staying the night with her. She'd been moved from the cardiac care unit to a step-down floor where family wasn't limited to specific visiting hours. And somehow, Alyssandra had convinced her parents to allow them this time together.

He'd brought Chinese food and three boxes of Godiva chocolate to thank the staff. The floor was unusually quiet when he stepped off the elevator. Lissy's nurse waved him toward her room as she opened the first bag of takeout.

Patsy and George sat by Alyssandra's bedside, talking quietly, and looked up when he entered. Their acknowledging nods were cordial, but justifiable tension hung in the air. Alyssandra sat cross-legged on the bed in her Hello Kitty pajama pants and hospital gown. Her hair was pulled into a loose bun held by a drinking straw. Plugged into her phone, her head bopped up and down as she thumbed through a *Vogue* magazine.

When she looked up, her face brightened with her huge smile. Rising onto her knees, she threw her arms around his neck and kissed him on the cheek. His face flushed hot, and he didn't dare look at her parents as he set the food down on her bedside table. Yanking out the earbuds, she turned the phone off before tossing it aside.

"Oh, thank God. I'm starving. The food here sucks. And what could be better for my last meal than moo goo gai pan?"

"Lissy, I don't think referring to this as your 'last meal' is appropriate. You're going to be fine," George scolded.

He stood, offering his hand to his wife. They kissed her good-bye with assurances they would return early in the morning before her procedure.

"Call us if you need us." Her mother's look meant business. "I don't want to leave her, but this is what she wants. The staff has been very kind allowing someone to stay with her." Her voice choked, and she turned to give Alyssandra another hug.

"I'll be okay, Mother. I love you." Lissy kissed her cheek. "And thank you."

Her mother shot him a look as she walked past him.

"Good night," Grayson said politely as they closed the door. "They hate me."

"They don't hate *you*. They're just not sure what to make of *us*." She opened the Chinese food and inhaled, smiling. "It makes it easier, really, if you think about it. Now we can meet when we want and not have to hide—that is, if you still want to…" Her voice trailed off, and as she took a bite, her eyes closed with a look of pure bliss.

"Mmmmm. O-M-G, Gray. This is the best, *ever!*"

"You're the only person I know who can make eating Chinese takeout look almost orgasmic." Grayson chuckled as he dug into his triple delight.

He ignored her unstated question about their relationship. He couldn't think about it. Not now, not when he was still reeling from nearly losing her.

"It's close. Chocolate would definitely be orgasmic." She laughed, but it sounded forced and slightly uncomfortable. "Gray?"

He paused, his chopsticks in midair, and waited.

"I—never mind."

"Are you okay? Is it your heart?" He put his food down and moved from the chair to the side of her bed. His gaze moved to her heart monitor.

"No, no. I'm fine."

She pushed the food away and curled up on her side to look at him. She looked so damn fragile, and it terrified him.

He'd listened with her and her parents to the explanation of the surgical procedure she would be undergoing, and he felt confident it was the right thing for her to do. *It had to be.* But it still scared the hell out of him.

He stroked her hair. "Talk to me, Alyssandra."

"I'm okay, just really tired. Eat your food."

"You eat, and I'll give you the present I brought you."

Her eyes sparkled. "Bribery will get you everywhere."

She sat up and ate a few more bites. Grayson remained on the side of the bed eating his dinner but not really tasting it. It was a wonder he could swallow at all with the lump in his throat. He gave her a bite of his food with his chopsticks, and she did the same. It felt oddly intimate, and he leaned in and gave her a quick kiss, tasting the soy sauce that lingered there.

She deepened the kiss, putting her food down as she cupped his face in her hand. The door opened and they separated quickly as the nurse peeked in, both of them blushing like teenagers.

The nurse smiled. "Her heart rate went up, and I was just checking on her. I understand why now. Let's not get too crazy." She backed out and shut the door.

He wondered if all nurses were this understanding or if the free Chinese food was the reason.

Lissy began to giggle. "I bet you have that effect on all the cardiac patients."

"Good God, I hope not. I think the other patients on the floor are elderly men." He joined her laughter.

"May I have my present now? I really can't eat another bite." She closed the top of her takeout box.

Grayson reached into the bag and brought out a box of Valentine's Day chocolate. "Lucky for me, the local pharmacy has this stuff out early." There was an envelope of pictures attached to it.

"It's a heart." Lissy blinked rapidly and smiled at him, her eyes shining. "A whole heart. And full of chocolate."

"My heart is yours." He gazed at her, taking in her trembling lower lip, her shining eyes, and the pulse beating at the sensitive spot on her neck.

"You have mine, too. Sorry it's kinda broken." She opened the envelope of pictures, and her tears turned to an excited squeal. He'd printed pictures of the family at the christening, the one of him holding her as she put the angel on their Christmas tree, Noëlle playing with the yarn, her cartwheels in the snow, and the series of them making funny faces at the camera in front of the snowman. The last photo was the one where she'd surprised him with a kiss in the snow.

He pointed at the picture of them kissing. "This is my favorite."

"Mine, too. But there seem to be a few pictures missing…" She flashed him a sly smile.

"I'll give them to you in private when you're recovered. I didn't want to set your heart monitor off again." Actually, *those* were his favorites. "Nor run the risk of your family finding them. I've been warned about Travis's right hook."

"Thank you, Gray."

"You're welcome." He watched her as she thumbed through the pictures again, lingering on the one of them kissing. She put them down and opened the box of candy. He laughed as she took one, bit it in half, and wrinkled her nose.

"Yuck. I always get the nougats."

He leaned forward and opened his mouth, and she popped the other half between his lips, her eyes widening when he sucked seductively on her fingers. He winked at her.

"S-Stop. That will definitely bring the nurse back," she whispered.

The pulse in her neck beat visibly faster, making him feel guilty. He stood and threw the Chinese food away.

"We forgot our fortune cookies." He handed her one as he cracked his open. *The one you love is closer than you think.* Well, damn.

Alyssandra cracked hers and read it out loud. "*Love is the only medicine for a broken heart.* You know, to make it more interesting, you're supposed to add 'in bed' at the end of the fortune. So mine would say *Love is the only medicine for a broken heart, in bed.*"

She frowned and added softly, "How weird that I ended up with one about a broken heart. Did you plan it? What did yours say?"

"*The one you love is closer than you think, in bed.*" He looked at her pointedly and raised his eyebrows. She laughed and took another candy from the heart-shaped box. "Those things are so silly but remarkably accurate, don'tcha think?"

He didn't reply.

She yawned, and he insisted she rest. After she brushed her teeth, he turned out the light and tucked her in bed. The room wasn't totally dark, as the lights from outside filtered through the blinds. They could hear the muffled sounds of the nurses softly talking and laughing at their station. He leaned over and kissed her good night, his lips lingering on hers.

"Good night, my darling."

She scooted over in the bed. "Please? Just hold me."

Stretching out beside her, he placed his hand over her heart. It comforted him to feel it beating. They were silent for several minutes. Softly he asked, "How did you convince your parents to let me stay?"

It was a few seconds before she confessed, "I pulled the dying kid card and told them if I was going to die, I wanted my last few hours to be with you."

"You're not going to die." He spoke firmly. "I forbid it."

"I'm scared," she said.

"I know. Me, too." A tear slipped down her cheek, and he kissed it away. "Please don't cry or get upset. You're going to be fine."

She sighed. "There are so many things I wish I'd done. Almost-dying really does make you appreciate how short life is and that you should live each day as if it's your last. I want to slow dance and make love with you again. I want to go back to Paris. When I was little, my parents took us there. To me, it was better than Disney World. I told my mother that someday my boyfriend would propose to me in front of the Eiffel Tower." She quickly added, "Before you panic, I was six. I realize now marriage is *so* not necessary."

"And the Eiffel Tower is crowded with tourists," Gray murmured. "What other dreams do you have?"

"I want to watch Lee and Grace grow up. I'd like to walk on the beach at sunset, learn to snow ski, and I even want to go back to school."

"Still in nursing?" he teased.

"No way. I'm going to convince my parents to let me go to fashion design school. Your father was very encouraging. He and your stepmother video chatted with me earlier, wishing me well. He said I have talent and offered to let me do an internship with his company. Then if I like it, he said he'll write a letter of recommendation for school. Do you think he might have offered just because I'm sick?"

"*Papa?* No. He's always brutally honest."

"I talked a little bit to my parents about it earlier. Daddy says there's no money in it. That's why he pushed me into nursing after I hated education."

"He's right, for the most part. But if you aren't passionate about your profession, it becomes drudgery."

"I *like* money. But I *love* fashion. I just want to find something to do in the industry…" Her voice broke into a sob. "But what if I die? It happens, you know. I don't want to die and leave you and my family."

"Shhhhh…You are not going to die. All these things will happen. You're getting worked up, and it isn't good for you." He sat up and smiled at her. "What if I can make one of your wishes come true? Tonight. Will you stop crying?"

"Here?" she gasped, her eyes darting to the door.

He laughed. "No, not *that* one. I'll be right back."

Lissy sat with her knees pulled to her chest and her arms wrapped around her legs. Convincing her parents to give her this evening with Gray had been difficult, but so worth it. She looked at the photo of them kissing in the snow. His look was one of surprise, joy, and passion. The picture blurred, and she wiped her tears away. Would she live to see another night? The doctor had said this was almost a routine procedure, but her mind kept focusing on the words *small risk of death*. What if tonight really was her last night?

Her heart pounded, the annoying beeps compounding her fear as she took several deliberate, measured breaths. *Please, not again.* Her chest was still sore and bruised from the last round of CPR and getting zapped like Frankenstein's monster.

The heart monitor slowed, and the nurse didn't come to check on her, so she must be okay. Would she always live in fear? She undid her bun and shook out her hair, wondering where Gray had disappeared to. What dream could he possibly make happen tonight, in the hospital? She plugged in her phone and hit shuffle, hoping music would soothe her.

The door cracked open, and she immediately felt calmer. Even in his faded blue jeans and long-sleeved T-shirt, Gray looked as if he'd just stepped out of the pages of *GQ*. Only the creases around his eyes betrayed his worry. A nurse followed him in and unhooked her IV and capped it, assuring her she wouldn't have to be re-stuck.

"Come with me." Gray took the phone from her and tucked it in his jeans pocket. He held out a hand. Putting her heart monitor in her robe pocket, she glanced at the nurses at the desk, who smiled and nodded their okay.

"Where are we going?"

"To the waiting room at the end of the hall."

"Why?"

"You'll see."

It was dark in the waiting room, with only the streetlights filtering through the windows. All of the chairs had been moved out of the way. Gray took her phone out of his pocket, fiddled with it a moment, and placed it on the window sill.

"May I have this dance, Alyssandra?"

He smiled down at her, and she thought her heart would burst with happiness. She nodded, and he drew her close. Edith Piaf's "La Vie en Rose" began playing.

"Is this our song?"

He frowned. "I hope not, but it does bring back happy memories."

"If I were chocolate, I'd be a melted mess of goo right now," she mumbled.

"I love melted chocolate."

"I love this song."

"So does my grandmother," he teased.

"C'est la Mort" by The Civil Wars was next on her Grayson playlist. When she'd added it a week ago, she hadn't been on death's door. Now the words hung like a funeral pall. She looked up, and in the dim light, his eyes were shiny. She opened her mouth to speak, but he shook his head.

Holding her cheeks in his hands, he lowered his mouth to hers. The kiss was gentle at first but deepened. She wrapped her arms around his neck, her soul crying for him. If her heart was broken, he was the one who could fix it, not any doctor. Her love for him was so intense her knees almost buckled. She hid her face in his chest; terrified he'd leave on the first jet for Paris if he realized the depth of her feelings.

"What would I do without you?" he whispered.

Maybe he feels it too? "Live a quiet life?" she teased.

"There is that." He chuckled.

She kept her head tucked under his chin, listening to his steady, strong heartbeat. Life was short. And that thought gave her the courage to admit the depth of her feelings.

"I love you, Gray. I can't die without saying it."

"You're not going to die."

"I don't expect you to say it in return. I know you may think I'm being overly dramatic, but I wanted you to know this, in case something does happen. I think I fell in love with you the first time we met."

"Alyss—"

She pressed her fingers to his mouth. "Let me finish. You've always been there for me. I know there's an age difference, and that you've done more with your life than I have. But I know what I feel. Our time at the cabin was the happiest of my life. And it's more than great sex—fantastic sex, really. You see me as a person. You've encouraged me to fulfill my dreams. Tomorrow, when they put me to sleep, I won't be counting backward. I'll be counting snowflakes and the paper cranes I plan to make so my wish comes true.

"I'm the luckiest girl in the world. I have my family, my friends, and you. If something happens, I just wanted you to know you were the best part of my life. You don't need to answer me. I don't expect you to declare your love or get down on bended knee. I don't want lies or platitudes, just honesty. Please, don't say anything unless you mean it."

"You won't die. I can't live without you. Nor would I want to."

It wasn't a confession of love, but it was more than she'd expected. She kissed him, pressing in close to him, feeling his response to her.

"We need to stop, my darling girl, or one of your other wishes will happen. It could be quite embarrassing if the nurses come running in with the emergency cart," he whispered against her ear. "One last dance."

He thumbed through her phone and hit play: "Last Dance" by her favorite group, The Raveonettes.

It was a catchy tune, not really a slow dance, and she laughed as he twirled her around the waiting room, even moving her up onto the chairs and letting her slide down his body for one last searing kiss.

"I'll always save the last dance for you," she whispered.

"I'll always be there for the last dance," he whispered back.

Chapter
Twenty-Two

"I've never been so happy to be home in all my life."

Her groin was sore from where the catheter had been inserted for the ablation yesterday, and she was totally exhausted and a little out of it from her new meds, but she was home.

Lissy paused outside her sister's old bedroom, the one where Gray had been staying. The bed was made, and his things were gone. Had he left for Paris already?

"Where's Gray?" she asked, following her mother into her room.

"He's staying with Jessica and Frank." Mother placed her overnight bag on her bed.

Lissy frowned. "Why? What did you say to him?"

"I didn't say anything to him," her mother snapped. "He has enough common decency left not to flaunt your affair under our noses now that we know about it." Her face flushed as she hastily unpacked Lissy's suitcase, opening and slamming drawers. "Did you know there were paparazzi hounding him?"

"It's because of that bitch Candie. The things she's saying are lies." Lissy picked up her phone and started scrolling. She blinked, and her mouth dropped open. "They were at the hospital?"

"Yes." Her mother snapped a pair of pajama pants and folded them. "They were rude and pushy. First the christening and then when our daughter is facing death. You don't want to live like that. We don't want you to live like that. We're a respectable family. We've had our minor transgressions but—"

"Please stop. I can unpack my own things. I'm not twelve. I'm an adult and perfectly capable of putting away my things *and* choosing the man I want to be in a relationship with."

"You may not be twelve, but you're *only* twenty-one. You're a *young* girl, and he's a grown *man*. An *older* man. You recently flunked out of college, and you're still recovering from a serious illness and surgery. Maybe some counseling would help. Tell Grayson to go back to New York, Paris, wherever. You need time to think about your future. If you don't, your father and I will."

"Will what?" she screeched. "Did you only act like you were okay with my relationship while I was in the hospital? Why? *To give the dying kid whatever she wants?* Does Daddy feel this way, too? Can't you please let me have the time with him before he goes back to Paris? Please, Mother? Please let him come back and stay here." She knew she'd failed miserably in keeping the begging whine out of her voice.

"I am not condoning this relationship. No." Her mother's voice wasn't as harsh but remained firm. She sat on the bed, and Lissy knew this wasn't going to be over anytime soon.

Tears never worked with her mother, no matter how justified. "Don't you remember how you felt when you first fell in love with Daddy?" she asked softly.

"Lissy, sit down." She patted the bed beside her.

With a huff, she did as she was told.

"Has he ever actually said he loves you?"

She couldn't answer her mother or look her in the eyes. "Not in so many words, no. But he said he thinks he's falling in love with me."

"Men will sometimes say things to get what they want…" Her mother's voice gentled as she rubbed her back.

"He isn't like that. You *know* him, Mother."

"Oh, Lissy, I know this is hard. This is your first love, and that's always emotional. I'm not saying he intentionally set out to break your heart. He's *older,* and you're beautiful and *young.* You've always looked up to him. He obviously didn't think about how you're not emotionally mature enough to handle this sort of thing. He's on the rebound from Candie. I think he's a decent man, but he's gotten caught up in this—"

"Stop," she croaked. "Why doesn't anyone think I know my own mind?"

"Lissy, you haven't demonstrated that you do—with school, then Josh…Pulling that stunt with Eddie posing as your boyfriend at your party and the lies? In my mind, all you've done is prove you aren't as mature as you think you are. And you've been sick. You need time to make this kind of decision."

"I want to go see him."

"He'll be here this afternoon. He had things to handle. You have no idea how rude and intrusive the press has been. I believe his father is helping with the situation." Her mother sighed. "I know you don't believe me, Lissy, but I didn't say those things to hurt you—far from it. I don't want to see you devastated. I love you and would do anything in my power to protect you. Now rest until he arrives." Her mother left the room, closing the door behind her.

Lying down, she attempted to gather her scattered thoughts, but found she couldn't. Surely once she spoke to him, everything would be better.

Patsy opened the door before he could ring or knock, surprising Grayson. She looked as exhausted as he felt.

"Is Alyssandra okay?" he asked.

"She's resting upstairs. Please, come into the study. George and I would like to speak with you." She stepped aside, and he mentally prepared himself for a difficult conversation.

Lissy's father sat at his desk, smoking his pipe and looking out the window. The sun had set an hour ago. It was a well-known fact George Carlton only smoked when stressed.

"Is Alyssandra okay?" he repeated. The dull roar of fear pounded through his body, leaving him slightly nauseated. *She has to be okay.*

"Physically, yes," Patsy responded and motioned for him to sit in the chair facing the desk. She perched on the arm of her husband's chair, her arm around his shoulder. It seemed a calculated move to provide an image of solidarity.

"Would you care for a drink?" George asked, his voice even and non-threatening.

Grayson relaxed a fraction and nodded. He gratefully accepted the scotch Patsy handed him. He wanted to throw it back and ask for another but refrained.

"Grayson, we consider you part of our extended family, and we care about you," Patsy started.

"Let's just cut to the chase," George interrupted. "This is the *what are your intentions toward my daughter* conversation. And what the hell are you going to do about the paparazzi that have been calling non-stop and hounded us like vultures at the hospital?" He sat back in his chair, puffing his pipe.

"I care deeply for your daughter. And I apologize for the unwanted attention. It amped up after someone in Candie's camp found out I was here. It should die down as soon as something more newsworthy comes along."

"Or when you leave," Patsy snapped.

Gray took a sip of the scotch, letting the warmth seep through his body. The air in the room was certainly turning chilly. He'd spent the afternoon with Frank and his father on the phone going over the same issues. His father had hired a publicist for him.

"Do you love her?" she continued.

"I have yet to discuss this with Alyssandra."

Tears filled her eyes. "She's *only* twenty-one. You're *forty*."

Inwardly he flinched. "I'm fully aware of the age difference."

George continued to puff on his pipe, silently assessing. "What if she wants to return to college?"

"If Alyssandra wants to continue with college, by all means I would support her in doing so. I have no intention of harming your daughter or standing in the way of her dreams and aspirations. However, as much as I respect and care for both of you, I truly believe this is something I should be discussing with *her*. Then, if we have plans for a future together, we will discuss this with both of our families."

"Are you going to ask her to marry you?" Patsy's voice grew sharp.

"I've never considered myself a marrying man. Alyssandra is aware of this," he conceded. Best to let her parents know right now.

The sound of the antique clock on the bookcase was magnified by the dead silence that followed.

Patsy's face grew redder. "How dare you use my daughter and abuse the trust our family has bestowed upon you!" she shouted.

"I am not using, nor am I abusing your daughter. As I have said, I made this clear to Alyssandra before we became involved." He remained calm and maintained eye contact with the Carltons.

"And just exactly how long has this been going on?" George set his pipe down and leaned forward.

Grayson could practically see the lawyer wheels turning in George's head. "Since Christmas," he said, meeting the prosecutor's gaze steadily, despite the trickle of sweat that slowly seeped down his back. "This relationship is new. We're still exploring where it might go."

"She was only twenty at Christmas," Patsy hissed.

"I like you, Grayson. But family is important to me. *Important to us.*" George glanced over at his wife and squeezed her hand. "Did you know what you wanted at her age? I sure as hell didn't. Add to that the fact she's been ill…She needs time to heal and think. I don't want you taking advantage of her youth—"

"What's going on in here?" Alyssandra stood yawning at the doorway, wearing a pair of yoga pants and a sweatshirt, her hair uncombed and hanging down her back. Her eyelids appeared heavy.

"We're talking to Grayson," her mother replied stiffly.

"You've been crying." Lissy's troubled eyes scanned the room. "And Daddy's been smoking. I can smell it."

She walked over and put a hand on his shoulder. Grayson didn't move, fully aware that everything he said and did was being judged.

"Is this about me?" she asked.

"We're concerned about you, Lissy, and trying to determine Grayson's intentions." Her father emptied the old tobacco from his pipe, repacked it, and resumed smoking, creating a cloud of smoke.

"*His intentions?* What the hell? Is this 1820? Geezus, Daddy!"

"Lissy, watch your language," her mother admonished.

"Come on, Gray. Let's get out of here." Lissy patted his back.

"Sit down, Alyssandra," her father commanded, pointing to the chair next to his.

She sat and glanced nervously his way. He kept his face impassive.

"Look at me, not him." George's tone must've been the one he used to intimidate someone on the witness stand. "Has he taken advantage of you in any way? Are you aware he has no plans to marry?"

"He has *not* taken advantage of me. And yes, I'm aware he does not want marriage. This is the twenty-first century. We're a modern couple; marriage is just a piece of paper." She lifted her chin, but her knuckles blanched as she held onto the arms of her chair.

"Do you see how this upsets her?" her mother snapped, glaring at him. "And marriage is *not* just a piece of paper. It's a *commitment*."

George puffed on his pipe.

Grayson crossed his arms but gave a quick, resigned nod.

Lissy leapt to her feet. "You're mistaken as to why I'm upset, Mother."

Grayson sat still, watching her. She tossed her hair as she faced her parents.

"I'm upset because you and Daddy obviously don't think much of me or my ability to know my own mind. You raised me to think for myself, to be my own person. And yet you're implying that Gray is some sort of Svengali who's seducing me and using me for his own evil purposes.

"That is so far from the truth it's laughable," she continued. "He's been nothing but *honest* with me from the beginning. I'm aware of the difficulties we face, but we haven't exactly had much time to sort through the specifics of our relationship. Now if you'll excuse us, we have things to talk about. As a matter of fact, I won't be home tonight."

"What? Where do you think you're going? You just got out of the hospital." Patsy stood up as well.

"Anywhere but here. I don't care if we go spend the night in his rental car."

"You are not leaving this house, young lady," her mother snapped.

George stood and wrapped an arm around Patsy's shoulders. He took another puff on his pipe as he looked at them. "You two go and discuss whatever it is you need to discuss. Take a walk, go out to eat, or go to a movie—whatever. But I agree with her mother. She needs to stay home tonight. And stay clear of those vultures hounding all of us." He looked at Grayson. "Her mother and I have made our point."

"But, George, she just got out of the hospital. She's sick—"

"Patsy, stop. This is a compromise." He looked at Lissy. "I'm actually quite impressed you were able to speak so eloquently about your feelings, and even more so that you know who the hell Svengali was," George replied with a wry smile. "Maybe you should consider a career in law, my dear." He turned his gaze back to Grayson. "I meant what I told you at the hospital. Hurt her, and you'll answer to me."

Grayson stood, put his glass down, and shook George's hand. "Thank you," he said calmly.

He turned, placed his hand on the small of Lissy's back, and walked her back upstairs to her room.

She shut the door and threw herself into his arms.

"I'm so sorry, Gray—"

"Shhh. Your parents love you. They're concerned. I understand. I would be too if you were my daughter." He sighed. "And let's face it. You're almost young enough to be my daughter."

"I really need to get away from my crazy family." She sighed and looked at him. "I can't have strenuous activity for a week. Just my stupid luck—how embarrassing to have to tell you I can't have sex." Color rose in her cheeks.

"I think Svengali can rein in his passion," he replied with a chuckle. "And no way in hell am I touching you in this house again. Why don't you take a shower? I'll go be the dutiful boyfriend and ask if I can take you out to dinner. I'll meet you downstairs."

He gave her a kiss and went down to the kitchen.

Patsy stood silently weeping at the sink.

"Patsy?"

She wiped her eyes and turned to face him, crossing her arms. She didn't say a word, her manner cool, though more defeated than hostile.

"I know this is hard for you, and I never meant to abuse your hospitality. This thing between us, it's difficult to explain. She's the lens of my soul, making me view life differently. I think we bring out the best in each other." He looked out the kitchen window. "That night she collapsed…" He couldn't continue for a moment, the pain and fear still too fresh in his memory. "I can't bear the thought of losing her," he said.

"And yet you don't want to marry her. *I don't want to lose her, either.* Or pick up the broken pieces when you leave. I have to do this to protect my daughter."

The look on her face drew his guard go up. It was the look *Grand-mère* gave when she played her trump card.

"I have one request, and if you don't agree, I'll resort to desperate measures." She looked away. Picking up a dishtowel, she haphazardly wiped a platter and placed it on the counter. She brought her eyes back to him, twisting the cloth in her hands.

He wondered if it was a subliminal threat. She was definitely nervous. The clock on the wall ticked thirty long seconds as he waited for her to continue.

"Go away and leave her alone for a year. Give her time think about this, to finish school—no matter what major she decides on. She's young and has been through a lot emotionally and physically…" Tears sprang to her eyes. "She nearly died, Grayson! Please, I'm begging you. I need this assurance as her mother that she's making the decision that's right *for her*, not *for you*."

"And if I say no?"

Patsy lifted her chin, and her eyes snapped with a mother's determination. "I'll go to the press. She was fifteen when you met her, and only sixteen when you photographed her…"

The threat both surprised and angered him. "I never acted inappropriately when she was underage," he replied through clenched teeth.

Her eyes dilated to dark pools, and her nostrils flared. "I know," she whispered. "But the publicity damage will be done."

He narrowed his eyes and clenched his fist, as if doing so would contain his rage. "But it's a lie. This is blackmail. I assure you, I've fought this thing between us. You'd really do this to me? To her?"

"Yes." Tears coursed down her red cheeks. "I want you to end things with her. Tonight."

"She won't stand for it. She won't believe me if I break up with her."

"That's your job. To make her believe it."

He paced as the ramification of her threat sunk in. It would affect his ability to work. Not that he needed to work financially, but he enjoyed his job. And then it could filter down and possibly affect his father's and Frank's business.

"You have no proof, nothing inappropriate ever went on!"

"I won't need it. People will read all sorts of things into those photos that are already out there."

"I need to talk to her—"

"You know she can't have relations. She just had surgery—"

He slammed his fist on the counter and hissed, "That isn't why I'm asking. She needs to understand I'm not leaving her forever."

"Don't make promises you can't keep. Do you honestly think I've made this threat lightly? There's a reason you say you're not interested in marriage. Do you still have feelings for Candie? I read the tabloid headlines, and I looked at the calendar. You were with Candie right after you were with Lissy. I don't think you really know what you want. You're not truly committed to my daughter, are you? This separation is as much for you to figure out your feelings as it is for her. You can have tonight only. And have her home by ten."

She quietly walked out of the room, leaving Grayson stunned silent—and at a total loss as to what to do.

Chapter
Twenty-Three

Lissy looked around the Sonic Drive-In and smirked. "Fine dining at its best."

Grayson had thought it a better option than going in somewhere with paparazzi possibly lurking. Thankfully, the vultures seemed to be gone.

Distracted, Gray didn't laugh at her joke. He was busy staring out the window.

"Will you be staying with your grandmother in Paris?"

He nodded but didn't appear to have any idea what she'd asked.

"I'm going to strip off my clothes and dance on the hood of the car. Think anyone will notice and give the poor sick girl a dollar?"

He didn't answer, still staring at the parking lot like it was the most interesting place in the world.

"Gray!"

At last he drew his eyes to hers, and the depth of pain she witnessed in them unnerved her.

"W-What's the matter?"

He shook his head. "Nothing." His deep sigh said otherwise. "Sorry. I have a lot on my mind. What were you saying?"

She narrowed her eyes. "What happened while I was showering? Your mind has been a million miles away since then. Did my parents say something else to you? They're so old-fashioned."

"I'm leaving for Paris, not quite a million miles." His smile didn't reach his eyes.

Lissy put her cheeseburger down, no longer hungry. "I wish you didn't have to go. Maybe I could fly to New York when you return—you know, for a weekend. I'll save my money for the ticket, since I'll have a job working at Travis's stupid bank. I could maybe set up a tour of Parson's while I'm there. It's the school of my dreams. Plus, I'd be close to you if I get accepted."

Gray covered his face with his hand. "No."

She stared at him. *Something's wrong.* Her chest felt heavy, but not because of her heart, or the bruising left from where they'd brought her back to life. Glancing down so he wouldn't see the hurt in her eyes, she realized she had a stain on her sweatshirt and wasn't wearing any makeup. The man lived his life surrounded by beautiful women. Why would he want someone like her?

Daddy was wrong; she'd never make it as a lawyer because at this moment, words escaped her.

"I know I don't look very sexy…I'm black and blue with a side order of green and purple."

"If you had those clip thingies in your hair, you'd be perfectly color coordinated," he replied with a wan smile.

"I don't understand. I thought, I mean…Do you love me? Did you change your mind?" she blurted.

He sighed. "Sometimes love is not enough."

"No, you're wrong! Love is always enough."

He didn't respond, and she closed her eyes. "Answer me. Do. You. Love. Me?"

"Honestly, I don't know. There's a fine line between lust and love, and considering the circumstances under which we got together, it's hard to say."

She flinched, his answer making her greatest fear real. "Is this goodbye?" Her voice hitched as she searched his face. "I thought we were going to give this a go. I mean, we don't have to be discreet anymore. My parents know…"

He sighed, looking lost.

"Is it the money? I don't want your money."

"What?"

"The reason you don't want me. Do you think I'm after your money?" she asked. "I know it was presumptuous of me to ask if you were rich. I wasn't asking with any ulterior motive."

"Alyssandra, you're overwrought and exhausted. I'm taking you home. I just think we need time apart to figure out our relationship." He gathered their trash and bolted from the car as if he needed to get away from her.

She bit her lip watching him, not believing this was happening.

When he returned to the driver's seat, he turned to her. "Listen to me very carefully. First, do you remember me saying I wasn't a marrying man?"

She nodded. "And you want a relationship with no strings attached."

"Exactly. When I'm in Paris or New York, what would your reaction be if I'm photographed with another woman?"

His face swam, and she stared out the window at the car next to them. How could people be laughing and enjoying their food when her world was falling apart? She shrugged, unable to speak.

"It will happen—even if I'm just with a co-worker or a friend for dinner. And you'll always wonder, won't you? Alyssandra, I'm leaving, and I won't be back for a while. This thing between us has happened too fast; it's like being on a rollercoaster. It's time to get off and catch our breath. This will give us time to see if we want to go on another ride. It will also allow time for the press to die down and the paparazzi to find some other poor bastard to hound."

"What if I don't want to get off this ride?"

Gray tucked a strand of her hair behind her ear and cupped her cheek. "All rides come to an end."

"So this *is* goodbye." She searched his face for answers but found only resignation. "Am I not enough? Is that it? You need something from other women that I can't give you?"

"Sometimes things aren't as they seem."

"And sometimes they are." She stared at his face, unable to read it. In her heart, she knew he cared for her…

Her emotions were pinging all over the place like a pinball machine. She wondered if it was her medication. Or perhaps they hadn't fixed her heart after all; it certainly felt broken. "You're scared. That's why you're saying goodbye."

"Not goodbye, *à la prochaine.* "

"What's that mean?"

"Until we meet again."

"Tell me why. Tell me why you're such a coward," she bit out. "Because I'm too young for you? Are you ashamed to be seen with me? Were you just using me all along? You felt something; I know you did. You told me so. You promised me the last dance! Was that just because you thought I wouldn't make it through surgery? And now you feel trapped? I don't believe that. I can't…You showed me in so many ways…Why?" She shoved him as hard as she could, but he didn't budge. "Tell me why, you jerk!"

He hung his head.

"I love you," she croaked. "I love you enough for both of us."

"I want you to take time to consider whether you want to be with me. You've been ill, not yourself. Even your family has said so. First the pregnancy scare and then this heart problem."

"I don't need time. I know what I want. What you're really saying is *you* need time to decide if you want *me* in your life. So why have you stuck around since New Year's, Gray? Feeling sorry for the sick girl? How's this for sorry? I'm sorry I'm physically not up for the goodbye pity-fuck."

He couldn't have looked more stunned if she'd slapped him.

His eyes narrowed. "Don't be ridiculous. I don't pity you. You need to think through this decision. This would be a move to a new city. You won't know anyone but me. You'll be leaving your family and friends. My work requires me to be surrounded by beautiful women. Candie was jealous all the time…This isn't a choice to be made lightly. I'm doing what's best for both of us. I'm the adult here."

"*I'm. Not. Candie. Fontaine.* Are you fuckin' kidding me? You want me as much as I want you. Why do you keep pushing me away? What is your commitment phobia about, Grayson?"

Lissy slammed out of the car and began pacing, afraid she might hit him in her anger.

He followed her.

"Get back in the car. I'll take you home."

"No! I'm not getting in that car with you. I'm too angry. What more do you want from me? I love you! I don't want to get married, so have no fear on that issue. I don't want your money. I just want to be with you. But that's not enough for you. You stupid bastard."

"Alyssandra, calm down. This isn't good for your heart—"

Lissy whirled on him and pointed her finger into his chest, punctuating each word through clenched teeth. "Don't. You. Dare." She closed her eyes and held a hand to her chest as her heart broke into a million pieces.

"Getting this upset isn't good for you."

"Why should you care? I obviously mean *nothing* to you."

"That isn't fair—"

"Too bad. Life isn't fair. Nearly dying does strange things to you. It prioritizes life's problems. *I* don't need to take the time to know what *I* want. *You're* the one who needs to decide what *you* want."

She dug in her purse, looking for her phone. She had to get out of here. Finding it, she hit speed dial and walked away. "Call me if you ever decide you want me in your life. But I'm not making any promises that I'll be waiting on you. Life is short, and I plan to live mine. I deserve better than this."

She paused. "Hey. Come get me. I'm at the Sonic. I'll be waiting outside. Now!"

"Where the hell do you think you're going?" Gray grabbed her arm and swung her around to face him.

"I'm leaving." Lissy looked into his face and cupped his cheek, her thumb resting in the cleft of his chin. "I love you, Grayson. I always have, and I always will. I don't know what your problem is, but I suggest you figure it out."

"I'm not explaining this well. I wish we could be together, but—"

"I called Travis to come get me…" She paused. "Maybe I should've called Josh. Josh fucked with my mind, but at least he didn't fuck with my heart."

Gray flinched and stepped back.

"I suggest you leave if you value your life. Trav will be here in about two seconds."

"Alyssandra, listen to me—"

"I'm done listening to you. You should try listening to *me* for a change. Oh, wait. Why would you? I'm just a dumb kid who doesn't know what she wants. Have a nice lonely, boring life."

They both looked up when a car squealed to a stop. Travis shot out of the car, and Gray experienced firsthand his fabled right hook.

Chapter
Twenty-Four

Six weeks later

Tired, Lissy sent up a small prayer asking the Almighty to keep her from killing the next customer who came in with fifty gazillion transactions and a screaming kid. Thank God it was almost time to close *and* her weekend off. Her feet hurt from standing in heels all day, and she was sick of being dressed up. No casual Friday for this bank—not with her anal, uber-professional brother running it.

Without looking up from the computer screen, she called out, "Next." Plastering on her fake, customer-friendly smile she asked, "May I help you?" She gasped when she looked up into the startling blue eyes that had haunted her dreams the past six weeks.

"*Oui.*" A hesitant smile lingered on those perfect lips.

Gray stared at her like a hungry panther. Impeccably dressed in a white long-sleeved shirt, his sunglasses hooked in the collar, he had the attention of every female in the building.

Next to her Rhiannon whispered, "Holy god of sex and sin."

"I'm sorry, sir. You don't have an account with us. If you'll step over to your right, Meka will be able to help you." Her heart slammed painfully in her chest, reminiscent of the way it had raced before her ablation. She attempted to look around him and called out, "Next."

His easy grin spread as he turned, revealing himself to be the last customer in line. He leaned one arm on the counter, propping his face on his hand. "I believe only you can provide the help I need, not Meka."

Lissy leaned across the counter and whispered for his ears only. "I sincerely doubt you need any help. You haven't needed anything for six weeks. Now if you'll excuse me, I need to finish so I can go home." Her hands shook as she started counting down her drawer.

"Alyssandra."

She squirmed, still loving the way her name rolled off his tongue like warm, rich honey. *Goddamn him!* "Leave me the hell alone," she hissed.

She started over, re-counting her drawer.

"I have something for you."

She stopped counting and looked up. He shoved a red, heart-shaped box across the counter.

"Lovely. It's the day after Valentine's Day, and you bring me left-over chocolate? No thanks. I'm not interested." She went back to counting her drawer.

"Open it, *mon chaton.*"

"No. And don't call me that." She wanted to burst into tears. At this rate it would be midnight before she could leave. "Go!"

"Is there a problem, Lissy?" Danny, the security guard, walked over and stood next to Gray, his hands on his hips.

"No. Thank you, Danny. Mr. Deschanelle was just leaving." She refused to look at Gray as she concentrated on closing down for the day.

"I'll wait for you outside." Gray grabbed the red heart box and walked away with Danny, talking casually about the weather and sports.

"Wow, Lissy. Was that who I think it was?" asked Rhiannon, the teller to her left. "His accent alone made me weak in the knees."

"Oh, I agree! I was hoping he really did want to open an account. He could read the telephone book and make it sound pornographic," Meka added with a dreamy sigh.

Lissy refused to tell them anything. *What is he doing here?* And why was she so damn glad to see him?

Grayson leaned against his car and waited. He'd waited over a month—another few minutes wouldn't matter.

Lissy had surprised him. After he left, she'd blocked his number and all access to her social media accounts. He'd even bought a new phone and texted her, but she'd blocked that number as well. Remembering the hurt in her eyes when she'd said he'd fucked with her heart had stopped him from trying again by phone.

Two days after his arrival in Paris, an unlikely ally had phoned. Apparently Patsy regretted her threat of blackmail and had confessed to her husband. George had assured him no so such action would ever take place, but he agreed with his wife that Lissy needed time to heal and settle down. As a concerned father, he'd asked him to stay away for a few weeks and then come see her in person. This, he'd said, would appease Patsy and keep him out of the doghouse. But before he'd hung up, he'd told Grayson that if he wasn't serious about his daughter, not to come back.

Grayson had agreed, because as much as he hated to admit it, Patsy had been partially right. He'd used her blackmail threat as an excuse to escape the snare Alyssandra held over his heart.

He'd never had close friends, and although he and Candie had been together for two years, it had been more convenience than romance after the first six months. Looking back, he'd come to realize that had been extremely unfair to her. The latest tabloid news reported that Candie and Antonio had reconciled and were now engaged, and he wished them well. Thankfully, this meant the press was now leaving him alone.

He really had no clue where his fear of commitment came from. When he was fourteen, *Papa* had remarried. At first, he'd resented the new family members. He'd been a lonely boy raised by an absent father, a demanding, emotionally distant grandmother, and servants. Was that why? His stepmother, Lynn, had loved him despite his surly teen behavior and Frank, who was only four at the time, had looked up to him as an older brother. *Maman* and *Papa* had been married for twenty-five years. And he now shared a good, loving relationship with his family. But he still had a tendency to keep everyone at arm's length.

Even Candie had said so, and she wasn't known as being insightful. His stepmother liked to describe him and Frank as "total opposites." Frank was like fire, burning wild, whereas he was like a rock, unmoving and steadfast.

Once, as a boy, he'd been caught in a riptide, and the fear of drowning had nearly killed him as he struggled to take control. *Papa*, wading toward him, had shouted for him to float with the current, rather than fight it, and that had saved him in the end.

This attraction to Alyssandra was also a riptide, and for weeks he'd struggled to be free as he dodged the paparazzi and lay low. When he couldn't sleep, he'd obsessively worked on his project to win her back. His last night in Paris, he'd sat on his balcony, staring at the nightlife as he finished his gift for her, praying she'd take him back. This had to work.

Without Alyssandra, there is no future.

Her parting comment had damn near eviscerated him. He'd broken her heart—a heart that was both fragile and strong. He should've fought for her and stood up to her mother, but fear of the repercussions had kept him silent.

Now he could only hope Alyssandra would forgive him and let him spend a lifetime making it up to her.

Grayson snapped out of his reverie as she walked out of the bank, waving goodbye to her co-workers. She wore a tight black skirt and a navy blouse under her light suit jacket. It was unseasonably warm for February. His mouth went dry at the sight of her sheer black stockings and heels.

She stopped, confused when she realized her car wasn't in the parking lot. She turned to glare at him.

"Where's my car?" Her lips pursed with annoyance.

"Frank and Jessica picked it up for you." He motioned to his Jaguar.

Her lips curled in a small smile when she saw the sweater on the hood ornament, but it didn't last. "No thanks. I'll just catch a ride home with one of the girls. Aren't you the least bit worried my brother might whoop your butt?"

"No. He's playing golf with *my* brother." He smiled, thankful for Frank's help. They hadn't been kidding when they'd said Travis had a mean right hook. He was about the only one in the family *not* in on his current plan.

"Get in the car, Alyssandra." He opened the door and waited. As if on cue, Noëlle meowed from the carrier in the backseat.

Lissy gasped and peeked in the backseat. "You kidnapped my cat?"

"More like catnapped, I would think."

"How long ago did you plan the catnapping?"

"Since the day we parted."

"Give me my cat and go back to Paris or New York and live your lonely life. You don't deserve me."

"You're right. I *don't* deserve you. But I'm not leaving without you. Now, we can stand here and argue all evening, or you can get in the car." He leaned against it as if he had all the time in the world.

With a loud huff she threw herself in the passenger seat and fastened her seatbelt. "Why do you have Noëlle?"

Grayson gave her an amused look before pulling out of the parking lot. "Don't we share custody?"

"Ha, ha, Mr. Funnyman. Keep your day job. Wait, where are we going?" She twisted in the seat, looking out the window as he passed the turn to go toward her house.

"Sit back and relax, *mon chaton*. We're going to talk."

"No, we're not. I'm not speaking to you." She crossed her arms and closed her eyes.

"Alyssandra, wake up."

Lissy stirred and stretched, not wanting the dream of Gray coming for her to end.

Warm lips pressed against hers, and a tongue teased her bottom lip. He tasted like lemon drops.

"I thought I was dreaming." She stretched, not quite awake, and unbuckled her seatbelt. She froze. "We're at the cabin."

She stepped out of the car and remembered she was angry at him. "Wait, we're at the *cabin?* When did I fall asleep?"

"You weren't speaking to me, so it was quiet. I guess the car motion lulled you to sleep," he teased. "Come inside. You don't have a coat, and it's cold in the mountains."

"You worry about me and coats at the weirdest times," she grumbled, grabbing her purse.

Gray followed, carrying Noëlle's carrier and the box of candy.

"I didn't realize I'd fallen asleep. Wait, I'm mad and not speaking to you. You're sleeping on the couch." Lissy stopped when she stepped inside. Her mouth fell open. A fire crackled in the fireplace. On the coffee table were a bottle of champagne and a plate of cheese with crackers and fruit.

"How did you do this?"

"Would you believe me if I said magic?"

Lissy nodded. "Probably." She looked up at him. "Don't do this to me. If you have any feelings for me, don't do this."

"I do have feelings for you. I also have good friends and family that have helped me. Mrs. Seales is my housekeeper. She cleans for me and did the grocery shopping. I texted her when we left Pine Bluff. And I'm not going to do anything you don't want. I brought you here to apologize and start over."

Noëlle stepped out of the cat carrier and wove between his legs, purring and butting his shin with her head. Lissy glared. *Little traitor.*

The cabin was the same, but different — more like a lived-in home. On the mantle were framed photos of their families. To her astonishment, the largest frame held the picture of her surprising him with the kiss in the snow.

"I don't understand."

"Welcome home. I purchased the cabin from Frank and Jessica."

"Welcome home?" she croaked, wanting to smack the self-satisfied smirk off his face. "You are the most obnoxious, condescending, controlling bastard I've ever known! What makes you think this can ever make up for the horrible way you've treated me? I haven't heard from you in almost six weeks!" She walked over to the mantle, staring at the pictures, trying to remember she was angry.

"You blocked me from accessing you," he reminded her. "*Je t'aime.*"

She whipped around to face him. His disarming smile was like a ray of sunshine through a dark forest.

"What did you just say?"

"I love and adore you, Alyssandra."

"I — I don't know what to say…How? How did you get Noëlle? How did you do this and why? You love me? What about just sex, no strings attached? What about the fact you don't think I'm capable of knowing my own feelings? You don't get to seduce me and think everything will be okay. You hurt me, Gray. Badly."

He pulled her close and cupped her face in his hands. His eyes crinkled as he brushed a soft kiss across each cheek. "I love you. Do you love me?" He kissed her forehead, sending a shiver of desire down her spine.

"*Sometimes, love isn't enough*, remember?" She threw his words back without much conviction. It was hard to concentrate with his lips and hands on her heated skin.

"And sometimes love is more than enough. I'm sorry I hurt you. I was scared, and I ran."

"Scared of what?"

"Everything."

"Could you be more vague?"

"The paparazzi, my feelings, our families."

"Our families? What do our families have to do with this? I mean, my family knew we were together, and Frank was okay with us…Did your father object?"

"He was concerned, but I didn't tell him until a few weeks ago," Gray replied. "I'm placing the blame on me. I was conflicted, confused. I didn't fight for you, for us. And I should've. For this I will be eternally sorry. I'm humbly asking your forgiveness. Let me make it up to you."

He got down on one knee and held out the heart-shaped box. "Make my wish come true, Alyssandra. Forgive me."

She took the box and opened it. "Oh," she whispered, picking up one of the folded paper cranes.

"A thousand paper cranes. Will my wish come true?" he asked softly.

Moved beyond words, she nodded and sank to her knees in front of him. "This is the most beautiful gift I've ever received." Grasping his face, she stared into those fathomless eyes. "I love you, Gray. I always have, always will."

"Each crane has something written on it — a wish, a dream, or a reason I love you."

"All different?"

"Yes, but toward the end, I was getting desperate. I used three different languages, and I think one says I love the fact that you're embarrassed to pee in front of me."

She giggled and tossed the box aside, showering cranes around them. Launching herself into his arms, she pushed him backward. "You silly, stubborn man," she murmured against his lips.

They made out like teenagers as Noëlle scampered over them, batting at the cranes. When the cat bit his earlobe, he laughed and stood up, pulling Lissy to her feet.

"Take off your clothes, Alyssandra."

He kissed the sensitive spot behind her ear that made all rational thoughts dissipate. *He loves me.* For the first time since he'd left, she could breathe. Did he still have explaining to do? Yes. But not now. She unbuttoned her blouse with shaking hands. She belonged with him. Period. She'd known it since she was a teenager. Her fingers fumbled at her buttons.

As her blouse fell to the floor, his gaze seemed to brand her skin. Feeling both powerless and powerful, she slowly unzipped her skirt and let it drop, kicking it out of the way with a toss of her hair. She stood with her hands on her hips before him, taunting him with her black demi-bra, thong panties, thigh-high stockings, and heels.

"Those aren't *Papa's* designs."

"No, they're mine. Do you like?"

He pulled her roughly to him, one hand fisting her hair and the other cupping her ass. His lips marked her as his, and he murmured in French as he trailed kisses down her neck and undid her bra.

She tore at his shirt buttons, ripping three off in the process, wanting nothing between them. He was her soulmate, the part of her that had been missing while they were apart. She wanted to feel whole, complete.

Gray dragged his lips from hers, his ragged breathing fanning across her cheeks. He rested his forehead against hers, his long fingers wrapped around her neck where her pulse pounded for him. Confused, she stared at him, silently questioning.

"Alyssandra…I'm sorry."

"Sorry?" She held her breath, fearing he was going to say this was all a mistake.

"For losing control…" He paused and stepped back, gesturing as if searching for words. "I wanted this to be special. I wanted to explain and then make love to you—"

Lissy slapped his chest. "Don't do that to me. I thought you were dumping me again." Moving back to him, she grabbed his face with both hands, pulling him close. "Stop talking and let go. I *want* you to lose control. Take me. Now."

"Does this mean I don't have to sleep on the couch?"

"Who said anything about sleeping?"

"You're certainly my kind of girl. But not here. There's one more surprise." He swept her into his arms and carried her upstairs. Lissy nibbled his lower lip, her arms wrapped around his neck. He kicked the door to the bedroom closed and whispered, "Close your eyes."

Grinning, she squeezed them shut.

"No peeking." He lowered her feet to the floor and turned her to face the door.

She heard the click of a lighter, but kept her eyes shut.

He returned to her and turned her back around. "All right, Alyssandra. Open your eyes."

She did and burst into tears. Candles flickered all over the room, and more paper cranes were scattered everywhere. But it was the picture over the four-poster bed that moved her most. It was the photo she'd taken of them, with his naked back to the camera as she peered over his shoulder.

Lissy wrapped her arms around his neck, trying to speak through her happy tears.

"It was supposed to be a nice surprise, not make you cry, my darling." He held her tight.

Laughing and crying at the same time, she replied, "Oh, Gray, it's perfect. So we're good, right?"

He backed her to the bed and leaned over her, kissing down her neck as he removed her thong.

"No, *mon chaton*, we are definitely *not* good." Raising her legs, he kissed behind her knees, rubbing his cheek on her stockings.

He placed her legs over his shoulders. "We are about to be very, very bad," he whispered with a glint in his eyes.

Chapter
Twenty-Five

"There is no physical way," he murmured the next morning.

"Party pooper," she teased as she ran a hand down his bare back before smacking his firm ass.

Lying on his stomach with his head on her shoulder, his right leg trapped hers. As always, his hand rested protectively over her heart. He hadn't moved since they'd fallen into an exhausted sleep a few hours ago.

"Gray?"

"Hmm?" He didn't open his eyes or move.

"I'm curious. Why are you against marriage?"

"You want to discuss this now? Before coffee?"

"Do you realize how often you put off talking to me? You just said we can't have sex, so let's take the time to have a real conversation."

"If I had the energy, now would be the time I'd spank your ass." He rolled over and cursed again when Noëlle protested being awakened.

Lissy giggled and petted the persistent cat.

"You did that last night. Don't worry. I'm not asking you to marry me. I just wonder why you're so against it. Your parents have a good marriage. So do mine. And Frank and Jessica are disgustingly in love."

"I'm not necessarily against it. I've just never thought it was for me. Why ruin what we have? You're my lover, my best friend, my muse, and my reason for living. But I've had more life experiences than you. Trust me—what you want at age twenty-one can be vastly different than at age forty. Statistics say we won't make it. Marriage would make it harder for you to get out of it."

"We both know I'm pathetic at math. Does that even our odds somewhat? And how condescending of you, to already anticipate I'd want out of it. I know what I want, Gray. And it's you."

He laughed and pulled her into his arms. "Have you decided about school?"

"I want to be with you, and you travel a lot. But I would kind of like to visit Parson's in New York. Or Paris. I've filled out my applications."

"I think that's a wonderful idea. *Papa* says you have talent. I'd curtail some of my traveling."

"Or we could just stay here forever." She sighed wistfully. "I could live here and be a mountain woman. I've watched those survival shows. I could make us loincloths from the skins of dead animals. Only I wouldn't really want you to kill them. Maybe we could find some that died from old age?"

He laughed. "I'd think you'd need to learn how to cook with a stove before we forage in the forest."

"Details, details."

"I long for a quiet life, with you all to myself, but that's not possible. I can't lock you away. And I'm terrified of losing you again. You nearly died…"

Lissy positioned herself on top of him and cupped his face in her hands. "I could die walking across the street, Gray. All we can do is take each day and be grateful for it. And just so you know, you're not getting rid of me again. Not even death could keep me from you. I'd haunt you forever."

He stroked her cheek. "My mother died having me. After my birth, my grandmother said *Papa* was a shell of a man who threw himself into work, leaving me to be raised by *au pairs* and servants. He wasn't unkind; he was just…distant. I'm afraid I'm a lot like him. It wasn't until *Maman* came into our lives that he became a true father. And he goes overboard sometimes trying to make up for the lost time. I worry I'm being unfair to you. Now is the time for you to live your life, make mistakes, and learn from them."

"Then let me. How will I know if we're a mistake if we don't try?"

"I love you, my darling."

"And I love you."

"I'm not saying I'll *never* marry you. And just so you know, when I propose, it will be in Paris, to fulfill your childhood wish."

"The city of love." She smiled happily and didn't point out that he'd said *when*.

"I love you," he murmured as he nibbled her ear. He rolled her over, his erection teasing her entrance.

"I thought you said there was no physical way!"

"Never say never."

The sun filtering through the trees highlighted Grayson's two obsessions perfectly. "A little more to the right, I want the shadow on your nipple…perfect." He snapped the picture of her lying naked on the hood of his car.

"You know, it would be nice to have a few photos we can actually put in a photo album for our families."

"You have a beautiful body, Alyssandra. I think when we move to New York I shall insist you go naked at all times."

"You're kidding, right?"

He raised an eyebrow. "Am I?" His thumb brushed over her lower lip. She turned her head into his palm. Leaning in, he nipped her lower lip.

"You're really a depraved perv, Grayson Deschanelle."

"It's one of my more endearing qualities."

He watched her slip into her clothes. Once dressed, she laughed when he took another picture. He showed it to her on the camera. Love shone in her sparking eyes. Her hair was tousled, her lips still swollen from his kiss.

"My hair's a mess."

"I love it. It's almost sexier than the nude ones. You look as if you've been thoroughly fucked."

"Because I have. I can barely walk," she replied. Her smug smile told him she didn't mind a bit. "I'll never be able to sit casually on the hood of a car again." She walked with him through the woods, holding his hand. "Do we have to leave?"

"For now. We'll be back soon."

They walked in silence for several minutes, soaking in the sun and the peacefulness.

"I know Paris, New York, and London are beautiful. But I can't imagine them being any better than this."

He smiled. "I agree. But someday soon I want to show you Paris."

The next morning, they left to return to Pine Bluff. Unfortunately, she had to be at work on Monday.

"I wish we could've just stayed at the cabin." Lissy smiled in the general vicinity of Gray. It was hard to tell with her eyes blindfolded.

"Me too, but totally impractical. We were bound to run out of scotch and toilet paper at some point in time."

"I don't understand why we had to leave before the sun was up and why I have to be blindfolded to go home."

"I can add a ball-gag to the equation if you don't hush," he muttered.

Noëlle began protesting from the backseat in her cat carrier.

Lissy snickered. "Even Noëlle thinks you should forego comedy and keep your day job, Gray."

"I was joking?"

Lissy hushed—just in case he wasn't. The movement of the car and the soft music from the radio soon lulled her into a trance-like state. The entire weekend had been a dream. But they still had to face her parents. They were pretty liberal as far as parents went, but she knew her mother, especially, would be devastated that Gray wasn't offering a solidified commitment in the form of marriage.

"You know, someone might think you're kidnapping me with this blindfold on. I'm getting hungry. Is it lunch time?"

"But of course. All kidnappers put their victims blindfolded in the front seat of their Jaguar. We'll eat soon."

"You're laughing at me."

"*Moi?*"

"*Oui.*" She smiled when he took her hand in his and kissed it.

"*Tu es mon amour, mon chaton.*"

"You know, half the time I don't know what you're saying to me in French. For all I know you could be telling me I smell like liver and onions. But I know what that meant, and I love you too."

A few minutes later, the car slowed, and the road noise changed.

"Is it time to eat?"

"No. Be patient. Good things happen to patient girls."

At last the car stopped, and Gray opened her door, helping her out of the car.

"When can I take off the blindfold?"

"Soon."

He placed something on her head as he guided her like a Seeing Eye dog.

"I'm in heels. I could break my neck. Please take the blindfold off." She wore the raspberry-colored mini dress and matching coat over the sexy raspberry lingerie and heels he'd surprised her with last night.

"Not yet, impatient girl. Although I do love when you beg," he replied.

"I think I've been pretty damn patient considering I have no idea where we are, or what you're doing. If this is some kinky sex thing, okay—super, even." She thought she heard a stifled snicker.

"Take off the blindfold, Alyssandra."

Lissy ripped the blindfold from her eyes and gasped. Gray was on one knee, holding a small blue box with a white bow. Taking what seemed to be forever, he opened the box.

"*Veux-tu m'épouser*, Alyssandra Georgina Carlton?" he asked, slipping the biggest diamond solitaire she'd ever seen on her finger.

She stared at the ring and then him. His eyes crinkled with his sexy, sinful smile. A gentle breeze blew a strand of his hair onto his forehead.

"Did you just ask me to marry you?"

"Yes."

"This isn't a dream?"

"No. There's a rock digging into my knee and one on your finger to prove it."

Lissy managed to nod and whispered, "You're serious?"

He stood and held her face, gazing into her eyes. "I love you and want you to be my wife. I can't imagine sharing custody of an obnoxious cat with anyone but you. I will spend the rest of my days moving heaven and earth to be the man you deserve. And your burned toast is divine." He kissed her lips. The raspberry beret he'd placed on her head blew off, and he caught it.

"We're really getting married?" she asked.

"If you'll have me."

She screamed and threw herself at him. He staggered a bit and kissed her soundly, smiling against her lips. Her eyes widened when she noticed the huge Eiffel Tower behind them and a photographer taking their picture.

"Gray? Where are we?"

"Paris. Now let's see if we can get a decent engagement picture for our families."

"Paris?" She pinched herself to see if she was dreaming. There really was an Eiffel Tower behind him, all right. She couldn't help but steal another look at the diamond glittering on her finger.

"Paris, Tennessee." With a wink and a smirk, he twirled the raspberry beret.

Chapter
Twenty-Six

Four months later

"I know you wanted to plan a big wedding, Mother, but this is what we wanted—a small, intimate gathering at home." Lissy looked at her mother's reflection in the mirror. She looked beautiful in her pale, shimmering gray dress.

"At least you didn't elope like Jessica and Frank. Maybe Travis will marry an orphan and I can plan his wedding." She placed the pearl and diamond comb in Lissy's hair and gave her a kiss on the cheek.

"I'll tell you what, Mrs. Carlton. My mother is deceased, and when I get married, I want the biggest, over-the-top wedding in the world. You can be my stand-in mother." Eddie flashed his megawatt smile as he straightened his tie.

"I would be honored and happy to plan your wedding, Eddie." Her mother smiled and patted him on his cheek, seeming somewhat mollified.

Mouthing *suck-up* behind her mother's back, Lissy laughed as she applied a pale pink lipstick, thinking about her mother arguing with drag queens over color schemes. She'd double-down on a bet her mother would win.

"You should've let me wear the dress and heels. I so could have rocked them, Liss," Eddie complained, handing her a tissue to blot her lipstick.

"I know, but you look really handsome in your suit."

"Well, duh! I'm going to give the groom a run for his money in the looks department." He gave her a kiss on top of her head and fixed one of her curls, staring at her in the mirror. "Half a chance and I know I could convince Gray to come play for the other team." He winked and walked to the door as her sister entered.

"Stay away from my future husband," Lissy yelled.

"No promises," Eddie replied as he left.

"Oh, Lissy. You look stunning." Jessica's eyes filled with tears. She wore a pale blue chiffon dress with a drop waist. To complete the classic 1920s look, her blond hair was styled in finger waves.

Lissy smoothed her own vintage Chanel dress, a Deschanelle heirloom. "Thank you. I'm terrified of ruining this dress. I've heard Gray's grandmother can be intimidating."

It was cream silk chiffon with a sheer lace yoke and a dropped waist. Sheer lace ruffles completed the skirt and overskirt. It was simple and elegant.

"I have to admit, the thought of meeting *Grand-mère* terrifies me. I hope she approves since this was her mother's wedding dress."

"Of course she will! You look beautiful, Liss! Eddie did a beautiful job on your makeup and hair," Jessica said.

Lissy laughed and stared at her reflection. Her hair was styled in a loose chignon with tendrils of curls. "I should've added a blue streak for my something blue."

Her mother groaned.

Jessica smiled. "Mother and I have your something blue and your something borrowed covered." Her mother roped a long strand of pearls around her neck, tears in her eyes. "This is your something borrowed. One day they will be yours." She gave Lissy a kiss on the cheek. "My baby girl is getting married."

"Please don't cry, Mother. If you cry, I will, and my mascara will run. I don't wanna look like a raccoon on my wedding day."

"I need to go check on the caterer, anyway." Her mother sniffled and left, leaving Jessica behind.

"Here's your something blue." Jessica presented Lissy with two blue garters. "One to keep and one to toss. Olivier designed them for you."

"Thank you." Lissy pulled them up her silk-stocking-clad legs and bit back her smile. Gray was going to love this part. He had such a thing for heels and stockings. She had her own personal surprise for him, too.

"I gave Gray strict instructions to aim the garter toward Travis and hit him square in the eye." They laughed and hugged.

"Jessica?"

Jessica's brows knit together. "What's the matter, Liss?"

"He is here, isn't he?" Lissy nervously fingered the pearls.

Jessica laughed. "Yes, indeed. Frank made sure of it."

Lissy blew out her breath and grinned. She still couldn't believe Mr. I'm-Never-Getting-Married was marrying her.

Another knock sounded.

"Come in." Lissy beamed when her father entered, a big smile on his face.

"Ah, both of my beautiful girls." George gave each of them a kiss and Jessica stepped out, closing the door.

"Your mother told me you looked beautiful, and she was right. Where is my little tomboy with the skinned knees and baseball cap?"

"Desperately wanting out of these heels," Lissy replied, hugging her father tight. "Thank you, Daddy. And thank you for supporting my decision. He's the man of my dreams. I love him."

"I know you do. And he loves you. It impressed the hell out of me when he asked for your hand in marriage. And your mother has come around. After your operation, it was such a stressful time, Lissy. W-We damn near lost you."

His eyes filled, and she handed him a tissue, hugging him tight.

"I know, Daddy."

After she'd returned from the cabin an engaged woman, her mother had tearfully asked forgiveness from her and Gray for her interference. Lissy had been livid at first, but as Gray and her father had pointed out, Mother had acted out of love and concern, not meanness.

"Now, now. We can't cry. Your mother will never forgive us if you look less than perfect going down the aisle."

Lissy dabbed at her eyes and nodded.

"Grayson's a good man. He's older and can handle you." Her father pinched her cheek. "But he will also take care of you. He didn't even want a pre-nup."

Lissy laughed. Her father was ever the lawyer. "I don't want his money, Daddy."

"I know that. He knows that. Even Olivier knows that. His grandmother, on the other hand, well, she's a formidable woman. But Grayson even bucked her. I damn near thought she was going to hit him with her cane when he refused to allow her to see you. Apparently, she brought the pre-nup with her."

"I see." She wrung her hands.

"She's waiting to meet you. Yell if you need reinforcements. I'll be close by." He gave her a kiss on the forehead.

Lissy smiled. "I love you, Daddy. Thank you."

She gave herself one last onceover in the mirror and squared her shoulders. Time to beard "the old dragon," as Grayson and Frank called *Grand-mère*, in the den — or in this case, her father's study.

The house was a flurry of activity with the caterer setting up for the reception. She could hear raised voices speaking in French through the closed door. Gray sounded angry, and she was fairly sure there were a few choice curse words flying between him, his father, and his grandmother. She quietly opened to door and caught her breath at how handsome her future husband looked.

Lynn Deschanelle looked at her and gave a startled gasp. "No! Grayson can't see you before the ceremony. It's bad luck!" She grabbed Gray and turned him away from her. Dressed in a beautiful peach dress, Lynn glared at the older woman seated on the couch.

Lissy laughed. "When have Gray and I ever done anything appropriate?" She looked around the room at her new family. Frank stood next to Gray, his hands stuffed in his pockets, his face red, as he, too, shot angry looks at *Grand-mère*.

"Grayson, you need to leave. You can't see the bride!" Lynn insisted.

"I'm not leaving."

"He can stay. It's fine, honestly," Lissy said. If his grandmother was as horrible as everyone claimed, she kind of wanted his support.

"Okay, but you can't look," Lynn warned her son.

Olivier wore a charcoal gray suit, but his white hair was disheveled. Lissy bet he'd run his hand through it, just like Gray did when exasperated. He stepped forward and kissed her on both cheeks. Taking her hand, he brought her forward to meet his mother.

"*Mère*, this is Miss Alyssandra Georgina Carlton, Grayson's bride."

Without thinking, Lissy gave a curtsy and then blushed when she realized how ridiculous she must look. For a brief second, she thought she saw a hint of a smile on the old woman's austere face. *Grand-mère* found the glasses at the end of a diamond rope around her neck and set them on the edge of her nose to peer at Lissy. Her snow-white hair was swept elegantly off her face, and although she was petite, the strength emanating from the physically frail woman was unmistakable.

"You may call me *Grand-mère,* and there is no need to curtsy, although you did it quite nicely." Her English was heavily accented, much more so than her son's and grandson's.

"Yes, ma'am. Thank you. My mother taught me how." She smiled as she withstood the woman's perusal.

With his back still toward her, Gray called, "Okay, introductions have been made. Let's get this wedding started."

Beside him, Frank nodded, looking nervous.

"May I have a word alone with you, *Grand-mère? S'il vous plaît?*"

Gray spun around and the color blanched from his face. He shook his head, looking almost ill at the thought.

His grandmother shot him a dirty look and motioned for her family to leave the study.

Gray started to object but stopped when *Grand-mère* raised an eyebrow and frowned, shaking a bony index finger. Lissy had to bite her lip to keep from laughing. She'd never seen Gray this flustered or cowed by anyone, not even his father.

When they were alone, Lissy smiled at the stern, beautiful woman. "Thank you for allowing me to wear this dress. It's magnificent and means a great deal to me and to Grayson."

"And well it should. It is an heirloom and priceless. Don't spill on it." *Grand-mère's* haughty tone went nicely with the imperious gesture she used to indicate Lissy should sit beside her.

Lissy swallowed her nervousness as she perched on the edge of the couch and faced Gray's grandmother. "I love your grandson with all of my heart."

"What would you know of love? You are a mere child," she scoffed.

"I may be young, but I've been close to death. I know it was my love for Gray that kept me here. I need him, and I rather think he needs me." She took a deep breath and looked the old woman square in the eye. "I want to sign your pre-nuptial agreement."

Grand-mère raised one eyebrow. "Why would you want to do that, foolish girl?"

"Because it's just a piece of paper. It means nothing to me. I'm not marrying your grandson's money. I'm marrying your grandson."

"You realize if you end up divorced it would mean you get nothing."

Lissy held her gaze. "If I were to end up divorced, I would have nothing anyway. Gray is my everything."

Grand-mère pulled the pre-nuptial agreement from her purse. "You will want your father to read this first?"

Lissy took it, walked over to her father's desk, and signed. "No, there is no need. As I said, I'm marrying the man, not the money. If he was to lose everything, and we had to live in a cardboard box, my life would still be complete as long as he was in it. With him, I'm the luckiest girl in the world, and also the richest. I don't want your money or his money. Just him."

She handed the signed pre-nup back and gave *Grand-mère* a gentle kiss on her parchment-like cheek. "I look forward to getting to know you. I hope you'll give me at least a little chance, for Gray's sake. You mean the world to him and therefore, to me, too." Lissy paused at the door and smiled back at her. "Plus, I would love to know every horrible thing Gray ever did as a child. I'm sure he was quite *l'enfant terrible*." She gave the old woman a wink and blew her a kiss.

"*Oui, mon petite monstre*." *Grand-mère* nodded, and Lissy was positive this time a hint of smile brushed the corner of her mouth as she placed the pre-nup in her purse.

Gray paced and tried three times to enter the study, only to have his parents and Frank stop him. When Alyssandra finally opened the door, he looked for any sign his grandmother had upset her. Seeing none, he resisted the urge to check her for teeth marks and stepped back, taking in her beauty.

Taking her hands in his, he kissed her fingertips. "You are stunning, my darling. Are you okay?"

"I'm fine, Gray. Chill. Go have a scotch or something." She straightened his tie and smoothed the lapel of his black suit. "You look very handsome. You liked the cufflinks?"

"Thank you, and yes. They're perfect." He glanced down at her feet and smiled. "I can't wait to see you in just the stockings and heels."

Frank walked by and punched him on the arm. "Save it for the honeymoon, Trip."

Lissy giggled, and Gray scowled.

"This is precisely why I never wanted to marry. It has nothing to do with you and everything to do with my family," he muttered. "Was *Grand-mère* at least pleasant? Did she say anything untoward?"

"Untoward? Is that a word used in this century? Everything's fine. I introduced myself, signed her silly piece of paper, and we parted best of friends."

"What? You didn't. Alyssandra, I had nothing to do with that pre-nup. I will tear it up myself."

"Don't be silly. She loves you and is protecting you. I told her I didn't want your money — just your sexy body."

His mouth dropped.

Her eyes sparkled. "I'm joking about the sexy body. I mean, I do want it, but I didn't tell her that."

He needed a really stiff drink.

"Let's go get married. They're waiting on us." Lissy nodded toward her father and the minister. "We don't have to go through with this if you're not sure, Gray," she whispered.

"I've never been more sure of anything in my life."

Chapter
Twenty-Seven

"Obey?" she asked as he stood behind her, posing for a wedding picture.

"You agreed." Grayson gave his typical grimace, knowing there would likely be one out of hundreds of wedding photos in which he looked halfway pleasant. He hated being on this side of the camera.

"I thought you were kidding. No one has 'obey' in the wedding vows anymore. That was positively archaic."

"We did. Everyone heard you agree to it, too. You should know me well enough to know I meant it. Now let's go cut the cake so I can spank your sweet ass."

"It's wedding cake, not birthday cake, Gray."

"Pity."

"I overheard some of the guests speculating I'm pregnant."

"Why would they think that?" Strangely, the idea didn't leave the usual distaste in his mouth.

He hurried her toward the cake. He was beyond ready to get through the festivities and let the real fun begin, alone with his bride. He wanted to initiate her into the Mile-High Club on board the private jet that would take them to Paris — the one in France — for their honeymoon.

"I guess because the dress has a drop waist. They'll figure it out when we're a childless, crazy old couple in fifty years with thirty-five cats." She grinned up at him.

"Now there's a depressing thought. I'll be ninety."

She looked at the camera as he held his hand over hers on the knife. He attempted a smile as the flash from the camera burst in their face.

"Please don't smash the cake in my face, Gray. *Grand-mère* will kill me if I spill on this dress."

Leave it to my grandmother to spoil all the fun. "I wouldn't dream of it. Is licking the icing off your fingers permitted?" He wiggled his eyebrows, causing her to laugh.

He gave her a petite, neat bite of cake, and she did the same for him, much to the dismay of everyone but *Grand-mère*. To appease them, he leaned in and kissed her, enjoying the taste of the icing on her lips.

"How much more do we have to endure?" he whispered after the obligatory toast with champagne.

"Dance and make nice conversation with everyone — two hours, tops."

"I'm not a patient man. I want to make love to you all night."

"All night?"

"I'll pace myself." He walked her to where the first dance was to occur.

"You know I didn't choose anything normal for us to dance to this first time, right?" She wrapped her arms around his neck as he encircled her waist.

"I would expect nothing less." He laughed as the band played an acoustic version of The Raveonettes's "Aly, Walk With Me."

"I suppose our first song should've been 'La Vie en Rose,' but it was so predictable." She kissed him, and he pulled her closer, enjoying the kiss, not giving a damn that everyone watched.

"True, and we are anything but predicable or appropriate," he said as he nibbled her ear.

"I should hope not. I have a wonderful surprise for you tonight. Do you think married sex will be boring compared to illicit sex?" She gazed at him with a look that nearly took his breath away.

"Only if we let it get boring." Something he didn't foresee happening until she was in the nursing home and he was dead in the grave. "I have a small confession."

"What?"

"I despise 'La Vie En Rose.' *Grand-mère* used to play it all the time."

"I have a confession to make as well."

"Oh?"

"Guess which song will be playing when you dance with *Grand-mère?*"

Lissy had changed into a form-fitting, belted navy silk dress she'd designed for her going-away outfit. She clipped in the fake strand of blue hair and smiled at her reflection in the mirror. She had first planned to leave in jeans and a T-shirt with tennis shoes, but Gray had sided with her mother, so here she was in another pair of heels.

She left her room, looked over the railing, and smiled when Gray looked up at her with a relieved expression. He appeared as ready to get out of here as she was. Lissy turned in surprise at the thundering sound of her nephew, Lee, running down the hall in hot pursuit of Noëlle. The cat was hell bent on getting away from the child reaching for her tail. Lissy attempted to move out of the way, but as she shifted back against the handrail, Noëlle darted through her legs. Her last cognizant thought was the fear that Grayson would kill her nephew *and* cat as she sailed backward over the railing.

"Where am I?"

"Your home away from home. The hospital, *mon chaton.*" Gray kissed her hand and held it to his scruffy cheek.

Dark circles surrounded his beautiful eyes and the laugh lines appeared more pronounced. His tie was loose, and the top button of his shirt undone.

"You're in a suit." The pounding in her head made it difficult to think. "Did my heart start racing again?"

"No, but I damn near had a heart attack when you fell over the banister. I knew I was too old for you. You're going to kill me with worry."

"I fell?"

"Yes, backward over the railing from the second floor just outside your bedroom down into the foyer."

"Was I at least graceful in my descent?"

"Not particularly. Thank goodness the area was full of people or it could have been worse. Frank caught you, but you still managed to hit your head on the corner of the table. You were unconscious for what seemed like an eternity, but they say it was only a minute."

She looked at her other hand, where he'd placed her wedding band, and gasped. "We're married?"

Grayson chuckled. "Yes. Disappointed?"

It started as a sniffle and soon escalated to an all-out wail.

"I was joking. See? You always tell me to keep my day job. My jokes are never funny. What's the matter? Are you in pain? Let me get a nurse." He hit the call button.

"Today was the most important day of my life, and I can't remember a thing. It's so unfair!"

"Shhh, Alyssandra. There will be hundreds of photos showing how beautiful you were with me scowling or looking like I'm wanted for armed robbery. Plus, we have video. Calm down, my darling."

The nurse bustled in to check on her. "May I get you anything?"

She kept looking between them, appearing to be trying hard not to laugh.

"When can I go home?" Lissy asked.

"In a hurry?" The nurse giggled.

Gray shot her a dirty look.

"Yes, I don't want to be here. Apparently I got married."

The nurse laughed. "We got that impression. The doctor will be in shortly." She ran through her nursing duties and asked her the date and time before leaving.

Gray swore softly in French.

"What's going on? Why can't I remember?" Lissy closed her eyes. Her head throbbed. Although cheeky, the nurse had been nice. *Why is Gray so upset?*

He raised an eyebrow and shook his head. "I'm afraid everyone knows about my wedding present."

Lissy looked at him, confused, trying to remember. "The cufflinks? So?"

Gray laughed, and Lissy was relieved to see some of the stress ease from his face, but it didn't explain a thing.

The door opened, and her parents rushed in to see her. Her mother had obviously been crying.

"What's wrong? What happened?" Lissy asked.

Gray chuckled and spoke to her parents. "She doesn't remember and is having problems focusing, but she's okay."

The nurse came back in and cautioned them that she could only have two visitors at a time. Panic raced through her when Gray stood and kissed her forehead.

"I'm going to go find some coffee. I'll be back."

"Promise? You've left me before." She held tight to his hand.

He pointed to his wedding ring and smiled. "Just try to get rid of me now; you're mine with no strings attached." He winked at her and stood. Daddy snorted, and Mother smacked him on the arm, her face as red as the needle disposal box on the wall. Grayson left the room grinning.

"We got here as soon as we could. Some guests just don't know when to leave," her mother huffed.

"How long do I have to stay here?" Lissy asked. "I'm slowly remembering some stuff. Getting ready, dancing with Gray…"

"Just a few more hours. They don't want you flying overseas for a few days, but Grayson has a room reserved for your wedding night tonight and plans to take you to the cabin. You have a mild concussion and with your recent heart condition, it's just a precaution." Her mother sank into the chair Grayson had vacated.

"Was it a lovely wedding?"

"Yes, Lissy. Up to the end, everything was quite lovely. Maybe not conventional, but you always were my rebel." Her mother fussed with the sheets and straightened the things on the bedside table.

"I can't remember much of it." She wiped away a fresh batch of tears.

"Maybe the photos and video will jog your memory later," her father offered gruffly, patting his pocket, which Lissy knew was an unconscious signal he needed to smoke.

"I'm sorry to have ruined everything."

"Nonsense. We're relieved you weren't seriously hurt. Besides, now you can tell your mother you were right. You should've been in tennis shoes and jeans. You might not have fallen, and it certainly would've saved the embarrass—"

"That's enough, George!"

Her mother's sharp rebuke surprised her. A knock at the door signaled it was time for them to let others visit. She wondered if the entire wedding party was waiting to see her.

Jessica and Travis walked in, and Jessica began crying. Her parents kissed her goodbye and left. Lissy turned to Travis for an explanation as Jessica stood sobbing into her hands.

"See? I told you nothing could harm that hard head of hers. Liss is fine. Now, can you stop blubbering?" Travis asked.

Sniffling, Jessica grabbed her hand. "I'm so sorry, Lissy. Oh my God, if I hadn't been so scared, I would've torn Lee's butt up, but he was terrified."

"Why would you spank him?"

"Lee was chasing Noëlle, and you dodged them, lost your footing, and fell." Jessica wiped her tears away.

"Hey, it's okay. It was an accident. Like Travis said, I have a hard head. I'm fine."

"But it ruined your wedding."

"I'm still married. I got him to the altar, and he's mine. That's all that matters. Although I wish I could remember more of it. It's this headache."

"Oh yeah, we all know you're his." Travis's smirk turned into a quiet guffaw and ended up a whoop of laughter.

Jessica glared at him, and he coughed into his hand, still grinning. "I'm glad you're okay, Liss. Your wedding was beautiful. Trust me, *everyone* will be talking about it for years to come." He grunted when Jessica elbowed him in the ribs.

"What's so funny, Trav?"

"Uh, nothing. Here's Frank. See ya, sis." He darted out the door as Frank entered with Lee in his arms.

"See? Aunt Lissy is fine."

Lissy waved at her nephew and smiled. He hid his face in his father's neck. "Where's Grace?"

"Mama and Pop are at home with her. They send their love." Frank handed Lee off to Jessica.

"There's so much I don't remember…" She frowned.

Frank looked all around the room—everywhere except directly at her. She was going to ask him what the hell was going on but got sidetracked when Jessica leaned over and kissed her goodbye.

"Again, I'm so sorry, Lissy."

"It's okay. I promise, I'm fine." She wished Gray would come back. *Why is everyone acting so weird?*

"Uh, Liss, there's one more person here to see you. I'll stay in here with her," Frank said, sounding serious. He left for a moment and returned, gently guiding *Grand-mère* to the chair next to her bed.

Lissy struggled to sit upright.

"*Non,* do not get up," she instructed in her thick French accent.

Lissy squeezed the hand *Grand-mère* offered. The old woman told Frank he should leave. He paused, but exited when Lissy nodded it was okay.

"I'm sorry I ruined the wedding."

Grayson's grandmother smiled. "*Au contraire*, it was a beautiful wedding."

"But I fell…Oh no! I didn't ruin the dress, did I?" She bit her lip.

"The dress is fine. I like you, Alyssandra."

"Oh." Lissy blinked. "Um, thank you. I'm afraid our meeting is kind of hazy. I'm sorry."

"That's fine, my dear. I remember meeting you, and anyone who would quite literally fall head over heels for my grandson will make a lovely granddaughter."

She smiled, and her eyes twinkled. Lissy smiled back. *Why is everyone so afraid of this sweet old lady?*

"I would do it all over again. He's worth it."

The old woman cracked her cane three times on the floor. Lissy jumped.

Frank threw the door open, eyes wide.

He helped *Grand-mère* to her feet, and she leaned over, kissing her on the cheek. She smelled of lavender, and Lissy found it strangely comforting. *Grand-mère* pressed an envelope into her hand.

"I want you to have this. No strings attached and no regrets. I will see you when you arrive in Paris." She paused, and her smile widened. "That is, if my grandson lets you out of his bed."

Lissy felt the heat rise in her cheeks, and Frank seemed to choke as he gently led *Grand-mère* out of the room.

Eddie bounced in, giving the old woman a sloppy kiss on the mouth as she passed.

"You still owe me a dance, Hélène!"

"You would never be able to keep up with me, Edward." *Grand-mère* chuckled, patting his cheek.

Chapter
Twenty-Eight

Eddie threw himself into the chair and propped his legs up on the side of Lissy's bed.

"What?" he asked as she stared.

"You called her *Hélène?*"

"So? That's her name. She's marvelous. If I was straight I'd want her to be my sugar mama." He looked Lissy over. "At least you didn't bruise your face. Your hair will cover the lump on the back of your hard head."

"Why does everyone say I'm hard-headed?" Lissy grumbled.

She slapped Eddie's leg when he gave her a look that said, *Are you serious?* He pulled his feet to the floor and leaned toward her, his chin resting on his hand.

"So, your little present to Grayson will be the talk of the town for years to come. Centuries even." He grinned and waggled his brow. "Brilliant, Liss."

"Why is everyone so enthralled with Gray's cufflinks?"

"Cufflinks?" Eddie's whoop of laughter was reminiscent of her brother's outburst.

"What's so damn funny?" she asked sharply as the door opened and Gray returned with a cup of coffee.

Eddie jumped up so Gray could sit. "I take it she doesn't remember much before her swan dive?"

Gray laughed as he took a sip of coffee and shook his head.

"Ah, well, I'll let you recount the interesting post-fall events. I'm going to see if I can catch up with Hélène. Grayson, you wouldn't mind calling me *Grand-père*, would you?" He blew them a kiss as he left, smirking.

Gray dabbed at the coffee he'd spilled on his white shirt.

"I'm glad the two of you find me so amusing." Lissy struggled again to sit up. She gingerly felt the goose egg on the back of her head. "Your grandmother gave this to me." She handed the envelope to Grayson.

His lips thinned with annoyance. "Did the old dragon upset you? Eddie was kidding about me calling him Grandfather, right?"

"Not at all. She's lovely, and Eddie said if he was straight, she'd be his sugar mama."

Grayson choked on his coffee and used a napkin to dab at the second spill.

Lissy laughed. "Go on, open the envelope."

"You don't suppose she's laced it with poison, do you?" he muttered as he slit it open. He emptied a pile of shredded paper onto the rolling table by her bed. "I'll be damned."

"What is it?"

"The pre-nup she had you sign prior to the wedding. It's torn in eight pieces." He looked up at her. "You really did make an impression on her."

"Of course I did. What's not to love about me? I'm your trophy wife. So what's the big secret joke everyone is alluding to about my wedding gift, Gray? Didn't you like the cufflinks? Mother helped me choose them. I thought they were quite elegant." She reached out and ran a finger over the gold discs engraved with *Property of Lissy Deschanelle.*

Grayson laughed. "Totally elegant, and they are perfect. But not nearly as perfect as my other gift."

"What other gift?"

Grayson put his coffee down and kissed her soundly as he pulled her covers down. Slowly, he raised the hospital gown to reveal her recent Brazilian wax job, and her eyes widened. She had totally forgotten her homemade, non-permanent tattoo. Written on her bikini line was *For Gray, No strings attached. All my love, Alyssandra.*

"It was quite the gift…But my family is in the underwear business. Next time at least consider wearing a thong."

The End

Author's Note

If you or someone you know has fallen in love… enjoy the journey. It isn't always a smooth, flat path. You will stumble. You might even fall. But if it's true love, it is so worth it.

Acknowledgments

It's hard saying goodbye to Pine Bluff. And who knows, there may be more at some point in time. (Never say never is my motto.) Many thanks to my critique partner, Jill Odom. Your red trackers of doom put me on the right path all those years ago.

I will have to keep writing and self-pubbing just to work with my amazing editor, Jessica Royer Ocken. She makes editing my favorite part of the entire process.

Coreen Montagna, thank you for putting up with my last-minute changes and always making the inside of my book as beautiful as the outside.

Shannon M. Lumetta, my amazing graphic designer who nails it every time. This cover is perfect.

To my proofreaders, Michele and Chantell, thank you for catching the little details for me! And to my special Cain Girls, thank you for reading, reviewing and promoting my books. Y'all are the best book friends, ever.

Blu Bird saved me with the French translations. (Without her, Grayson would've been calling Lissy a very unflattering name!)

My family has been through a lot the last few years, but their support has never wavered as I've gone after my dream. I couldn't do it without them.

And to my readers. Thank you for reading and loving my characters as much as I do. I write because I have to. I publish for you.

About the Author

During the day, Nancee works as a counselor/nurse in the field of addiction to support her coffee and reading habit. Nights are spent writing paranormal and contemporary romances with a serrated edge. Authors are her rock stars, and she's been known to stalk a few for an autograph, but not in a scary, Stephen King way. Her husband swears her To-Be-Read list on her e-reader qualifies her as a certifiable book hoarder. Always looking to try something new, she dreams of being an extra in a Bollywood film, or a tattoo artist. (Her lack of rhythm and artistic ability may put a damper on both of these dreams.)

Website: nanceecain.com
Blog: nanceecain.com/blog
Goodreads: goodreads.com/Nancee_Cain
Facebook: facebook.com/NanceeCainAuthor
Reader's Group (Cain Raisers): facebook.com/groups/Cain.Raisers
Twitter: twitter.com/Nancee_Cain
Pinterest: pinterest.com/nanceecain
Instagram: instagram.com/nanceecain
BookBub: bookbub.com/authors/nancee-cain
Newsletter: eepurl.com/bhFMtX
YouTube Channel: bit.ly/2xsU6Ad
Spotify Playlists: open.spotify.com/user/12184539074

Books by Nancee Cain:

Paranormal Romance (Angels)
Saving Evangeline
Tempting Jo
Loving Lili (novella)

Contemporary Romance (Pine Bluff Novels)
The Resurrection of Dylan McAthie
The Redemption of Emma Devine
The Rehabilitation of Angel Sinclair
The Redirection of Damien Sinclair
The Reinvention of Jinx Howell
The Reintroduction of Sammie Morgan
The Realization of Grayson Deschanelle

Contemporary Romances

pine bluff

Although each of the titles in this series can be read as standalone stories, this is the preferred reading order:

The Resurrection of Dylan McAthie
A Pine Bluff Novel

Maybe You Can Go Home Again

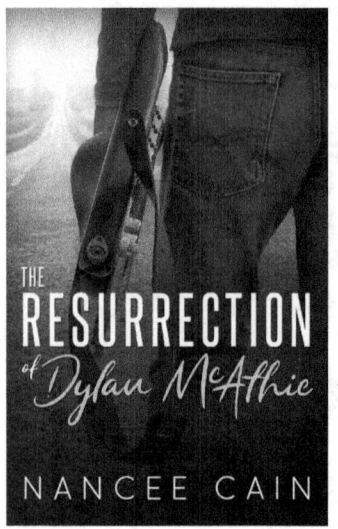

Hounded by paparazzi, Dylan McAthie — the former lead guitarist for Crucified, Dead and Buried — craves quiet anonymity to regroup and sort out his life. An accident leaves him dependent on the family he once ran from, with no choice but to return to the small town of Pine Bluff, Alabama.

Hired by Dylan's estranged brother, private-duty nurse Jennifer Adams remembers the charming boy Dylan was before fame and misfortune. And she notices he's developed a knack for blaming everyone else for his problems, rather than bothering with introspection. She's not having it.

Despite their clashes, as her patient heals, the chemistry between them grows undeniable — until scandal finds Dylan again, threatening to destroy the progress he's made and the couple's growing respect and affection. Can Dylan fix what fame has so easily broken? Or will his public resurrection mean the death of any relationship with Jennifer?

The Redemption of Emma Devine
A Pine Bluff Novel

A Little Shake-Up in Life Can Be Devine

Emma Devine is on the run and fighting to survive. Her tortured past makes trust difficult, especially where men are concerned. But she has no choice other than accepting the help of the man who catches her shoplifting on Christmas Eve.

When not stopping shoplifters, David Patterson leads a quiet life in Pine Bluff, Alabama, working as a high school teacher. His random act of Christmas kindness brings unexpected joy to his life, as he finds himself drawn to the mysterious Emma. When she leaves, his world is turned upside down, and his dreams are changed forever.

Four years later, Emma returns in search of long-overdue redemption. But despite an undeniable attraction between the two, trust is an even greater issue now — for both of them. Can they find their way to a place of understanding? Or have yesterday's mistakes destroyed their chance for a future together?

The Rehabilitation of Angel Sinclair
A Pine Bluff Novel

Love — the Hardest Addiction to Kick

Angel Sinclair arrives in Pine Bluff, Alabama, determined to make amends for his past and move on. But that changes after a chance encounter with a beautiful inn owner, and instead he finds himself pursuing two things that haven't been in his life for years: love and trust.

Still reeling from a bitter divorce, Maggie Robertson wants to focus on making her business a success. Getting involved with anyone in this gossipy little town is the farthest thing from her mind...until she finds herself tempted by a younger man.

Neither Angel nor Maggie can ignore the sizzling heat between them. But Angel's secretive nature soon fills Maggie with doubts about the man she's allowed into her heart.

Was she wrong to believe love could conquer all? Is their age difference an obstacle they can't overcome?

The Redirection of Damien Sinclair
A Pine Bluff Novel

Sometimes You Get What You Need

Acclaimed divorce attorney Damien Sinclair has witnessed more than his share of love's ugly aftermath. He keeps things black and white, preventing anyone from getting too close. But his illusion of control fades when an attempt on his life leaves him struggling with PTSD.

Enter Damien's childhood friend, the free-spirited Harley Taylor. Shrugging off the awkwardness of their teenaged fling and her broken heart, she appoints herself his caregiver. The man needs to learn not to take himself so seriously, and she's hellbent on snapping him out of his brooding funk.

After a decade apart, Harley and Damien find their attraction is stronger than ever. Could Harley's sunny disposition be the bright spot Damien needs in his life? Or will their differences overshadow any hopes of a future together?

The Reinvention of Jinx Howell
A Pine Bluff Novel

Can Love Unmask Their True Selves?

Hiding behind her wigs and heavy makeup, Jinx Howell masks her insecurities — which even she doesn't understand — with bravado, slashing through life with reckless abandon. Lonely, but unwilling to get close to anyone, she finds the ideal solution: a hook-up with the campus's most notorious heartbreaker.

In similar fashion, Mark "Two-Time" MacGregor protects his heart and keeps himself unencumbered through a string of one-night stands. A chance meeting with the edgy Jinx in a dark alley seems like destiny. She claims to want sex with no ties, making her perfect. *Like attracts like.* But this girl with a switchblade has more hang-ups than he does, which is a hell of a lot.

When tragedy strikes, Mark's hit-and-run lifestyle takes a backseat to his need to protect the broken girl whose secrets are unraveling. Along the way, both of them will find their truths unmasked. Can they forge a real relationship, or will they give up on their romance as jinxed?

The Reintroduction of Sammie Morgan
A Pine Bluff Novel

Can Life Get Any Crazier?

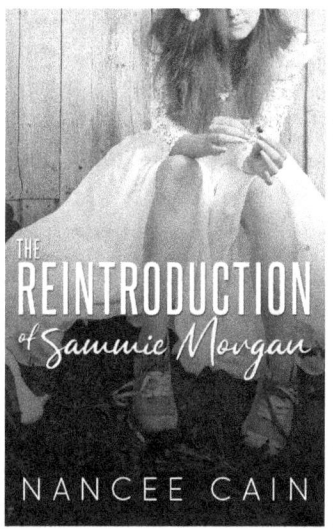

Still reeling from the tragic deaths of his wife and daughter, Matt Tyler trudges through life, caring for his young son, managing his cantankerous father, and working as much as he can. Despite his best efforts, bills are piling up and his vindictive in-laws seem determined to take Luke away from him.

Things change when he stumbles upon Sammie Morgan — with a car that won't run and her mother's ashes in the backseat. Best friends growing up, Matt and Sammie have spent years apart following very different paths. Now they've both run out of options. Without a dime in her pocket, Sammie has nowhere to go. And Matt lacks the stable home life he needs to fight his former in-laws.

Their hasty solution? A marriage of convenience.

But how convenient will this reintroduction be if it means Matt and Sammie have to relive the most painful parts of their past?

The Realization of Grayson Deschanelle
A Pine Bluff Novel

Sex, No Strings Attached

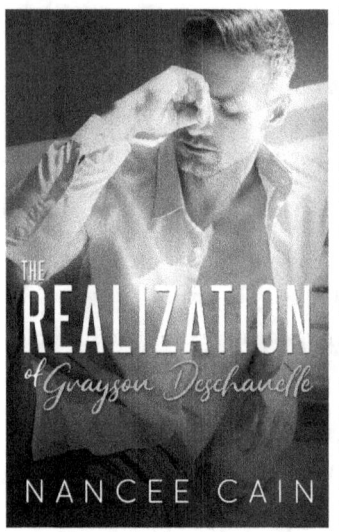

Despite a high-profile clientele, fashion photographer Grayson Deschanelle prefers being behind the lens, away from public scrutiny. After his movie star girlfriend dumps him, he flees to his stepbrother's remote cabin to hide from the paparazzi.

Caught by surprise, Grayson finds Lissy much different than the girl he's known for years. She's no longer a child — though her teen-aged crush is still very much intact. Snowed in with her, he tries to fight his growing attraction. But being with Lissy brings what his life is lacking into sharp focus.

The ice melts, and they return home. When their families discover their secret, Grayson must decide what kind of life he truly wants — and whether he'll fight to keep Lissy by his side.

Paranormal Angel Romances

Although each of the titles in this series can be read as standalone stories, this is the preferred reading order:

Saving Evangeline

Tempting Jo

Loving Lili (novella)

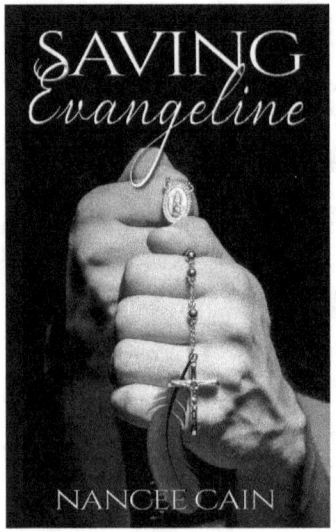

Evangeline is the town pariah. Everyone knows she's crazy and was responsible for the death of her last boyfriend. Even her mother left her and moved cross-country. Lonely and desperate, Evie decides to end her life.

Rogue angel Remiel longs to return to Earth, but there's just one problem. He tends to invite trouble and hasn't been allowed back since Woodstock. The Boss sends him to save Evangeline, but there's a catch: he can't reveal his angelic nature, and he must complete the task as *Father* Remiel Blackson.

Forced together on a cross-country trip, a forbidden romance ignites and love unfolds. A host of heavenly messengers tries to intervene, but Remiel and Evangeline are headed on a collision course to disaster. Will his love save her, or will they both be lost forever?

Tempting Jo

Forbidden love is hell…

Confident and quirky, Jo Sanford thinks her boss is God's gift to women — and she couldn't be further from the truth. Devilishly handsome, Luc DeVille will stop at nothing to lure his administrative assistant right into his arms — and bed.

Over Rafe Goodman's dead body…

Rafe, Jo's best friend, refuses to sit by and watch as Luc tries to win the heart of the woman he's always protected. After all, Rafe is her guardian angel. Suddenly, Jo's caught in the middle of a battle between good and evil. But the closer she gets to the fire, the hotter it burns. Now, Jo's going to learn that when love battles lust, Heaven and Hell collide.

Loving Lili (novella)

Their lovemaking is hot and dirty. Their break ups are nasty and epic.

Tired of taking the blame for every wicked thing that happens on Earth, fallen angel Luc DeVille decides to write a tell-all-book exposing The Boss.

Sharing a long and passionate history, Luc is shocked when Lili Nix arrives to interview for the job as editor. Immediately the verbal sparring begins, but the sexual chemistry remains combustible. Fascinated by this heavenly creature, Luc changes his game plan. After all, she's the only angel who has ever held his attention and understood his intentions.

Being in this world, but not of this world, is a lonely business. Can two lost angels connect and make it last this time?

www.ingramcontent.com/pod-product-compliance
Lightning Source LLC
Chambersburg PA
CBHW060529260626
47161CB00003B/818